REMEMBER NO MORE

REMEMBER
NO MORE

by
Jan Newton

HONNO MODERN FICTION

First published by Honno Press in 2017. 'Ailsa Craig', Heol y Cawl, Dinas
Powys, South Glamorgan, Wales, CF64 4AH
1 2 3 4 5 6 7 8 9 10
Copyright: Jan Newton © 2017

The Author would like to stress that this is a work of fiction and no
resemblance to any actual individual or institution is intended or implied.

A catalogue record for this book is available from the British Library.
Published with the financial support of the Welsh Books Council.

ISBN 978-1-909983-56-4 (paperback)
ISBN 978-1-909983-57-1 (ebook)

Cover design: Annika Faircloth/Trustfund Graphics
Cover image: © Giles Bennett
Text design: Elaine Sharples
Printed in Wales by Gomer Press

For Merv, who taught me how to fly

There are so many people who have helped me to make this book a reality – from its very beginnings at Tŷ Newydd, when Janet Thomas guided me gently but firmly in the right direction, to the wonderful people at Honno who have continued to steer it on its course. Along the way there have been so many others who have encouraged and supported me. To all of them my grateful, heartfelt thanks.

A special thank you to Poppy Peacock, who has been cheerleader and mentor through every stage of the process, and to Nigel Jenkins and Chris Kinsey, both wonderful, inspirational tutors who between them taught me how to weave non-fiction and fiction, and that a sense of place is just as important as character and plot.

To Kevin Robinson, retired West Yorkshire Police Inspector, huge thanks for his wonderful course for crime writers and for his subsequent support in ensuring that my facts were factual. Any mistakes in any aspect of the novel are, of course, entirely mine.

Thanks too, to the lovely people of mid-Wales who have made us so welcome since we arrived in 2005. The place is breathtakingly stunning, but its people are even more amazing.

Lastly, but most importantly of all, without Mervyn none of this would have been possible. For over thirty years, he has supported everything I have ever wanted to do with insight, patience and pride. I will always be grateful.

'And their sins and iniquities will I remember no more.'
Hebrews Chapter 10, Verse 17

PROLOGUE

From his perch high on a sandstone outcrop, the buzzard watched the silver motorbike zigzagging along the narrow strip of tarmac. The road was hemmed in either side by reeds and grasses, which had been bleached by the winter's snow and were still untouched by the spring sunshine, so that the bike looked like a salmon, darting through weed-laced water. The buzzard began to lose interest. He had to find food for his chicks. He scanned the flock of mountain sheep, checking for stricken lambs – easy pickings out here in the open. A red Land Rover had turned off the road and was bouncing along the rutted track, which led towards his vantage point.

A sharp crack startled the bird. Gunshot. He launched himself from the rock as the motorcycle swerved and left the road. For a second, it too was flying, suspended above a shallow ravine before it plummeted into the stream below. The growl of the engine was silenced by the water, but the back wheel continued to spin, slowing and finally stopping as the buzzard began gliding lazy circles overhead. The Land Rover slewed to a halt; its engine still running. The driver clambered out and there was a flash of light as he focused his binoculars. Then he climbed back into the vehicle, hurled it into a ragged three-point turn and sped back along the track, disappearing beneath the folds of the hill.

CHAPTER ONE
Thursday, 21ˢᵗ April

DC Julie Kite logged out of the computer system and watched the familiar Manchester Metropolitan Police logo fade from the screen. She stared at her reflection, as though the face looking back at her might somehow appear more confident than she felt inside, might convince her that she was doing the right thing.

'That it then?'

Frank Parkinson's face appeared in the top corner of the screen as he leaned over her shoulder.

Julie sighed. 'Yes, Sarge. That's it.'

'Sarge yourself from Monday eh?'

'In name at any rate.'

'You'll be grand. Just take your time. Anyway,' he thrust out his hand, 'you know where I am if you need anything. Just give us a bell.'

'Thanks, Sarge.'

'Well, all the best then.'

Parkinson ambled off and Julie looked around the office. It was all so familiar; the bright blue fabric of the chairs, the clock which was always three minutes fast, the view of ornate sandstone swirls on the hotel across the square, even the rows of lever arch files with their enigmatic labels on the shelves on the far wall. She would probably never see it again. There were still a dozen officers in the open-plan. Nobody looked up as she walked over to the DCI's office and knocked quietly on the door.

'Sir, I …'

'You all done then, Kite?'

'Yes, Sir. I've left everything with DC Mitchell.'

'Right you are.' DCI Hargreaves came out from behind his desk and shook her hand. 'Well, Julie, good luck with the new job. And you know where we are if you get bored.'

'Yes, Sir.' If only he meant it. If she could come back if things didn't work out. But she knew that particular boat had sailed.

Hargreaves walked back round his desk, pausing on the way to look out of the window and over the city's seemingly endless skyline. Building after building – brick, glass and limestone jostling for space. Julie knew every street down there. All that local knowledge and here she was, starting again with a clean slate.

Hargreaves seemed to have forgotten she was there. She crept out of his office and closed the door behind her. One or two people acknowledged her with a wave but nobody got up to talk to her, nobody slapped her on the back and said they'd miss her. She picked up her coat and her bag and made her escape to the Ladies.

Locked in the cubicle she dabbed her face and blew her nose. What the hell was she doing? It wasn't even as if there were any guarantees that Adam would turn over a new leaf. What if she hated it? What if she was allergic to the countryside, what if …

The outside door had opened. Julie pressed the flush, straightened her hair and unbolted the door. It was Helen Mitchell, Julie's partner for the last three years, peering at her mascara in the mirror. She watched Julie's reflection walk over to the hand basin and press the soap dispenser.

'You OK?' She rummaged in her bag and extricated lipstick. 'Do you fancy coming into town,' she said, almost unintelligibly, as she applied a slash of scarlet.

'I don't know. I think I'll just go home and get an early night.'

Helen rolled her eyes and sighed. 'Oh come on, Jules, keep me company.'

'I'm not in the mood.'

'But we've got to celebrate.' She swivelled the lipstick back into its lid and threw it into her bag.

Julie dragged a comb through her blonde hair, glancing at herself from beneath her fringe. She shrugged.

'You did say you didn't want any fuss.' Helen smiled at Julie's reflection.

Julie nodded. 'Yeah, but I didn't think it would be quite so low-key.'

'Maybe they think you'll be back. City lass like you.' Helen zipped her bag. 'Parki's probably running a book on how long you'll last in wellies.' With a last glance at herself in the mirror, she shepherded Julie towards the door. 'Come on. I'll take you to The Roebuck. You can totter home from there.'

'I'm not going for a session.' Julie said. 'I've still got loads to do. I'm moving to the back of beyond on Monday morning, remember?'

The Roebuck was tucked away in the web of narrow streets behind the police station. Away from the trendy wine bars and clubs on the city's main arteries, it had resisted any form of refurbishment. Helen led her through the grubby assortment of mismatched tables and chairs towards the bar.

'Soda water and lime, if I really must,' she said, plonking herself down on a threadbare brocade-covered stool. Helen had insisted they walk to the pub. There had also been a detour to the Chinese supermarket, where she had weighed up every make and size of dried noodle before glancing at her watch and hastily putting everything back on the shelf. She bought Julie a box of fortune cookies from a rack by the checkout and thrust it into her hands.

'Open them when you get to your new house,' she'd said. 'And think of us up here.' Now she handed Julie her soda water and lime, complete with a chunk of lemon and a pink umbrella balanced on the thick rim of the tumbler. As she lifted the glass to her lips Julie could smell the gin. So much for keeping a clear head.

'Fancy a game of darts?' Carrying a large glass of cold white wine and two sets of darts, Helen tottered off on fabulously high stilettos towards the function room where the log end dartboard was kept – in a bucket of water. Julie sighed and followed her. Adam would have been home for hours, his bag bulging with presents and cards from the kids and the staff. They should be celebrating their new start together. Maybe she would just stay for half an hour and make her excuses. Helen would be well gone by then in any case, or chatting someone up, if her luck was in.

As Helen flung open the door to the function room suddenly there was cheering and party poppers and a huge sea of grinning faces. Everyone was there: friends from the station, her Mum, Dad and Adam, all raising their glasses in her direction. A gaudy foil banner strung between a light fitting and the glitter-ball over the tiny dance floor said 'Congratulations Sergeant Kite' and two sheep-shaped balloons bobbed in the opposite corner of the room.

Adam was chatting to Sophie, the very young DC who'd just been appointed to replace Julie. Helen watched them, watched as he held her refilled glass for a moment too long before letting it go, how he leaned one hand on the wall and bent down towards her as he listened to her.

'He really does like them young doesn't he?' Frank Parkinson came to stand beside Helen. 'Is she doing the right thing, following him out to the arse end of nowhere?' He sipped his pint. 'She's a city girl, and far too good to spend her career on sheep rustling and illegal diesel usage.'

'I hope so. But it's meant a promotion sooner than she'd have got one here. Besides,' she watched Sophie smiling up at Adam, 'she says he's changed.'

Frank Parkinson said nothing, just looked at Helen over the top of his glasses.

By the snooker table Julie was trapped in conversation with DCI Hargreaves and her parents.

'We shall be very sorry to see her leave us.' Hargreaves beamed at Julie. 'Our loss is the Principality's gain,' he said.

'We'll be sorry to see her go too.' Julie's father sounded gruff, but her mother squeezed Julie's arm.

'You have to know when to let go, don't you?'

'Where is Sergeant Kite?' The familiar voice on the microphone lifted them out of their conversation, and Julie was ushered onto the dance floor where two parcels in sheep wrapping paper were waiting for her.

'There's a bit of a theme here, Sarge.'

'We weren't sure what to get you.' Frank Parkinson handed her a large oblong package. 'But we knew you'd need these in Wales.' Inside was a pair of bright red Hunter wellingtons. She lifted them out of the box to a round of applause. In the other parcel was a dark green waxed jacket and matching hat with a maroon tweed band which ended in an understated bow. She put the hat on to a barrage of wolf whistles and she smiled.

But Helen could see that the smile didn't reach her eyes.

CHAPTER TWO
Friday 22nd April

Ella Watkin lifted the kettle off the stove and filled the teapot. 'You should try to be more patient with her. Like it or not, she is your aunt. We all have to try to get on together.'

Gareth sighed. 'Why do you always take her side, Mam? You of all people know what she's like.' Except she didn't know the half of what went on at work did she? Not really.

'Yes I do know what she's like, believe me, Gareth. And antagonising her won't help one little bit, will it?' She opened the pantry and lifted out a large chocolate sponge dusted with icing sugar. 'Will you take some of my baking back to the bungalow? I've done some Welsh cakes and this chocolate sponge Dylan likes.'

'You're changing the subject. Don't think you can change my mind with chocolate cake.' Gareth sighed. 'She even told me off for being late. I felt like a kid. I'm surprised she didn't put my name in the late book.'

'She's a stickler, that's all. It's not just you, you know, we all feel the sharpness of Catherine's tongue.'

'But I don't get any support from Dic either. He's the senior partner and he still lets her pull his strings as though she's some sort of demented puppet master.' Gareth went to stick his finger in the buttercream filling of the cake, but Ella swatted his hand away.

'I know, *cariad,* but she's desperate for Dic to retire. She just wants everything to be organised in advance. She has plans.' Ella

8

bundled Welsh cakes into a clean tea towel. 'She's beginning to think he doesn't want to retire at all.'

'And you're surprised?'

'Gareth, please. Try to see things from her point of view. She thinks you and Eurig are running away with the company that she and Dic started.' Ella twisted the tea towel closed and put it next to him on the table.

'We're not running away with anything, and if she keeps talking to Eurig the way she did yesterday then he won't be sticking around long enough to sign Dic's leaving card. We have to move with the times, Mam, keep up with new developments. There won't be a business at all if they don't modernise and find more work. She thinks they can keep things as they've been for thirty years.'

'But there are ways of handling a situation, Gareth, especially where your Aunt Catherine's concerned. She's already been on the phone about yesterday's meeting – as if I can do anything to influence you.' Ella thrust the biscuit tin under his nose. 'Eat. You look as though you're fading away. You don't get enough fresh air stuck in that office the whole time. Have you thought about what I said about helping Milos with the farm a couple of days a week?'

'I'm fine, Mam. I'm running more again, that's all. He patted his stomach. 'It helps with the side-effects of all those business lunches.' He watched his mother as she flitted round the kitchen. 'Farming's just not my thing, it never has been, you know that. And Milos is more than capable of managing this place on his own.'

'It was good enough for your father.' Ella banged a mug down on the table and the contents slopped onto the plastic tablecloth. 'And we could do so much more with it if the two of you pulled together.' Gareth said nothing. This argument had been running for twenty years or more. Ella shook her head and set about trying to squeeze the sponge cake into a plastic container. 'Catherine told me you were being difficult and having ideas above your station.' She laughed, with a mischievous sideways smile at her son. 'You really know how to upset her, don't you?' She squeezed the lid onto the container and pushed it across the table towards him. 'Why can't you just humour her? Just let her think she's winning.'

Gareth laughed. 'Is that what you do?' He shook his head. 'Don't worry, Mam. It'll sort itself out. Her bark's worse than her bite. For a Rottweiler.' He ducked as she pretended to cuff him round the head.

'Just apologise. For me. I hate it when you two argue.'

'I know you do.' Gareth smiled at her. 'We're just one big happy family aren't we, Mam?'

'Don't be cheeky to your mother, Gareth Watkin. What's wrong with wanting you all to be happy?'

'We are happy, Mam. And I'll phone Catherine and apologise if you think it'll make a blind bit of difference.'

'Good. Drink your tea and go home, it's Friday night. You spend too much time working. You shouldn't be spending your weekend in here with me.'

'You know I'm not being awkward deliberately, don't you, Mam?'

Ella gave him one of her looks. 'I do know, but you need to make allowances. And Dic needs to take charge and decide what he's doing.' She smiled at her son. 'I know you're carrying the can for him not being brave enough to tackle her.'

'The last thing Dic wants to do is to spend more time with Catherine. She'll have him running around after her like a puppy. And there's no way she'll keep out of the business, even if he does retire. You know she'll still interfere. She can't help herself.'

Ella waggled her hands at him. 'Shoo, go and see your family. And take this for Dylan.'

Gareth smiled. His mother always had known how to make him behave. He tucked the Tupperware container more firmly under his arm, patted one of the collies by the gate and strolled down the rough track towards the bungalow. If this deal came off they would be able to tarmac the drive for Mam and go on a decent holiday for a change. Mind, Mam wouldn't be happy with him, and Catherine would be more than incandescent if she found out about that particular possibility. If only Dic would retire, or even just admit they needed to change the business plan, they could all move forward. Then there might be no need for such drastic action. He stopped and gazed out over the hills and valleys, the farms clinging to the hillsides, the hedge-lined lanes winding their way between them. Perhaps he was making a huge mistake. Maybe there was another way to make it work.

Seren and Dylan were in the front garden of the bungalow. She was reading, while Dylan ran his toy tractor round the little wooden farmyard Gareth had bought him in the Royal Welsh Show. When he saw his father he ran to the gate.

'You've got the John Deere on the yard then,' Gareth nodded towards the little green tractor.

'The Massey's in the garage,' said Dylan. 'It needs new tyres and an oil change. Can you help me set up the ramps?'

'Nana sent chocolate cake.'

'Can we have some now?'

'No, Dylan Watkin, now you can go and wash your hands. Dinner's ready.' Sarah shook her head. 'Honestly, your Mam thinks I can't bake.'

'That's not true.' Gareth handed the Tupperware over to his wife. 'She was trying to get round me. She wants me to apologise to Catherine for daring to get some new literature printed.'

'I don't know which of them's worse. Why does Ella make excuses for the old witch?'

'She just wants a quiet life. You know she hates us fighting. She likes us all to play happy families and pretend everything's rosy. Anyway, it'll all be sorted soon, one way or the other. Dic can't hold out forever, he'll have to make his mind up soon.'

'Will you phone Catherine?'

Gareth nodded. 'I promised. And anyway,' he grinned at Sarah, 'she's babysitting tonight.'

Sarah shook her head and sighed. 'Seren, get your nose out of that book and come and wash your hands.' Seren rolled her eyes and wandered into the bungalow and Sarah waited until she was out of earshot before she laughed. 'Honestly, where does she get it from?' She followed the children indoors. 'Best behaviour tonight, mind, your Auntie Catherine's babysitting,' she shouted at Seren's retreating back. 'Provided Daddy does as he's told,' she said to Gareth with a smile.

CHAPTER THREE
Monday, 25th April

Julie Kite looked slowly around her living room. The carpet was its original dark blue where the sofa and chairs had been and the room looked a half-decent size without furniture. In the middle of the carpet a small ginger cat sat, watching her.

'Don't look at me like that, you never know, you might even like it.' She picked him up and walked to the window. They both looked across the street to a low block of flats, which mirrored exactly the one they were standing in. The cat purred and rubbed its head against her shoulder. Elaine was letting herself into number 36, straight off the night shift at Manchester Royal. She waved and gave a thumbs-up as she disappeared into the flat. An old man and an ancient dog wheezed their way along the pavement. Julie could just make out the rumpled stripy legs of pyjamas poking out from beneath the man's trousers. Even now, just past six in the morning, there were commuters forcing their way impatiently through the roads made narrow with parked cars, like furred arteries.

Julie stroked the cat under his chin. 'There won't be all this traffic. You might even be able to stay out at night if you fancy it.' She opened the metal grille of the cat basket by her feet. 'And you might even find the odd mouse or vole, or … something.' Avoiding his stare, she tipped the basket on its end. She felt his body stiffen. Quickly, she dropped him in and closed the grille. The cat, having righted himself too late to escape, scowled.

'That's us then,' said Julie. As she reached for the lock on the front door, she had to blink back tears yet again. What was wrong with her? It was just a poky flat in the place where she'd lived all her life. It was time for a change, a fresh start and, as her Mum had said, it wasn't as if she was moving a million miles away, was it?

'You'll be back to see us won't you?' Julie's mother hardly ever cried, but she had last night. 'And you'll come home if he … if there's any nonsense.'

'He won't, Mum. It's a last chance, he's promised. Clean break, away from…'

'Temptation?' suggested her mother. She knew all about Adam and his liaisons. People were only too keen to share gossip, especially when your daughter was in the police force. She probably had a shrewder idea of Adam's intentions than Julie did. How long would it be before Julie was back, after Adam had run out of luck, or excuses? And where was he tonight? Was he really driving the lorry to Wales, or was he saying his own fond farewells?

As, at last, they said their goodbyes her father had barely spoken; he had just hugged her, while she wept in the driveway.

CHAPTER FOUR

Manchester City Centre had been busy even at six-thirty, but Julie had wanted to see it all for one last time. Cheetham Hill was alive with people and colour. Piccadilly Gardens greeted the new working day by depositing jay-walking pedestrians from trams and buses, and gathering up others to sweep them off to Salford Quays or Trafford Park. Just three hours later she had crossed the bridge over the broad river into Builth Wells and turned left onto Castle Street and the tree-lined A470 where it flirted with the River Wye. Where was everyone?

Julie drove for a further twenty minutes on virtually empty roads, then turned the nose of her Fiesta into the police station car park. There was a rank of reserved slots, with unfamiliar and important names she would know by the end of the day. She settled for a space in the visitors' section.

She climbed out of the car and was suddenly aware that a CCTV camera was pointing straight at her, its red light blinking slowly. She closed the door and locked the car, slung her bag over her shoulder and straightened her jacket. First impressions.

The desk sergeant was talking to an elderly man who trailed a collie on a piece of orange twine. The man was shorter than Julie, an oblong in a well-worn tweed jacket. His cap, greasy with wear, was pushed up, away from his forehead, showing a pale stripe of unweathered skin.

'I was only lending the tractor to him. He's no right.'

'It's just not a police matter, Joe. Unless you want him charged with stealing it, then it's your word against his.' The sergeant waited. 'I don't suppose your Meg would be too pleased with that idea?'

'Too soft on him, she is. It was probably her idea in the first place. She thinks I'm too old for farming.'

'She's just looking after you I expect. Now, do you want him charged, or will you go and talk to him?'

The old man shook his head and muttered something Julie didn't catch, but the sergeant smiled. 'That sounds like a plan. He'll be old enough to retire himself in a few years anyway. Then you'll both have to let the grandsons take over.'

The sergeant watched the man and the collie as they carefully negotiated the automatic doors, then he turned to Julie.

'Now then. What can I do for you?'

'I'm Julie Kite. I was told to report to DI Swift. I'm a bit early.'

The sergeant checked the diary. 'Here we are. Detective Sergeant Kite.' He lingered on the first word and raised an eyebrow as he appraised her. He reached for the phone, turning away as he spoke into the receiver.

'Detective Inspector Swift is on his way,' he said, turning back to face her. '*Croeso i Gymru.*' She was confused. 'Welcome to Wales,' he added with a grin.

DI Swift was powerfully built, stocky and immaculately dressed in a dark blue suit. He thrust out his hand as he approached her.

'Punctuality is my watchword, Sergeant Kite. I can see we're going to get on.' He pumped her hand. 'You've met Sergeant Hughes … Brian. He's been here for donkeys' years and there's nothing he doesn't know about this area. If you need local knowledge he's your man.'

'Thank you, Sir. The Sarge might be sorry you said that.' *If* she needed local knowledge? This felt like starting again from the beginning.

'Right, let's get you installed.' Swift punched a code number into the keypad by a set of swing doors and set off down the corridor. The doors to rooms on either side stood open, but the corridor was silent.

'Is it always so quiet, Sir?'

Swift slowed as he turned up a flight of stairs. 'It's normal for this time of year. May half-term's when things really get going.'

'What happens then?'

'Hay Festival happens, Sergeant. A great mass of velvet jackets and silk scarves.' He slowed for a second time, breathing in short, urgent breaths. 'Then there's the Royal Welsh Show in Llanelwedd. Less silk scarf, more stock coat and rosette.' He reached the top of the stairs and stood for a moment, gasping quietly for breath. 'And then there's the Jazz Festival.' He set off again, his breathing restored. 'And let's not forget the walkers, the cyclists and other random holidaymakers. Absolute bedlam it is in the summer.'

Julie followed Swift into a large open-plan office.

'You'll be just here with DC Williams.' Swift pointed to an empty desk.

A young, blond man was leaning back in his chair at the desk opposite Julie's, laughing into his phone. He was, thought Julie, about the same size as a second row forward. '*Wela i di wedyn.*' DC Williams put the phone down and reached over to shake her hand. Julie gasped at the firmness of his grasp, extricated her hand from his and slowly straightened out her fingers.

'I'm Rhys,' he said.

Swift looked at his watch. 'I'll leave you to get acquainted. DC Williams will take you through the outstanding cases, show you where everything is. He waved vaguely in the direction of ranks of tall cupboards. Come and see me after lunch once you're settled in and we'll go through anything you're not sure of.' He turned, signalling a conclusion to their conversation and ambled off to his glass-fronted cubicle at the far end of the office.

'So you're DS Kite, then?' DC Rhys Williams was still standing by his desk, watching her as she watched Swift. 'As in Mary Poppins or the bird?'

'I've no idea. Is there a difference?'

'What's your first name, Sergeant Kite?'

'Julie.'

'It's first names in here usually. There are that many Joneses and Evanses, not to mention Powells and Davises. Gets confusing, see.' He smiled, his head on one side. 'Mind you, we've never had a Kite before, or a Julie come to think of it. Come on, first things first, I'll show you where the canteen is.' He nodded as he passed the others. 'That's Morgan over there and this is Goronwy.'

The officers looked up. Morgan was on the phone. He stared at her, then swivelled in his chair, turning his back on her. Rhys frowned but Goronwy, oblivious of the snub, grinned broadly. 'Don't believe a word that Rhys tells you.'

'Sod off,' retorted Rhys, as he steered Julie towards the door. 'Don't mind Goronwy, he's my cousin. Right, the canteen's here on the left, IT Department on the right. If you want anything really technical doing, Maggie's brilliant, but she's at a funeral this afternoon.' He pushed open the door to the canteen. 'Here we are then.'

There were maybe a dozen people sitting around the pine tables in groups of twos and threes. There was something odd about it, something not quite right, but what was it? Was it just the newness of it all, the paranoia that came with knowing nothing and nobody? She took in her surroundings. There were the normal vending machines and a coffee machine, offering the usual Latte, Cappuccino, Black, White and Extra White, all of which, Julie knew, would taste exactly the same. She reached into her pocket for change.

'We only use the machine in cases of dire emergency, or on the night shift,' said Rhys. 'Which generally amounts to the same thing. Otherwise the lovely Nerys attends to our every need.'

Nerys shook her head. 'Cheeky bugger,' she said, from between two stainless steel urns.

'Kite … Julie,' said Julie. 'And is Rhys one of your relations too?'

'Good God, no,' said Nerys. 'Well, only by marriage. It's not genetic or anything. Now, what can I get you?'

'Two coffees, *cariad*, and two pieces of your splendid bara brith.'

'Not for me,' Julie said. 'Coffee will be fine.'

'Ah, but you have to try Nerys's bara brith. It's an initiation. Marginally better than having your head put down the bog.'

'You're all charm, Rhys Williams.' Nerys put one piece onto a plate and showed it to Julie. 'Well?' she asked. 'Will you risk it?'

'What is it?'

'Speckled bread, well that's the translation.' Nerys pushed the plate across the counter. 'More like fruit cake. It's lush it is. Just needs a bit of butter on.'

Julie smiled at Nerys. She knew when she was beaten. She took both plates and put them on Rhys's tray.

'My treat,' he said. 'Find us a table.'

Julie could feel twelve pairs of eyes scrutinising her as she crossed the canteen. She'd be exactly the same. It was an occupational hazard. She wished she could just look at someone and not judge, not pigeonhole them into a 'type'. Adam had refused to take her to his staff Christmas party at school last year. It was only at the last minute he'd relented, and only then after he had made her promise that she wouldn't interrogate his colleagues. Again.

She picked a table in the furthest corner and sat with her back to the wall. Through the window she could see the slated point of a church spire topped by a gilded cockerel and beyond it nothing but steep, jagged hills rising in the middle-distance. She watched Rhys collect cutlery and serviettes, heard knife against plate and realised what it was that had been bugging her. It was as though the mute button had been pressed. He plonked the tray down on the table.

'It's like being in a library,' Julie said.

Rhys shook his head and handed her a mug. 'Welcome to Mid Wales Police,' he said. 'I suppose it's a bit quieter than what you're used to in the big bad city is it?'

Julie sipped her coffee. Great, she told herself. You've moved to the middle of nowhere with a husband on his very last warning, for a promotion which will probably be majoring in bicycle theft and sheep rustling.

'Well,' said Rhys, 'what do you think of Nerys's baking skills?'

She bit into the dark fruit cake with its generous slather of butter. 'As initiations go, I've suffered worse.'

It was as they were walking back to the office that Swift approached them on the corridor at a half run.

'There's been a bad accident on the Epynt,' he gasped, 'it sounds pretty nasty. Some bloke's come off his motorbike. Uniform have asked for backup.'

'Right, Sir, we're on our way,' Rhys said with, Julie noted, a little too much relish.

'I think it might be an idea if I take Kite, just to show her the ropes,' said Swift. 'It won't need three of us.'

CHAPTER FIVE

The road snaked across the bleached moorland, a dark grey slash slicing the hill in two. Swift's fingers were white on the steering wheel as the powerful car shuddered into potholes. Julie gripped the edge of her seat and concentrated hard on the road ahead, conscious of a rising tide of bara brith and canteen coffee.

'Just round this next bend and you should be able to see the bike down there on your left.' Swift pointed past her out of the side window. 'Bottom of the ravine.' The car lurched to the right and he turned back to the road. Even the advanced driving course hadn't prepared her for terrain like this. She caught a fleeting glance of mangled metal before the road switchbacked.

'Do we know why he went off the road?' she asked.

'No details at all. The call came in about eleven-thirty. The caller said where he was and that the casualty seemed to be in a bad way, but then he rang off.' Swift glanced across at her. 'He must have been a local though.'

'What makes you say that?'

'This is one of the Army's access roads. They're not open to general traffic.'

'Army?' Julie scanned the moorland for signs of activity. Wherever they were, they must have been well camouflaged.

'It's an artillery range, has been since 1940.' Swift pulled the car out of a tight bend. 'And the caller knew the name of the farm where the bike went off the road. It was demolished in about 1942 and it doesn't appear on the maps now.'

'So would it be someone from the military who phoned?'

21

'Could be. Or it could be a farmer checking his sheep. Or maybe even a boy racer would know the names. They hold rallies up here now and again and the kids sometimes come back after the event.'

The car rounded a sharp bend and dropped towards the deep valley. 'That bloody woman,' said Swift. 'How does she do it?'

Julie frowned. What woman?

Swift stamped on the brakes, sending loose chippings skittering, then he flung the door open and rocked himself out of the car. 'Come on,' he said, 'come and meet our pathologist. Talks just like you she does.'

Julie fought to open the passenger door against the wind. It must have been five degrees colder up here. It felt more like February than late April and she shivered. Swift had charged off down the hill. Julie craned forward so she could just see the silver motorbike lying on its side thirty feet below in the shallow water of the stream. Just to the right of the bike, inside an oblong of fluttering blue and white tape, was the body of what looked like a man. Even from this height, she could hear the tapes thrum and crack as the wind pulled at them. Fifty metres further on, where the strip of tarmac widened slightly, an ambulance was parked in front of a black Alfa Romeo sports car and a marked police car. As she watched, the ambulance pulled away, slowly climbing out of the valley. But surely the biker was still down there, in the taped-off square by the stream?

'Come on Kite, we're not sightseeing,' Swift called. He stood, hands on hips, surrounded by half a dozen quizzical ewes, quietly cudding as they watched him. Julie followed Swift's squat, square frame as he picked his way between rust-coloured boulders and wispy grasses, which were bent almost flat by the wind. But surely the body was too far from the motorbike?

'Good afternoon, Doctor,' bellowed Swift, his words carried away by the breeze.

A woman, slender even in her unflattering white SOCO suit, turned towards them. She bobbed under the tapes and removed her hood, allowing waves of auburn hair to escape. Pointedly she looked at her watch.

'Good of you, Inspector,' she deadpanned, watching his face. Then she laughed; a deep, dirty chuckle at odds with both her appearance and the scene which confronted them. 'Your face…' she said to Swift. 'You should ditch that bus and get a proper car.'

Swift shook his head, but Julie noticed he was smiling. 'Doctor Greenhalgh, this is Detective Sergeant Kite. The doctor is a fan of speed,' he added as the two women nodded their greetings.

'Here,' said the doctor, handing them blue paper suits and shoe covers. 'Come and have a look.' She pulled her hood back on. 'Tell me what you think.'

Kite and Swift climbed obediently into the one-size-almost-fits-all garments and ducked under the tape held aloft by one of a brace of uniformed officers. They joined the doctor, a photographer and two further Scene of Crime officers, who were clipping reeds and grasses and bagging them. The wind moaned through the tapes.

'There's sheep shit everywhere.' The photographer stood up and stepped away from the body.

'Well? First impressions?' Greenhalgh folded her arms and watched as Julie looked at the victim's face.

'Shit.' Julie's hand flew to her mouth as bile rose in her throat. She'd seen more than a few bodies, but this… The victim lay on his back, eyelids open, but the eye sockets were empty. She swallowed. 'The eyes, are they, did they—'

That the bara brith and canteen coffee stayed outside the locus was entirely down to Swift's speedy reaction. One of the uniformed officers was trying, unsuccessfully, to conceal a smile.

'Sorry, Sir, I…' Julie wiped her mouth with the back of her hand, then she wiped her hand on the leg of her paper suit. Bloody hell. Now she looked like some wet behind the ears PC.

'That was unfair,' said Swift. 'You should have warned her.'

'Sorry.' The doctor raised a hand in acknowledgement. 'Didn't think. Sign of me having been here far too long. It's raptor damage.'

Julie looked at Swift.

'Birds of prey. Buzzards, kites, that sort of thing.'

'I can't say I've ever come across them in Central Manchester,' said Julie.

'Nah, Bradford were't same fer wildlife.' Greenhalgh's accent was pure Yorkshire. She smiled, and reverted to the more neutral tone. 'You'll get used to it. To be honest, it doesn't happen very often, even here.' She walked towards the corpse. 'What do you think of the wound?'

Julie bent down to examine the body, trying to keep her breathing deep and regular. The man was dressed in a suit and tie and what looked like a relatively new blue waxed jacket. Not the sort of thing you would wear on a motorbike. The back of his head on the right hand side was so damaged it was as though it had exploded.

'Well, gunshot wound, looks like shotgun. Single shot?' She looked up for reassurance and the doctor nodded.

'Probably point-blank range, there's residue around the wound and on the collar of his coat. He's been shot just behind the temple, which could indicate suicide.'

Julie stood up and looked down on the body. 'There's dried mud on the knees of his trousers and his right shoe is missing.' She frowned. 'Could he have been kneeling?'

'We've got the shoe bagged. It was over there.' Greenhalgh watched Julie move round the locus.

'From the state of his sock he hasn't walked anywhere without his shoe. Were there spent cartridges?' Julie paused. Just how much was the doctor expecting her to notice?

Greenhalgh shook her head. 'Nope, just a couple of old ones, rusty. We've picked them up but they're buggers for hunting up here.'

'But that's—'

'Illegal,' agreed Swift. 'Only sometimes. And it's almost impossible to police.'

24

'And you can't really expect the farmer to sit about and wait for foxes to eat his lambs, can you?' The doctor's face gave nothing away. Julie couldn't decide whether either of them was being serious.

'And the weapon?' she asked.

The doctor shook her head. 'No weapon.'

'Was there a note?'

'No note. What's your instinct telling you?'

Swift watched her as Julie weighed up the options.

'Well, I'd have said suicide initially, with the missing shoe and the location of the wound. It could account for the off-centre shot if he'd pulled the trigger with his foot.'

'Not bad,' said the doctor.

'But without a weapon,' Swift asked.

'So, it's either murder, and a feeble attempt to make it look like suicide, or it is a suicide, but made to look like murder.'

'That covers all the bases, then,' said Swift.

'Not quite, Sir.' Julie turned back to the doctor. 'He obviously didn't come off that motor bike, not dressed like that.'

'Well spotted, Sergeant, he didn't. The biker's in the ambulance. The poor lad's got a badly broken leg and severe concussion.' The doctor lifted the tape. Way up on the hill behind her there was a sudden flash of light, then another, and Julie watched as a figure darted away, quickly disappearing below the horizon.

'His face looks familiar,' said Swift, continuing to look at the victim, and ducking under the tape as requested. 'But I just can't place him. Do we know who he is?'

'Yes. There was a wallet.' The doctor pulled an evidence bag from her case and handed it to Swift. 'There's over two hundred pounds in it,' she said. 'I think we can rule out robbery as a motive.'

Swift pulled three credit cards from the wallet. 'Oh no. Of course.' Swift closed his eyes, then took another look at the body, as though this might have changed things. 'I know him. It's Gareth Watkin.'

A blood-curdling scream ripped the air above them. All but one of those people clustered in and around the taped oblong turned and looked up. A gigantic rust-coloured bird with a triangular forked tail rode the thermals, effortlessly flicking a wing tip to circle the scene playing out below him. Julie shivered.

'Sir, are there eagles up here?'

'No.' Swift shaded his eyes and scanned the sky. 'Oh, you should know this one, Sergeant. It's a red kite.'

'And could it have…?' Julie glanced towards the sightless corpse.

'It could,' agreed Swift.

'Sir?'

'Yes, Kite.'

'Who's Gareth Watkin?'

'Local solicitor, chairman of the Round Table, all round good egg.' Swift looked back at the corpse and shook his head. 'Sweet Jesus,' he muttered. 'Come on, Sergeant, we'd better go and break the news to the family.

As they climbed back into the Volvo, Julie glanced back at the bleak hillside, but the running figure was gone.

CHAPTER SIX

The farmhouse was set on the very edge of the hill. A thickset stone building with a grey slate roof, it blended into the hillside as though it had grown there. What trees there were had been permanently bent against the wind. Swift ended his call and steered the car down the long, steep drive. 'Rhys is at the hospital.'

'Where is the hospital?'

'Depends where you're picked up and whether they call out the Air Ambulance, but this chap's probably gone to Hereford or Nevill Hall.'

'How far's Hereford?' At last, somewhere she had heard of.

'About an hour and a quarter from here.' Swift braked as the drive bent round to the right and ruts either side of the grassy hump at its centre became much deeper.

'Is there nothing nearer?' Dear God, what would happen if you were having a heart attack or bleeding to death?

'They're about the same distance, Abergavenny, Hereford, Aberystwyth, we're slap bang in the middle really.'

'Middle of nowhere,' muttered Julie. 'How far away do you reckon the neighbours are?'

'There are a couple of farms just over the hill, maybe a mile.' Swift slowed down to a crawl as they entered the farmyard. A collie raced across the yard and chivvied the car into stopping. 'Then there's Llangammarch, about four miles down the hill.' Swift switched off the engine. 'Where will you be living?'

She knew this had to come up some time today. If she'd bothered to show the slightest interest and ask Adam, she wouldn't have felt quite so stupid now. 'It's near Builth Wells somewhere. Starts with an L.'

'Most places do, Sergeant.'

Julie blushed. 'I've never even seen the house. Adam – my husband – he only came to see it the once and decided it was perfect. He drove the lorry up last night and I came straight from Manchester, this morning. I had to sleep on the floor in a sleeping bag last night.' She rubbed her neck.

'So you've no idea where you live?' Swift laughed out loud. 'And you a detective.'

'I've got the postcode in the satnav, Sir.' Julie could feel her cheeks reddening still further as Swift chuckled to himself. He shook his head. 'Come on, let's get this over with. We can work out your domestic arrangements later.'

'If only it were that simple, Sir,' said Julie, under her breath.

The yard was tidy. There was no stray clutter, no rusting machinery. Hanging baskets bursting with miniature daffs swung gently in the breeze. Attached at right angles to the house, the barn was another wing in stone and slate and together they sheltered the yard. For the second time today Julie had the feeling of being watched.

'Does anyone live in the barn?'

'No, that'll be storage for hay and machinery. Gareth's mother and brother, Ella and Milos Watkin, they live in the house. Gareth and his wife and kids live in the bungalow just along there.' Swift pointed to another rough grey track leading out past the barn. 'Let's start with the house and see who's in.'

Swift pushed the gate open and knocked on the door, shading his eyes to peer through the frosted glass. Julie shivered. It was warm in the yard, but there was something about the place. It was brooding, watching. Even the rest of the dogs, chained to their kennels, eyed them silently. Swift knocked again, this time lifting the heavy brass knocker and letting it fall back onto the pitted plate beneath. As the door was opened, the dogs began to bark and one, a wall-eyed red and white bitch, howled like a banshee.

'Shut it!' The man at the door bellowed at the dogs, adding something in Welsh. Julie didn't need a translation to know it was a warning. Then he turned towards the police officers, but was silent. He was lean and as tall as Adam, six foot, six one. His faded cord trousers were almost worn through at the knees and the cuffs of his checked shirt were undone. His black hair was long and lank and fell into his eyes.

'Milos,' said Swift.

'What do you want?' the man replied, barring Swift's way with a thick, muscular arm thrust against the door frame.

'This is Sergeant Kite. We need to come in.'

'I've nothing to say to you.'

'We need to speak to Sarah.'

'She's not here.'

Swift looked straight at him. 'Look Milos, I know what you think of me, of the police,' he said, 'but this is serious. It's about Gareth.'

Milos Watkin glared at Swift and glanced at Julie before opening the door just wide enough for them to follow him into the dark hallway. There was an unmistakable odour of damp and stained wallpaper curled at the edges. The doors had curtain poles above them and heavy curtains slung to one side. At the far end of the hall, Milos opened a door and gestured for them to go inside.

This, thought Julie, must be what people meant by a parlour. It reminded her of visiting her great grandmother in Pendleton. Funny, she couldn't remember what the old woman had looked like, but she remembered the room, just like this, stuffed with fat sofas with floral covers, the mantelpiece loaded with china dogs and plates. There were photographs of stern relatives in starched collars and a grandfather clock punctuated the silence with a listing tick.

'Is Sarah in the bungalow?' asked Swift.

'Taken Mam to Builth. Annie Lewis's funeral.'

'Ah,' said Swift. 'Of course. Will they be long?'

Milos shrugged. Swift gestured to the chair nearest to Milos. 'Maybe you'd like to sit down?' Milos stayed where he was, folded his arms across his chest, but did not reply. Swift glanced at Julie. Did he want her to take over?

'Mr Watkin,' she began.

Milos shot her a look, which let her know she ranked just above the collies in the scheme of things. 'Spit it out then,' he said to Swift.

Swift scratched his ear. 'The thing is, Milos, we've found the body of a man out on the range.'

'Bastard army shooting each other are they?'

'Well,' Swift watched Milos carefully, 'that's possible I suppose.' The clock's lopsided tick emphasised Swift's reticence. 'The thing is, Milos… Well, we think it could be Gareth.'

For a second or two, Milos did nothing. Then he sat down slowly on the arm of the chair. 'Our Gareth?'

'I'm so sorry,' said Swift. 'He'll have to be formally identified, of course, but there's little doubt.'

Milos was shaking his head now. 'You must be wrong. Not our Gareth. He's at work. What would he be doing up there?'

'I don't know.' Swift sat on the arm of the sofa, which brought him back on a level with Milos. 'But we'll find out.'

'And you're sure it's him?' Milos was suddenly pale despite the weather-beaten skin.

Swift nodded. 'We'll have to ask you, or Sarah, to come down to the mortuary later to make a formal identification, but I'm certain it is Gareth. Can you phone Sarah, see how long she'll be?'

Milos nodded and walked to the door and out into the hall. They could hear the buttons being pressed on the ancient telephone.

'Don't they have mobiles yet?' whispered Julie.

'There's virtually no signal in here,' said Swift, checking his own phone and showing her the screen. 'These walls are about a foot thick.' They heard the receiver clatter back into the rest.

'They'll be back now,' said Milos. 'She's picking something up in Garth.'

'Go and put the kettle on, Kite, would you?' said Swift, gesturing to Milos that he should sit down again. Julie paused, but there was something dismissive in Swift's manner. She closed the parlour door on her way out and followed the sound of voices into the kitchen. She pushed the door cautiously, but it was only the radio. She relaxed and took the heavy kettle off the range and held it under the tap. The view from the window was amazing; great swathes of moorland and square stands of dark green pine trees, sheep wherever she looked. From here she could see right down into the valley with its tiny fields and even tinier houses. This was a bit different to the view from the flat in Manchester. As she gazed, water splashed from the spout and onto the draining board.

'It'll never boil if it's that full.' Julie jumped and the kettle bounced off the white enamel of the sink. A girl of about nine or ten was sitting at a small table in a cubby hole at the far end of the room. She had a book in her hands, a thick hard-backed novel, and she eyed Julie over the top of it.

'Dad says you should only boil as much as you need,' she said, putting the book down on the table and slotting in a bookmark shaped like a flat zebra.

'Is that your Dad in the other room?' asked Julie, emptying some of the water away. The child shook her head.

'Dad's at work,' she said. 'That's Uncle Milos.'

Oh dear God, this child's father must be the man with no eyes and half his skull missing out there on the hill. Julie carried the kettle to the range.

'Aren't you going to light it?'

'I'll be back in a minute.' Julie headed back into the parlour. Both men turned as she came in.

31

'Sir, there's a child in the kitchen. I think she must be…'

'That's Seren, she's off school today. She wasn't well last night. Mam said Gareth and Sarah had to come back early from their night out.' Milos got up and stepped towards the door.

'Back from where, Mr Watkin?' asked Julie.

'Out,' said Milos. 'They don't tell me everything they do.' Was it all women he had a problem with, wondered Julie, or just her?

'I think, maybe we should wait for Sarah,' said Swift. 'So when did you last see Gareth, Milos?'

Milos sank slowly onto the arm of the chair. 'God, the kids,' he said. 'What can we tell the kids?'

'Tell the kids about what?' The door opened slowly and Seren pushed her way past Swift and stood squarely in front of Milos. The two men looked at each other over the child's head.

'Come and show me how that cooker works.' Julie took Seren's arm and led her back towards the kitchen. This was so difficult. If she'd been working with Helen or even with Paul Mawson she'd have known how to play it, how to read the signs. She would have known which role to play. She'd only met Swift three hours ago. How did he like to run things? The collies began to bark and through the frosted glass of the front door, Julie could see the dark shape of a car turning round in the yard. Swift appeared briefly in the hallway behind her.

'Can you take Seren and her grandmother into the kitchen. I'll speak to Sarah in here.' He went back into the parlour and closed the door.

The front door opened and a slight, slim woman stepped into the hallway. She was maybe sixty-four or sixty-five Julie guessed.

'Mrs Watkin?' she asked.

'Yes.'

'And is Sarah with you?' She tried again.

'She's parking the car.' This Mrs Watkin wore a black jacket over black trousers and a grey silk blouse, with discreet silver

32

jewellery. The effect was sombre but immaculate. She examined Julie closely.

'Who are you?' she asked. 'Should I know you?'

'No, I'm with Man… Mid Wales Police. Detective Sergeant Kite. My colleague, Detective Inspector Swift is…'

'Young Craig? I've not seen him since he and Milos fell out about the foot and mouth nonsense in 2001.'

The front door opened again and a second black-clad woman, with close-cropped auburn hair stepped into the hall.

'Mam!' Seren barged her way through to her mother. 'Why are the police here? Have we done something wrong?'

Sarah Watkin paled under her perfect make up.

'DI Swift would like a word with you,' said Julie. 'He's in here with Mr Watkin.' She pushed open the parlour door.

'Gareth?' said Sarah, pushing past her. 'Has something happened to Dylan?' She stopped abruptly when she saw Milos and Craig Swift. 'Where's Gareth?' she said. 'What's happened?'

'Nothing's happened to Dylan,' said Swift. 'Dylan's fine. I think it would be better if you sat down, Sarah.'

CHAPTER SEVEN

'Do you think Milos really didn't know his brother was dead?' Julie closed the car door. A face peered out of an upstairs window, watching them. Seren. Swift had suggested they did not tell her and Dylan about their father until the body had been formally identified, but the poor child knew there was something very wrong. Julie could feel her stare even from this distance, pallid and intense.

Swift slid the gear lever into reverse. 'I'm pretty certain it was Milos who phoned it in this morning.'

'But why would he phone and then make out he didn't know what had happened to Gareth?'

Swift shrugged. 'The bike going off the road would have made it difficult for him to just walk away.'

'So he must have been down there and checked that the biker was still alive, or there would have been no need for him to phone at all, would there? He could have just waited for someone else to find both bodies.'

Swift nodded. 'Exactly. Even Milos wouldn't have left the poor lad out there to die.'

'But why would he not want to report Gareth's death?

They were back out on the road now. Swift had turned right, away from the remains of Gareth Watkin and the stricken motorcycle.

'Milos can be a funny bugger,' said Swift. 'He always was a bit...'

'Odd?' suggested Julie.

'Difficult,' replied Swift.

The car rattled over a cattle grid and a vista of villages and isolated farms opened up below them as the road hairpinned to the right, before descending along the edge of a steep valley. The tops of the hills were the pale browns of moorland, but the valley bottoms were already lush with meadows and hedges. It reminded Julie of a very old map book she'd been given as a child. Greens for low-lying land, through browns and heather-purples to snowy peaks; it was all laid out beneath them with ribbons of road and river winding their leisurely way through the vast landscape.

'Where are we now?'

'Coming into Garth. Llangammarch's down there on the left, then Llanwrtyd and Llanafan up there.'

Julie shook her head. Fat chance of getting anywhere in a hurry, it all sounded the same. Swift slowed as they passed a walker. Dressed all in black, he didn't look up as the car swept past, but continued to plod deliberately up the steep incline. Julie watched the man in the wing mirror. When he was almost out of sight he turned and waved at the car. Julie frowned. 'Do you trust Milos, Sir?'

Swift scratched his ear and considered. 'Before the foot and mouth I'd have said so, but he took it very badly. I'm not sure they ever quite got over it at Penrhiw.'

Julie watched him as he thought about it. Swift wasn't one to rush to conclusions then.

'What happened?' she prompted.

'You must have heard about foot and mouth.'

'Well yes, of course, but I was fifteen that summer and it wasn't cattle I was interested then.' She smiled at the memory. 'I guess it just wasn't quite so momentous in Manchester.'

'It wiped them out up here though. Some of the cattle had been in the family for generations. Bloodlines going back to the old farm which they lost to the government in 1940.' From his tone, Swift obviously didn't think this was a laughing matter and Julie's smile faded.

'I didn't realise it had got this far.'

'It was bad. We lost a million animals in Wales. The government in its infinite Whitehall wisdom decided everything had to be shot.' Swift turned the car onto the main road towards Builth. 'And worse than that, they decided that the Epynt was the perfect place to bury and burn infected livestock from all over the country. There were protests, even violence in some places. People were worried that the land would always be contaminated.

'And is it?'

Swift shrugged. 'Who knows? It all got a bit out of hand at the time. One of our lads was trapped in a police van which was crushed by a JCB.'

Julie's eyes widened. 'What happened to him?'

'He was lucky. It was madness up here for a while.' He waved at the driver of a car going in the opposite direction. 'But it was the fires that finally got to Milos. They smouldered for days, and the smell...'

'Fires, Sir?'

'The carcasses. Cattle, sheep, the odd pet goat. They built huge bonfires back there on the hill. You could see them for miles and the smell hung around for weeks.'

'That must have been...' Julie floundered for a suitable description. She vaguely remembered news footage, huge mounds of dead animals, of black and white cows lying on their backs, their legs sticking straight up into the sky as the flames engulfed them.

'Of course, it was the old man that put the lid on it.'

'Gareth's father?'

Swift nodded. 'He shot himself in the barn as the last cow was destroyed out on the yard. He wasn't the only one either. Things were desperate here then.'

Julie stared out of the side window. As far as she could see were small neatly-hedged fields full of sheep and cattle, grazing contentedly in the spring sunshine. She couldn't imagine anyone being so attached to livestock that they'd do something so devastating.

'Milos has a problem with authority?'

'That's not really fair. They've been unlucky. The army threw them off their land in the war with hardly any notice.' Swift raised a hand to the driver of a tractor, which was chugging slowly up the hill. 'They managed to buy Penrhiw, right on the edge of the range, and then sixty years on, the government took away their livestock.' Swift glanced sideways at her. 'It's understandable.'

She nodded slowly. 'Can they make a living up there?'

'Most people have two or three jobs. Milos does a bit for the Forestry Commission and for the auctioneers in Builth on market day.' Swift slowed down as they crossed the river and dipped under the railway bridge, then indicated right and pulled onto the main road. 'Digs potatoes for a bloke in Hereford.'

'They're grafters then.'

'But there wouldn't have been enough work on the farm to keep both lads. It's as well Gareth wanted to be a solicitor, not that it went down well with the family. He was expected to follow his father and Milos onto the farm.'

'Milos isn't a Welsh name, is it?'

'No, he's named after Ella's grandfather I think. They came from somewhere in Eastern Europe, but I can't remember where. I've lost the plot since they started changing all the country names.'

Swift's mobile rang and he passed the phone to Julie.

'We must get you sorted with a phone that works out here,' he said.

It was Rhys. She could listen all day to his accent, the way it lilted and lolloped. 'The biker's gone into surgery. They're putting a plate in his leg, poor dab. He'll be hours now. What does the boss want me to do? I'll meet you back at the station is it?'

'Tell him to get back,' said Swift. 'We'll sort out the biker tomorrow. You can have a word with Gareth's GP while I gee up the lovely Dr Greenhalgh.'

'She seems pretty switched on,' ventured Julie.

'She's bloody brilliant,' said Swift, 'but don't you dare tell her I said that.'

The GP's surgery was housed in a modern purpose-built complex. For some reason Julie had expected a converted Victorian semi with dog-eared magazines and hand-written notes, but this looked like a private gym, painted in pastels and pale greys with glass in the sloping ceilings and potted palms in the corners. The receptionist smiled as Julie approached the desk and asked to speak to Gareth Watkin's doctor. Julie spoke quietly so as not to alert the patients, who were beginning to drift in for afternoon surgery.

'Can I tell Doctor what it's about?'

Julie hesitated. The chairs closest to the counter were already full, their occupants feigning disinterest in their conversation. She slid her warrant card onto the counter.

'Background information', she whispered.

The receptionist consulted her screen.

'Dr Peters has just arrived,' she said.

By now everyone's attention had been drawn towards Julie.

'Let me just check.' She picked up the telephone receiver and pressed two buttons. A phone rang in one of the offices, and stopped as it was picked up. 'There's a policewoman out here, a Detective Sergeant.'

Doctor Jonathan Peters wasn't much older than Julie. He shook her hand firmly and offered her a seat.

'I need some background medical history on Gareth Watkin. I believe he's one of your…'

'I'm afraid there's not much I can tell you, Sergeant.' The doctor sat down and picked up a pen, which he clicked on and off as he spoke.

'Did Mr Watkin not consult you very often?'

'On the contrary, he is one of our regulars, shall we say, but I'm sure you understand about patient confidentiality.'

'Of course,' said Julie. 'But there's a possibility that a body discovered earlier today on the Epynt may be that of Gareth Watkin.'

The clicking stopped and the doctor frowned. 'Gareth? Dear God. Was it an accident?'

'I'm afraid it's too early to say. Once the pathologist…'

'Touché,' said Peters. 'Has he been formally identified?'

'Not, not yet.'

'Look, Sergeant, I know how difficult it is for you, but I make it a rule not to divulge personal information until I have confirmation that the patient is deceased.'

He took a card from a plastic holder next to the phone and slid it across the desk until it lay between them.

'Phone me anytime, once you're sure it's Gareth.' He stood up and grasped the door handle. 'Does Sarah know?'

'There will be a formal ID later today we hope. The family has been informed.'

The doctor sighed. 'So much has happened to them over the last few years. We'd hoped things had turned a corner.' He opened the door. 'I'm sorry I couldn't be of more help, but once you know for certain…'

The chairs were filling up now, and by the main doors a group of old men stood in a huddle – as though they were standing by the livestock pens at the local mart. Julie wondered whether succumbing to illness was considered a sign of weakness, and that by staying close to the outside world they were denying its impact. There were so many ancient people here, where did they all come from? Maybe in Manchester they had all been tucked up in old people's homes, always smelling vaguely of pee and hermetically sealed from the younger generation. She smiled at the old farmers and pushed the door.

'Sergeant Kite?' The receptionist waved a piece of paper at her.

'Would you like to sign up while you're here? Dr Peters is accepting new patients at the moment.'

Julie hesitated. 'I'm not sure where my surgery will be. I've only moved here today.'

'Yes, it's fine. Llanafan Fawr is within our catchment area. I've filled in your address, so all you have to do is sign. We can sort the rest out later.'

Julie was aware of the whole waiting room watching her as she crossed back to the desk and took the pen which the receptionist held out.

'I don't suppose you could do me a copy of that form, could you?' she asked.

As she got back to the car, Swift was just finishing a phone call.

'Did you get anything?' he asked.

'Not about Gareth Watkin,' said Julie, folding the photocopied form into her bag. 'But I know where I live now.'

Swift laughed, pulled out onto the main road and back over the bridge Julie had crossed earlier in the day. 'I'll drop you off at the station, and then I'll go back and meet Milos and Sarah for the ID. Greenhalgh reckons she's got him looking reasonable.'

'The marvels of medical science. Shouldn't I come with you?'

'Why don't you get off home, seeing as you still have to work out how to get there and there's nothing else we can do until morning. The full post mortem's scheduled for eight. You can join me there if you like?'

'I'd like to.'

'Really? You'd be the only one on my watch who enjoys PMs.'

'Not enjoy, exactly, but... no, that's not true. To be completely honest, Sir, I do. It's not as if it makes any difference to the deceased is it? And forensics is fascinating, don't you think?'

Swift smiled. 'Whatever floats your boat, Sergeant. I'll pick you up at 7.30am from the station.'

CHAPTER EIGHT

Julie watched Swift's Volvo slide back into the trickle of school traffic and waited for it to disappear before she crossed the road.

There was a row of four shops opposite the police station; a post office, a shop selling mountain bikes, a small café with two tiny tables outside on the pavement and an agricultural supplies yard. A hand-written sign had been tacked to the fence. 'Open to the Public' it read. She smiled at the distinction which made a farmer 'one of us' and resisted the urge to sit at one of the little tables outside the café and watch her new world go by. Instead, she pushed open the door of the post office. As expected, the magazines included *Farmers' Weekly, Farming Times,* and *Poultry World,* but she was surprised – and then embarrassed at her surprise – to see *House Beautiful, Period Living* and a whole range of local books and maps. The familiar pink and orange spines of Ordnance Survey maps stood to attention beside a large inflatable daffodil and a family of plush red dragons. Julie ran her finger along the shelf. 180, Builth Wells. That must be the one.

'Do you need any help?' A short, smiling woman tied into an old-fashioned wrap-around floral pinny appeared from behind the shelving.

'I do.' Julie nodded. 'Definitely.'

'Let's see what we can do then.' The woman picked up the map Julie had been contemplating. 'We're on this one, see, down at the bottom there.' She pointed to a huge bend in the River Wye, which seemed to be the only spot which wasn't crammed with contours.

Julie fished the photocopied surgery paperwork from her bag. 'Is… Llanafan Fawr on there?'

'Llanafan…' the woman traced the river north and then west up the map. 'You're just off the end of this one,' she said, scanning the shelf. 'You want the Llandrindod one. 200. Here you go.' She pointed to the bottom corner of the map. There's Llanafan.'

Julie bent down to look where the woman was pointing. 'There's nothing there, just a pub and a church.'

'That's about it – and the community centre. If you're on holiday there's plenty to do, but you'll need a car.'

'No,' said Julie slowly. 'Not on holiday, we've just rented a house, er…' she consulted her piece of paper once more. 'Cwm Nefal Cottage?'

'You'll love it up there, it's really quiet. You need the Beulah road, then turn off here.' She pointed to a tiny yellow road flanked by a line of hills on one side and a small stream on the other. 'Ignore this bit that says it's a bridlepath, it's been tarmacked now. Then you turn sharp left, here. There's a gate across the road, go through the gate and it's along there on the right. You can't miss it.'

'Where's the Epynt from there?'

'Here.' The woman flipped open the Builth map and pointed to a vast expanse of sepia hills and pale blue streams bordered by the solid red triangles which picked out the boundaries of the firing range. There were still fields and a few houses named on the map, defiantly remembering a long-lost community, but already Julie knew that things were very different on the ground.

Swift hated hospitals. Even this silent corridor way below the wards and operating theatres harboured that unique blend of surgical spirit and cleaning fluids, which turned his stomach. He could never decide whether the added waft of necrotising flesh existed only in his mind.

He walked slowly, his rubber soles squeaking on the highly-polished lino. He would never get used to this part of the job. What if it was Gwen or one of the kids in there, waiting for Doctor Greenhalgh to slice into them? He shuddered.

'They've arrived.'

Swift spun round. 'I wish you wouldn't do that. You could give someone a heart attack.'

'It's not likely.' Greenhalgh allowed her gaze to settle on Swift's midriff. 'There are other factors which could do the trick though.'

'Thank you, Doctor.' Swift pulled his jacket across his stomach. 'Let's get this over with shall we?'

Milos and Sarah sat on a pair of hard chairs at the far end of the corridor, under a gold-lettered sign that read 'Chapel of Rest'. Milos was leaning forward, elbows resting on his knees and his face cupped between his hands. He stared at the lino. Sarah, still wearing funeral black, sat tidily with her knees pressed together and her fingers laced, thumbs uppermost in her lap, looking unseeingly at the wall opposite. She reminded Swift of a small child who had been told to behave in church. As Swift and Greenhalgh reached them she looked up, willing them to tell her there had been a mistake.

'Sarah,' said Swift, reaching out to support her as she rose unsteadily from the chair. 'You don't have to... Milos could identify the... Gareth.'

Sarah looked up at him. 'I need to know. To be sure.' She took an unsteady step.

'If you'd like to follow me.' Swift was glad of Greenhalgh's detached manner as she shepherded the little group towards the door of the viewing room. It made it sound like a television lounge in a down-market boarding house, thought Swift, stepping aside to let Milos go before him.

'Let me know when you're ready, and my colleague will turn back the sheet. Just tell us if you think it's Gareth. Take your time.' Greenhalgh paused with her hand on the door handle. 'OK?'

Sarah nodded slowly and glanced at Milos. Suddenly Milos turned away from her and found himself facing Swift.

'Don't,' he muttered.

Greenhalgh stopped. 'It's fine, we can take as long as you need.'

'She doesn't need to see. It's him. It's Gareth.'

'Milos?' Sarah's voice was barely a whisper, her face so pale that Swift prepared to catch her if she began to sway. 'What have you done?' She yanked Milos's arm, forcing him to turn and face her. 'What have you done?'

Julie stopped the car in front of a metal gate that spanned the lane. The catch was held in place by an old horseshoe, battered into the thick gatepost. The gate had dropped and the road bore the scars of repeated opening and closing, an arc of damaged tarmac. By the time she had opened the gate, got back into the car, driven through and wrestled the gate back into position she was already cursing this unaccustomed road furniture. The single-track lane snaked behind her, and ahead of her it disappeared up into the hillside between stands of pine forest. She was standing in the bottom of a steep valley, its sides covered with banks of trees, vertical outcrops of rock and small fields which gradually gave way to moorland at the very top, where it was too steep to take a tractor. There was just one tiny cottage, off down a track to the left, but otherwise she was completely alone. Then someone coughed.

Julie whirled round. Above her, and peering through the fence, was a sheep. It blinked, and chewed thoughtfully.

'You frightened me to death,' she said to the sheep. 'I don't suppose you can tell me where Cwm Nefal Cottage is?' She climbed into the car and closed the door, so she didn't hear the muttering of the shepherd who sat in the trees on his quad bike, nor see him watching her as she drove away.

'Just along here on the right, it is.'

Barely into the shade of the trees, two freshly painted white stones stood either side of a driveway on the right hand side of the lane. A tall metal sign told her she had reached Cwm Nefal, exactly as the woman in the shop had said. Adam was on the drive, scraping mud from his cycling shoes. He put down the brush and clattered over to the car, cleats clacking on the tarmac.

'You found it!' He opened her door and as she stepped out he wrapped her in a hug.

'You've been out on the bike?' she asked, as the familiar waft of triathlete in training greeted her.

'You're not a copper for nothing. Just back. I didn't expect you so soon.'

'The DI's let me off early.' She locked the car. 'There was a suspicious death this morning, up there somewhere.' She pointed to the south.

'And you said it would be really boring here after the great metrop.'

'It's probably a suicide.'

'Oh well, you have to be thankful for small mercies.'

Julie shook her head.

'Joke, Jules.' Adam smiled as if to demonstrate. 'And Menna next door says you don't really need to lock the car up here.'

'Menna?'

'Neighbours. Menna and Gwyn.'

'Neighbours? You're joking. There's nothing here.'

'They're just up the lane, in a farm about quarter of a mile up that way.' He nodded vaguely in the direction of the lane. 'I'll show you later.'

'Right. You've obviously been busy unpacking then?'

'They were checking the sheep and noticed the lorry, so they came to introduce themselves.'

'I bet they did.'

'They're OK. You'll like them. Once you've run a background check on them.'

'Oh very good. Have you unpacked the kettle? I need a brew and a guided tour, in that order.'

A Land Rover swung into the drive and a middle-aged woman wearing working clothes and wellingtons clambered out of the cab, leaving the engine running.

'It's Menna,' said Adam. 'I wonder what the problem is?'

'You must be Julie,' Menna said. 'I've got a message from Craig Swift. He says can you get back to the station, there's been a development.' She climbed back into the Land Rover. 'Oh, and he says you need to get your phone sorted pronto.'

'Thanks,' shouted Julie over the roar of the engine, but Menna was already reversing down the drive at speed. She waved and was gone.

'I knew it was too good to last,' said Julie.

'I'll have unpacked the kettle by the time you get back.'

CHAPTER NINE

The interview room smelled of new paint – mushroom-coloured emulsion over woodchip wallpaper. The regulation orange plastic chairs and the plastic-topped table must have been relatively new. Milos sat on one side of the table. Julie was on the other side, checking the recorder. Swift was still standing by the door. Julie cleared her throat and pressed record.

'Interview with Milos Watkin. Monday, 25th April, 19.15 hours. Those present Detective Sergeant Julie Kite…'

'Detective Inspector Craig Swift.'

'And…' Julie looked at Milos who was concentrating at the matt grey surface of the table and refused to meet her gaze. 'For the tape, Mr Watkin.'

'Are you charging me?' Milos looked up at Swift like a belligerent child. 'What with?'

'Also present Mr Milos Watkin, Penrhiw Farm,' said Swift. 'Look, Milos, we'll know more tomorrow, after the inquest, but the pathologist has concerns.' He crossed to the table and pulled out the chair next to Julie. 'We just want a chat. You're not under arrest, you're free to leave at any time.

'Right then.' Milos shoved his chair backwards and placed both hands on the table. His nails, Julie noticed, were black with oil, his fingers split and cracked.

'But,' continued Swift, 'it might be easier to tell us everything you know while it's still fresh in your mind.' He took off his glasses and rubbed his eyes, then put them back on and looked directly at Milos. 'Just so there are no misunderstandings later.'

Julie attempted a small smile, but Milos cast her a glance of pure contempt. 'Misunderstandings?'

'So how did you know it was Gareth's body in the mortuary?' asked Julie, watching the frown cross Milos's face as the question landed.

'*He* said it was Gareth.' Milos gestured towards Swift with his pointed, unshaven chin. 'Sarah didn't need to see. That was the only reason I said what I did.'

'And there's no other reason?' Julie's face was all wide-eyed innocence.

'Don't be bloody stupid, woman, what other reason could there be?'

'We just need to get our facts straight,' said Swift.

Milos sat back in his chair. 'Facts?'

Julie opened the manila folder in front of her. She kept the flap of the folder over the photographs inside, so Milos was not able to see the damage to his brother's face. 'The pathologist says he was shot in the head, twice.'

'She can she tell that, can she?'

'It wasn't terribly difficult.' Swift said.

'With all that damage?' Milos replied.

'Damage?' asked Julie, closing the folder.

Milos shut his eyes. 'You said he'd been shot in the head. There had to be damage.'

'Milos,' Swift's voice was softer now. 'We know it was you who made the call about the biker.'

'I don't see how you could know that. And why would I phone you and not stay with Gareth if I'd seen what happened. He was my brother for God's sake.'

'The motor cyclist,' said Julie. 'You couldn't just leave him to die in the ditch, could you?' Milos was silent, staring at her.

'And then there's the problem of the gun,' said Swift.

'Or rather the guns,' added Julie.

Milos gripped the edge of the table and shifted in his chair, 'Guns?'

'As I said, Gareth was shot twice.' Julie opened the folder, again sparing Milos from the close ups of the bloodied mess that had been his brother. 'Once with what we believe to be a hand gun and then with a shotgun from point blank range.' She looked up at Milos, who looked away, then down at his hands.

'And how can they be sure about the hand gun?'

'Apart from the fact that most of the back of his head is missing from the shotgun blast, we've been informed that there's pitting on a bullet which was found in Gareth's temple. That pitting was caused by the shotgun pellets, which tells us that the pistol shot came first,' said Swift. 'We think the shotgun cartridge was home made, so it will be fairly easy to identify where it came from.'

'I didn't think it would still be...' Milos clenched the fingers of his right hand and clamped his mouth shut.

'And,' said Julie, 'the pathologist says that it's possible he may have already been dead when the shotgun was fired.'

'Shit,' said Milos. '*May* have been? You're winding me up, you bitch.'

Julie shook her head. 'No, Mr Watkin. I'm not.'

'But I thought... It was pretty obvious that... Oh Jesus Christ, I just wanted...' he wiped his eyes with the cuff of his jumper. 'For Sarah. And for Mam.' He shuddered and looked up at Swift. 'For God's sake, Craig, you know how things were after Dad. I didn't want them to think he'd killed himself.' Milos rocked in his chair and put his head in his hands. 'He was dead, Craig. I know he was dead.'

'Was there a note?'

Milos looked up at Swift and nodded.

'Did you keep it?' asked Julie.

'I shredded it. I didn't want them getting hold of it.'

'What did it say?' asked Swift.

'That it had come back. It was the bloody cancer. Gareth always said that if it did he wasn't going through it all again. Said

49

he wouldn't put the family through it. Not with the kids… seeing him like that. You wouldn't want a dog to suffer like he did.'

'I know, Milos. We were mates once, remember?'

Milos nodded and wiped his nose on his sleeve.

'Can you remember *exactly* what the note said?' asked Julie.

'Just what I said,' said Milos.

'Was it hand written?'

'I'd not have been able to read it if it was.'

Swift smiled. 'I remember. You'd never have been able to copy from him at school. I always said he should have been a doctor rather than a lawyer.'

'So the note might be on his computer?' said Julie.

'It's not on the one at the farm. I checked.' Milos was squirming now as he looked up at Swift from under heavy black eyebrows.

'So,' said Swift, 'you just happened to find him up there?'

Milos shook his head. 'I heard the shot. I'd just gone up to check the lambs and I heard the gunshot. I didn't see it happen.'

'But you saw something?'

'I saw the bike had gone off the road, I could see it through the binoculars. I couldn't see Gareth though, not until I got over there.' Milos closed his eyes. 'I thought they'd both killed themselves, but the lad was alive when I got to him. Is he… He's not dead, is he?'

'Thanks to you, he's still very much alive in hospital,' said Swift.

Milos sighed and stared up at the ceiling. 'Good. But he's not going to keep quiet about what he saw for too long, is he? How long will it be before everyone knows that Gareth killed himself?'

'So you really thought that Gareth had shot himself?' asked Julie.

For the first time, Milos looked at her and answered her directly. 'It was just like Dad, lying dead in the barn with that same pistol in his hand.'

'So where is the pistol now? Did you take it away with you?'

'We need that gun, Milos,' Swift said.

'I didn't take the gun home. I swear I didn't.'

50

'So what would be the point of shooting your brother in the head with a shotgun to make it look like an accident and then leaving the pistol with which you thought he had committed suicide near the body, Mr Watkin?'

'For Christ's sake. I don't know. Would you be thinking straight if you'd just found your brother's body out there on the hill? I was so angry with him. I must have picked it up and hurled it away from him if you say it wasn't there. I don't know where it went. But I didn't take it away from there, it must still be up there somewhere.' Milos had leaned across the table as he spoke, and he was shouting into Julie's face now.

'We have retrieved your father's pistol, Mr Watkin. Our officers found it at the bungalow. It is already being examined by ballistics experts,' she said, not backing away from him. She could smell his breath and his greasy hair, the stench of sheep on his shirt.

Milos stared at her. 'You're wrong, woman. I didn't take it from there. It's still out on the hill.' Milos sprang to his feet, knocking his chair backwards.

'All right, Milos.' Swift stood and picked up Milos's chair. 'We have to do this. Let's just calm down and sort it out.'

'Does she have to be here? What does she know about us?'

'Yes,' said Swift. 'She does.'

The canteen was deserted. Nerys was long gone and Swift plied the vending machine with ten pence pieces.

'Are you sure you want it black?' he asked as he put the plastic cup down in front of her.'

Julie peered into its depths. 'Thank you. Sir, can I just ask?'

'Yes, Julie.'

'Why did we let Milos go?'

'I don't think he's going anywhere, do you? Besides, Dr Greenhalgh has already confirmed that Gareth *was* almost certainly dead before the shotgun was used on him. We'll know for sure tomorrow.'

'So you're happy that it's suicide?'

'Happy doesn't really describe it.'

'Sorry, Sir. I meant…'

'I know what you meant.' Swift traced the rim of his plastic cup with a stubby finger. 'I'm pretty certain Gareth was already dead before Milos shot him. I'm absolutely certain that Milos shot him, or rather shot the body, and then I think he left, taking his shotgun from the scene. Maybe he was in shock and just can't remember picking up the pistol, but we scoured that area and found nothing. We'll just have to wait for ballistics to confirm what we already know.'

'So why did he do it?'

'My guess would be exactly what he said. To make it look like an accident. He probably thought we could blame the Army.'

'I wouldn't have thought the Army would use shotguns with home-made cartridges though, Sir?'

'I don't suppose he was thinking too rationally at the time, Sergeant.'

'So why was it so important that it was an accident?'

'Suicide's still got a huge stigma attached to it in some quarters, and as you know, it's not a happy place for the Watkin clan.'

'Old man Watkin.'

Swift nodded slowly. 'To make things a million times worse, Milos and one of the neighbours got into a really vicious fight at the father's funeral. The bloke called his father a coward, for leaving his wife and kids to struggle on in the aftermath of Foot and Mouth. It nearly went to court. Milos laid him out in The Feathers and threatened to kill him. I wasn't here when it happened. I'd been sent to work in Merthyr temporarily, after a slight misunderstanding with Gareth and a gang of his mates over a protest meeting. My DI thought it would be a good idea to keep us apart for a while.' Swift smiled. 'He was a good bloke, old Gwyn.' He scratched his ear. 'Apparently though, feeling was bad enough for the neighbour to bring charges for assault.'

'Did Milos get away with it?'

'I'm not sure of the detail, I only had it all second-hand, but it seems Ella Watkin had been good friends with the neighbour's brother at one time, and she went round to smooth things over and eventually he dropped the complaint.'

'Friends, Sir?'

'Let's concentrate on the little matter in hand shall we, Sergeant.' Swift grinned. 'It'll take you a while to get up to speed with local history and family trees, let alone any extra-marital shenanigans that might or might not be lurking out there.'

'Fair enough. But shouldn't we be charging Milos with tampering with the body at the very least?'

'I'm sure we'll have to eventually, but I don't want to bring him in just yet. They'll be struggling enough up there right now without having to sort out the stock without him as well.' Julie frowned. 'They're still lambing, Sergeant,' said Swift, leaving her none the wiser.

'So we still have to establish whether it was actually suicide?'

'Hopefully ballistics will sort that one out. I'll get another search started up on the hill if we don't find the other pistol at Penrhiw. And we'll go to Gareth's office straight after the PM in the morning. I'll phone his partners now and ask them not to touch anything of Gareth's.'

'Then there's the bloke on the motor bike.'

'He's not going anywhere either. He'll wait until tomorrow. Get yourself home, or it won't be worth going.'

Julie inched the car down the lane, which looked even narrower in the dark, until she found the gate. She wrestled with the catch for the third time in as many hours, barely able to make out what she was doing in the glow from the car's headlights. When she finally yanked the gate open it dropped on its hinges, hitting the tarmac and missing her foot by inches. She dragged it open and climbed wearily back into the car. She'd never appreciated how easy it had been to park outside her own numbered garage and saunter into the flat, floodlit every inch of the way by strategic street lights. She drove through the gate and sighed as she got out of the car to close it behind her. The hills glowered above her. It was pitch dark, but she knew they were there, closing in around her. It was a relief to turn into her drive and see the lights of the cottage glowing almost yellow from the windows set deep into the thick stone walls. It looked like one of the jigsaws her gran had liked.

She parked the car and crossed the yard. She noticed, with some satisfaction, that the kitchen door already had a cat flap. All she had to do was teach the cat how to use it. Maybe he wouldn't even know what to do with himself in the great outdoors. He wouldn't be alone in that department. She smiled to herself and pushed the door open. She could hear Adam's voice from somewhere in the house, in a one-sided phone conversation. At least Adam's mobile provider seemed to reach the parts hers didn't.

Julie filled the kettle and tried the cupboards. Unpacking the kitchen stuff hadn't been high on his list, then. There were two large boxes by the table, one marked 'Bedroom' and the other 'Bike'. She grinned. That just about summed him up. She was still smiling as she went into the living room.

Adam had his back to her, one hand resting on the low central beam which spanned the room, the other holding the phone to his ear. He laughed at whatever was said at the other end, then said '…working, you know how it goes.'

Julie stopped in the doorway. She felt as though she was eavesdropping, but she stayed where she was.

Adam laughed again. 'Yeah. Leave it with me, I'll work something out, we could always say …'

The kettle whistled. Adam spun round and saw Julie by the door. 'Yes, that's no problem,' he said, looking at her, rolling his eyes as if in exasperation. 'I'll call to make an appointment.'

Julie could hear laughing at the other end of the phone as he ended the call.

She stepped back into the kitchen. 'Mugs?' she said.

He scurried after her. 'Jules… I was going to…'

'You've got your mobile working, then?'

'Menna says some networks are better than others. You'll need to change yours. It's a black spot apparently.'

'You can say that again. Who was that on the phone?'

Adam disappeared under the table. 'Just work,' he said. She heard tape ripping and he reappeared with two mugs and a teaspoon. 'School Secretary. I'll have to go back to Manchester for a couple of days, maybe this weekend. To pick up some stuff I forgot at school. That cupboard in my old form room's like a black hole.'

Julie opened the fridge and scanned the empty shelves. 'Milk?'

'Ah. I was going to go shopping. I nipped out on the bike for another hour, I needed a bit of a leg stretch after driving that lorry and the day just went.' He rummaged in the box marked 'Bedroom' and emerged with a jar of instant coffee. 'I'll go tomorrow. Menna says there's a Morrisons in Brecon and a Tesco in Llandrindod, she says—'

'You're getting on well with the neighbours then.'

'You know me.'

'Oh I do.' She picked up her bag. 'I'm going to bed. Early start tomorrow, post mortem first thing.'

'Ah.'

'Go on.'

'I've not actually found the sheets yet.'

CHAPTER TEN
Tuesday, 26th April

It was still only 7.45 am, but there were ambulances already queuing outside the hospital's A & E entrance, and one or two white-faced relatives clutching plastic sacks containing crumpled pyjamas and half-empty bottles of barley water making their way back to their cars. The usual gaggle of patients in dressing gowns was having an illicit early-morning smoke by the door to the X-Ray Department.

Pathology was as far as it was possible to get from the action. The departmental equivalent of the bed by the door, thought Julie. Swift held the door open for her, and gestured down the corridor. She breathed in the clean smell of polish and surgical spirit and wondered, as she did every time she found herself in a hospital, why she hadn't concentrated on her A Levels. She could have been a pathologist herself, even a surgeon. Yeah, right, like she'd have kept her nose in her books for another five years. She smiled to herself. Swift, she noticed, looked pale.

Kay Greenhalgh was waiting for them. Even at this hour she was brisk and business-like. She wore green scrubs and short white wellingtons which, on anyone else, would have looked ridiculous.

'Morning, both. Oh dear, Craig, you do look peaky.' She looked at her notes. 'Shouldn't take too long. I won't keep you longer than absolutely necessary. Of course, you could always wait outside, if…'

'It's fine,' breathed Swift. 'Let's just get on with it, shall we?'

Greenhalgh looked up from her notes, her face serious. She

looked back at her folder, looked up at Swift and beamed. 'It's your lucky day.'

'You mean it's likely to improve?'

'We were in early. We've finished your Mr Watkin.'

Swift's shoulders relaxed and he exhaled slowly. 'Why didn't you say?'

'I didn't know if we'd manage to fit him in before you got here. There's been a bad smash on the Heads of the Valleys. I thought you'd like him out of the way, as it were, before they start arriving. I was told he was a friend.'

'We were in Young Farmers together, though he was a lot younger than me.' Swift let out a breath. 'Thanks, it's appreciated. So. What's the gist? How long did he have left?'

'With a fair wind, probably thirty years.'

'But what about the cancer?'

Doctor Greenhalgh flicked through her notes. 'Whoever did the surgery did a fabulous job. You can hardly tell. And there's no sign of any recurrence.' She turned the page. 'Slightly fatty liver, but no more than you'd expect from the age and profession.' She looked up at Swift. 'You're all a bit too partial to the liquid lunch aren't you, you chaps over a certain age.'

Julie stifled a smile. 'So we've got a suicide note which leads the victim's brother to say he killed himself because his cancer had come back,' she said. 'You think that's not true?'

'I haven't found any evidence of it, at the original site or anywhere else.'

Swift frowned. 'What about the head wound? Could you confirm the sequence of events?'

'Small bore pistol shot to the right temple. Point blank. Shotgun damage post mortem, also virtually point blank.' She looked up from the folder. 'It's a wonder there was any of his skull left at all, but there'd have been much more blood around if he'd still been alive. It was definitely a home-made cartridge by the looks of things, and with what was in it, well it could easily have stopped an elephant.'

'So it looks like suicide?' asked Swift.

'There's not much of the original wound left to go on, but from what I can make out from where the bullet was lodged, the angle looks right, but that's not to say it was suicide. It could just as easily have been murder. The bullet's interesting though. Not like anything I've seen before. Foreign, maybe Eastern European?'

'And the eyes,' asked Julie. 'Was it the birds?'

'It looks like it.' She looked up at Julie and smiled. It was probaby crows rather than kites, from the condition of the sockets. And of course we didn't find the eyes at the locus.' Julie swallowed and Swift thrust his hand into his pocket. 'And there were a couple of rather nasty cuts on the eyelids and around the nose.' Kay looked back to her notes. 'Where he'd obviously been pecked quite viciously.'

Julie shivered. 'The eyes,' she said, 'better than the alternative scenario.'

Swift dabbed his lips with his handkerchief, still folded, which he returned to his jacket pocket. 'Time of death?'

'From the stomach contents, which consisted of—'

Swift held up his hand. 'Just a time will be fine.'

Greenhalgh suppressed a smile and ran a finger down the page. 'From the stomach contents I'd say around eleven, eleven-thirty yesterday morning, give or take an hour.'

'And you're absolutely sure the shotgun didn't kill him?'

'Positive.'

'And the bullet from the hand gun?' asked Julie.

'I sent it to ballistics a couple of hours ago. It's a good job your rifleman wasn't quite on target or there'd have been nothing left. Maybe he was squeamish.'

'Thank you, Kay,' said Swift. 'I wasn't looking forward to…'

'I know.' Greenhalgh closed the file and looked up at him. 'It's different when you know them.'

Back outside on the corridor, Swift's colour had returned, along with his good humour.

'Thank God Milos is off the hook.'

'For murder, Sir, anyway.' What was wrong with him? Why was he so reluctant to charge Milos? At the very least he could be done for tampering with the body.

'Yes, Sergeant, for the murder.'

'So, what's next? Shall I go back to the GP and ask for Watkin's medical records?'

'We'll go on the way back to the station. I want to go into Builth anyway, and take a look at his office. They've been told not to touch anything of Gareth's until we get there.' Swift held the door open for her. 'So how was your first night in Cwm Nefal?'

'Dark, Sir. I woke up in the night and thought I was dead, it was totally black.'

'You'll get used to it. I'm guessing it was too quiet for you?'

'I've never realised how noisy the countryside actually is. I'm used to cars, buses and drunks, but how loud are sheep?'

Swift laughed. 'Only this time of year really, when the lambs are around. And when they're weaned of course. Then you'll hear them.'

They were outside now, and Swift's stride slowed.

'And there were owls. And then there was something scrabbling about in the loft about four o'clock this morning.'

'It might be a bit early, but it could be bats.'

'Bats? Oh my God. You're joking.'

'They'd only be pipistrelles, they're tiny little things.'

Julie squirmed. 'How do you get rid of bats?'

'You don't. They're a protected species.'

Julie sighed and Swift laughed again. 'You'll get used to it. My wife's from Swansea and it took her a while to get used to it up here. Twenty minutes to a decent supermarket she said.' He pressed the key fob and the Volvo squawked. 'You'll have to meet her. She says it's about time we had more women in CID.'

'Should we go and see if the motorcyclist's fit to talk, Sir, while we're here?'

Swift opened the car door. 'No, let's leave him to Rhys. They're probably still in the throes of breakfast up there. Besides, we wouldn't want DC Williams to feel left out would we?'

CHAPTER ELEVEN

Watkin's office was at the end of a long row of shops at the bottom of the High Street. It must have been a shop at one time too, and still had a large window on either side of the door. One of the windows had a few local small adverts and a large poster advertising a Young Farmers' rally. A row of highly polished brass plaques gave the names of the partners, Jones, Watkin and Powell.

A young woman was seated behind a desk just inside the door. She blew her nose on a damp, black-smudged paper handkerchief as they entered. Julie had her warrant card in her hand, but the receptionist didn't look at her.

'Mr Swift,' she said, her bottom lip beginning to quiver. 'Mr Powell's just told me.'

'I know, Bryony love.' Swift patted her hand, and Julie slid her warrant card back into her pocket.

'They're saying he was shot. Is it true? Why would anyone want to shoot Mr Watkin?'

'Well we're not sure what happened yet, but we'll find out. Do you think you can answer a couple of questions for me?'

Bryony blew her nose again and ventured a cautious nod.

'How did Mr Watkin seem yesterday? Was he in the office?'

'He was, but just first thing. He had an appointment with a client at the Metropole Hotel in Llandrindod at half past nine. Then he had a meeting at County Hall and said he'd be back here by three.'

Julie wrote down the names and times in her notebook. 'And what did he do before he left in the morning?'

'There was a partners' meeting. He was late for that and Mrs Jones wasn't pleased.' She gave a rueful little smile. 'Mrs Jones is never very pleased. The meeting didn't last long, and he left straight afterwards.' Bryony's face crumpled. 'He told me how much he liked my hair.' A huge sob choked her words. 'Just… had it… cut.'

'Did he collect his post as usual?' Julie persisted.

Bryony shook her head. 'There were just a few bits from Saturday's post. Yesterday's didn't arrive until after he left. I gave it to Mr Jones this morning.'

'Did you usually open his correspondence for him?'

Bryony blew her nose. 'Yes, he likes… liked me to get the client files out to go with the incoming mail.'

'And his e-mails?'

'I didn't look at his e-mails. He's been dealing with those himself for the past few weeks, even if it meant him working late at home.'

'Did he check them yesterday before he left?'

'I don't know.' Bryony sagged in her chair and sighed. 'He did go to his office, but he can't have been more than a minute or two in there, then he left for Llandrindod. That was the last time I saw him.'

'So he didn't mention receiving anything unusual or important?' Julie asked.

Bryony shook her head. Tears began to gather, and Swift dived in before she started to cry again. 'Is Mr Powell in, or Mr Jones?'

Bryony sniffed. 'Mr Powell's at the Mags, but Mr Jones is in his office.'

'Shall we go straight in?'

Dic Jones was sitting behind his desk. There was a beige folder on the blotter and his briefcase was on the corner of the desk, both unopened. He got to his feet, shook Swift's hand, nodded to Julie and sank back into his chair.

'Terrible business,' he muttered, almost to himself.

'Dic, this is Detective Sergeant Kite,' said Swift, lowering himself into one of the visitors' chairs and gesturing for Julie to sit. Jones did not acknowledge that he had heard. 'We need to have a look through Gareth's things. Take a look at his computer. Would that be all right?'

This appeared to bring Jones back to his senses. 'Have you got a warrant?'

'Do we need one?'

'Client confidentiality, Craig. You know how it works.'

'I can get a warrant, of course,' said Swift. 'But maybe you could help us to establish what Gareth was working on, whether there was anything in his e-mails which might have caused…'

'Do you think it was suicide?'

'We don't know.'

'Like his father.' Dic stared at the leather blotter on his desk. 'We just don't know at this stage. What we need is anything you can tell us about his state of mind.'

'He was the same as always. He'd finally got back into his running, signed up for the Cardiff half-marathon in October. He laughed about being back in peak condition when he brought in the sponsor form.'

'You didn't get the feeling he'd had bad news of any sort recently?'

'No, he was his old self. How he'd been before his illness.'

'And he didn't give you the impression he thought that the cancer was back?'

'No, definitely not.'

'Can you show us his computer?' asked Julie.

'Jones stood up and took a bunch of keys from the top drawer of his desk. The three of them walked out of his office, through Reception, where Bryony was surreptitiously attempting to repair her mascara with the aid of a small oblong mirror, and down a short, dark corridor towards the back of the building. He selected a large key from the bunch and jiggled it into the lock in Gareth's door.

The room was tidy. There wasn't a stray piece of paper or even a treasury tag out of place. The chairs had been pushed underneath the leather-topped partners' desk and the plants had been recently watered, Julie noted.

'Does he usually leave his office like this?'

'Well he wasn't untidy, but there were usually piles of things he was working on, correspondence he needed to reply to.' Dic shook his head. 'Maybe he's taken them home. He did that sometimes if he had to catch up.'

'And the computer?' prompted Swift.

'Of course.' Jones flipped open the lid and switched it on. Dic waited until the police officers had looked away before he entered the password. When they looked back, the screensaver had appeared. It was a photograph of Sarah and the children. Seren was laughing and the little boy clutched a threadbare soft toy, a horse maybe, in a pudgy hand.

'That was a couple of years ago,' Dic said. 'Young Dylan has started school now.'

They waited while he brought up the e-mail system and scanned the subject column.

'There doesn't look as though there's anything out of the ordinary here, just the usual… oh. That's strange.' He scrolled down and back up the page. 'He seems to have deleted all last week's e-mails.'

'What about documents?' asked Julie. 'Can you tell if there are any documents he may have written which might be missing?'

'Just a moment.' Dic pushed the mouse, clicking frantically. 'He files all his outgoing documents here in this folder… Same thing here. Nothing since a week last Friday.'

'Could they be in the recycle bin?' suggested Swift.

As they waited for Dic Jones to check the system, Swift raised an eyebrow at Julie. There had to be something worth looking at here.

'No. Nothing. He's emptied everything.'

'Maybe our IT boys can retrieve something,' said Swift. 'If we could take the laptop with us.'

'I'm not sure. There are records on here which will almost certainly relate to members of your staff. You know what it's like, in an area like this. How can I be sure that the information will remain confidential? It could compromise our position, our good name.'

'Dic,' said Swift quietly, 'I don't have to tell you how important this could be. There is a remote possibility that this wasn't suicide.'

'You can't mean murder?'

'We just don't know as things stand. The post mortem has raised as many questions as it's solved. It would really help us to know as much as possible about Gareth's state of mind just prior to the incident.'

'Can you guarantee that our files will remain confidential?'

'You have my word, Dic. Nothing which isn't relevant to this case will get out of the IT office.' Swift eased himself out of the visitor's chair and stood up. 'You know I could get a warrant.'

Dic Jones rubbed his temple and looked from the screen to Swift and back again. 'Yes, of course. If there's anything I can do to help you sort out this mess.'

'Thank you,' said Swift. 'We'll get it back to you just as soon as we can. Could you ask Eurig Powell to give me a call when he gets in? I just need to ask him whether he noticed anything unusual in the last few days.'

'He won't be back until late this afternoon probably, but I'll text him now and leave a message.' Jones zipped the laptop into its case and handed it to Swift.

'Just one more thing,' said Julie as she turned to leave. 'Did Mr Watkin usually take his laptop home with him at night?'

Dr Peters was apologetic. To the disgust of the patient who had been halfway to his door, having deposited her number in the little wooden rack by the reception desk, he ushered Julie and Craig straight past her and into his room. Watkin's file was already on his desk. He motioned for them to sit, but with only one chair, Swift left Julie to oblige.

'So, Doctor, was there any sign that Gareth's cancer had returned?' asked Swift.

'None whatsoever. He'd just had his six-monthly check-up and they were very pleased with him.'

'So he was in good health?' asked Julie.

'I'd say so. He'd worked extremely hard to claw his way back to fitness. He had even insisted on jogging while he was still on chemo, although I had advised him against it.'

'So he wasn't the sort to give in?'

'Just the opposite I would have said.' Peters tapped the fat bundle of notes with his pen. 'When you've been through all this, life has to be precious.'

'And there wasn't any history of depression?'

'If you're asking me do I think he was a candidate for suicide, then no, Sergeant. He didn't strike me as the sort of person who would take his own life.' He stood, bringing their consultation to a close. 'But suicide is not an exact science, of course.'

They left the doctor's room and his next patient jammed her number back into the rack and strode past them, muttering as she went.

'Who'd be a doctor?' whispered Swift, loudly.

'Oh I don't know, Sir, there are worse jobs.'

They walked out into the sunshine and Swift patted his pockets, looking for his car keys. 'I'd like you to go and have a brief chat with Dic's wife while we're here.' He climbed into the driver's seat of the Volvo. 'It will probably be a brief audience though. She's not an easy lady to work with apparently.'

'Aren't you coming?'

'I'd just like to see what you think of her. It's handy, you not having met any of them before.'

Julie nodded. 'Is she a solicitor too?'

Swift turned to look over his shoulder and reversed carefully out of the parking space. 'She's a paralegal I think. She used to run the office. When Dic started out on his own it was just the two of them. She did the accounts and the marketing, and he used his local contacts to build up the business.' He nosed the car out of the car park. 'They've been very successful too, over the years. Rather more successful than poor Ella up at Penrhiw.'

'Sorry, Sir?'

'They're sisters, Sergeant, but moving in slightly different circles these days.'

'Oh, right. Is everyone round here related, Sir?'

Swift nodded. 'Pretty much.'

'You've no idea why Bryony would say Mrs Jones wasn't happy with Gareth?'

'Sorry, I haven't, but I have every confidence you'll find out.' Swift indicated and turned onto the bridge across the River Wye. 'I'll drop you off at the house now and when you've finished with Catherine Jones, we'll head back to Penrhiw.'

CHAPTER TWELVE

Swift dropped Julie at the end of a sweeping gravel drive, which wound its way through manicured lawns and small groups of ornamental shrubs. As she approached the house there were neat flowerbeds with crisp edges and stone toadstools. The house was large, double-fronted and Victorian; warm, red brick walls with pale sandstone corners and lintels and artfully draped curtains in the deep bay windows. Julie pulled the bell and could hear it tinkling in the depths of the house, then footsteps clacking on a tiled floor.

Catherine Jones was the image of her sister, petite and dark-haired, but there the similarity ended. While Ella had shown the same sense of stylish flair in yesterday's funeral outfit, Catherine's clothes were the real deal, iris-blue linen ankle-grazers and a pale blue silk blouse with tiny diamante roses on the collar and cuffs. Her engagement ring, Julie noticed, had a single diamond as large as anything she had ever seen. She smiled, remembering the times in Manchester (when she and Helen were supposed to be working) that she had been diverted past Boodles in King Street to gaze at the sea of artfully-arranged rocks. It was Helen's ambition to have an engagement ring of at least those proportions, and the high flier to go with it.

Julie flashed her warrant card. If Catherine Jones was perturbed by a visit from the police it wasn't obvious. She opened the door wider.

'Do come in, Sergeant. What can I do for you?' She led the way down a long hallway lined with photographs. There was Dic

Jones, holding a golfing trophy aloft, Gareth and Sarah's wedding with a glowering Milos squeezed into a dark suit, the arms and legs of which were several inches too short, and there were various photographs of Seren and Dylan, school photographs and snaps taken on the farm and at the seaside. At the end of the corridor, Catherine led the way into a huge sunny kitchen, all Farrow & Ball creams and greys and pale oak surfaces. So this was what Elephant's Breath looked like in real life. How the other half lives, thought Julie. Swift was right. It was nothing like the damp and peeling wallpaper at Penrhiw.

'Do sit, Sergeant.'

Julie sat. Catherine spooned coffee into a cafetière and flicked the switch on a cream enamelled kettle.

'I was sorry to hear the awful news about your nephew, Mrs Jones.'

Catherine turned her back and reached up into a cupboard for china mugs. 'I can't take it in, Sergeant. Why on earth would Gareth want to kill himself?' She placed the cups on the worktop and turned the handles so they were facing in the same direction. 'He had so much to live for. It's such a waste.'

'Have you spoken to your sister?'

Catherine nodded. 'Of course. Dic and I visited the farm briefly yesterday evening. We went up as soon as we heard.'

'Who told you the news?'

'Ella phoned. Sarah was in no fit state to do anything.'

'Mrs Jones, I've come to ask about your relationship with Gareth.'

'Gareth was my nephew.' She frowned. Perfectly sculpted eyebrows knitted towards each other. 'What sort of relationship do you expect us to have had? Perhaps you could get to the point, Sergeant.'

'I understand you weren't very happy with Mr Watkin yesterday morning?'

'Oh for goodness sake.' Catherine's polished nails tapped on the worktop.

Julie smiled benignly. 'Just for our records.'

'Gareth was late for a meeting. It was nothing more exciting than that, I'm afraid.' The tapping stopped. 'So who told you about it?'

'That's not important. I wonder if you could tell me where you were yesterday morning, after the meeting in the office had concluded, say between 10am and noon?'

'I was in the office and then at a funeral at St Mary's Church.' Suddenly Catherine picked up her mobile phone from the counter. 'I'm phoning my husband, this is ridiculous. This sort of accusation could undermine the unblemished reputation of our practice.'

'There's no need for that, Mrs Jones. Nobody's accusing you of anything. I am simply trying to ascertain Gareth's state of mind yesterday morning. Was it usual for you to have words with him?'

'It was perfectly normal business banter. I'm sure you're *au fait* with banter, Sergeant, in your line of work.'

Julie made a couple of flourishes in her notebook. The kettle hummed discreetly and Catherine poured water into the cafetière, spilling some onto the pale worktop.

Julie traced a delicate knot in the wood of the table with her finger. 'Would you have any idea why anyone would want to harm Gareth?'

'Harm Gareth? Dear God, Sergeant, you're not actually trying to say he was … Do you honestly think he didn't kill himself?'

'We have reason to believe the death was suspicious, but we have no further information at the moment.'

Catherine reached for a pale grey jacket and a set of car keys on a Mercedes fob. 'I'm sorry, Sergeant, but I'm going to have to ask you to leave. I need to speak to my husband as a matter of urgency.'

CHAPTER THIRTEEN

Swift had pulled off the main road and they started to climb towards the Watkin farm. It was like being towed upwards in a glider, thought Julie. When you got to the top of the hill you half expected to be launched into nothingness, the white silence of riding the thermals.

A low metal barrier separated the car from a deep chasm where the rocks were twisted and folded. They were still in their layers, but dipping steeply away from the horizontal. Was this how Sarah felt now, stepping into the unknown on her own, everything tilted. Except she wasn't on her own, was she?

'Sir.' She turned to look at Swift who was concentrating on the narrow strip of zig-zagging tarmac. There was a shudder as the car crossed a cattle grid. 'Do you think there could be something going on between Milos and Sarah?'

'Going on, Sergeant?'

'You know, Sir.'

'I don't think I do.' Swift changed gear and swerved round a ewe who sat steadfastly in the middle of the road.

'Could they have been having an affair?'

'What, and Gareth found out and topped himself?'

'It does happen. And it would give Milos a motive for trying to cover up his suicide.'

'I can't see it. Milos? He's not exactly her type is he? Gareth and Sarah were close. They'd been together since they were kids.'

'All the same, maybe we could ask?'

'Let's leave it for now.' Swift slowed to turn into the lane to the farm and shot Julie a glance. 'Good idea though, it's always possible.'

A black-clad figure darted across the lane and disappeared behind the broad trunk of a huge oak tree.

'Who the hell…' Swift stamped on the brakes and the Volvo spluttered to a stop and stalled.

'I saw him yesterday.'

'How can you be sure it was the same person? He moved like sh… ' Swift turned the key in the ignition.

'How many people do you see dressed from head to foot in black – hat, gloves, the works?'

'Where was he when you saw him yesterday?'

'Back there, on the hill before the cattle grid. Shall I go after him, Sir?'

'He'll be long gone. Besides, you're not exactly dressed for fell running are you?' Swift glanced at Julie's beige wool jacket and pale suede boots. 'Very central Manchester, Sergeant.' He laughed. 'Don't worry, I'll get the local bobby to keep an eye open. He'll love the excitement.'

'Will they need a family liaison officer?'

'I'm not sure resources will quite run to that at the moment. Let's just see how they're doing. The neighbours will rally round.' Swift slowed the car as they approached the yard. 'Possibly too much.'

Seren was sitting on the low wall separating the tiny garden from the yard. Her arm was wrapped round the neck of the wall-eyed collie that had greeted them the previous afternoon. She watched them get out of the car and make their way over to her. The dog didn't move.

'Is it your dog?' asked Swift.

'It is now,' replied Seren.

'It was your Dad's, was it?' asked Julie.

The girl gave Julie a long stare. 'No. She was Uncle Milos's. He doesn't get on with her.' She pulled the dog even closer. 'He wanted to shoot her but Mam said I could keep her.'

Julie looked at Swift, but he kept his eyes on the girl and her dog. 'Does a lot of shooting then, Uncle Milos?' he asked.

'Just rabbits, foxes, injured sheep.' Seren jumped down from the wall. The dog followed her, all the while its head close to her hand. 'He says it's kinder to put some things out of their misery.'

Seren wandered off down the track towards the bungalow, the collie keeping close to her.

'Injured sheep and brothers?' Julie said.

Swift grimaced. 'We are keeping an open mind, aren't we, Sergeant?'

'Why don't they speak Welsh to you?' Julie asked, watching Seren disappear into the distance.

'They know you don't speak the language.' Swift scratched his ear. 'It goes back a long way. In the 1800s schools' inspectors introduced a rule that the children weren't allowed to speak Welsh in school. They said it led to immorality and ignorance.'

'But how could they do that, if it was their local language?'

Swift shrugged. 'The kids were punished for it. Even today, you'll find people who still accuse Welsh speakers of rudeness. They imagine Welsh is just a device to talk about strangers.'

'And do they use it that way?'

'Mostly they don't.' Swift smiled. 'But it makes them more cautious than they should be.' He shook his head. 'Maybe we should agree to steer clear of linguistic politics, Sergeant. This was a real enclave of Welsh at one time, this and the Elan Valley. And then the government cleared both of them. The workforce they brought in to build the dams over there was mostly from Ireland, so Welsh couldn't be used as a day-to-day language in the valley. Even for those whose homes hadn't been drowned to supply Birmingham with water.'

Julie nodded. 'So do you speak Welsh at home, Sir?'

Swift blushed and knocked hard on the farmhouse door. 'I know enough to understand what's going on.' He looked away from her as the door opened.

'You'd better come in,' said Ella. She seemed smaller than she had before and her face was more deeply lined than Julie remembered. Even from the back, as she led them down the narrow hallway, her shoulders showed the defeat Julie had seen in her eyes.

Ella showed them into the parlour. The clock still ticked, the room looked the same, apart from a sheaf of sympathy cards which already graced the mantelpiece.

'How are you?' Swift asked.

Ella shrugged. 'You have to carry on, don't you?' Carrying on, thought Julie, seemed far from Ella's mind at this moment, even as she mouthed the required words for the benefit of her visitors.

'How's Sarah?' Swift asked.

'How you'd expect,' replied Ella. 'Still in shock. We all are. I don't suppose you've any news for us?'

'No, not yet,' admitted Swift. 'There are one or two things which we need to sort out before we can be certain what happened out there.'

'It could have been the army, couldn't it, Craig?' Ella's eyes pleaded with Swift. 'Gareth was just in the wrong place at the wrong time?'

'So you've not spoken to Milos?'

Ella shook her head.

'There were no troops out on the hill yesterday, Ella.'

'No. I thought not.' She sat down heavily as though her legs would no longer hold her. 'So you think he killed himself.' It was a statement rather than a question.

'It's too early to say,' said Swift, sitting down next to her on the sofa. 'But we've a few things we need to check.' He continued to watch her face. 'Milos hasn't said anything to you about it?'

Ella shook her head. 'You know Milos, he never says much about anything. He didn't even tell me you'd been talking to him at the police station. Sarah told me.'

'Had Gareth seemed worried about anything lately?'

Ella picked at a loose thread on the arm of the sofa. 'I don't know whether it's anything. There was something in the post. About a week ago, addressed here instead of the bungalow.' She pulled the thread, which left a long snag in the cotton fabric.

'Did he say what was in it?'

'No. He just stuffed it into his pocket. But I could tell it wasn't good news.'

'Was it an official letter? A bill maybe?'

Ella shook her head. 'It was a small white envelope. Handwritten, with a first class stamp.'

'Do you remember seeing a postmark?'

'It was from Stockport. I only remember because that's where Phyllis's daughter moved to. Her son-in-law's from up there,' she jerked her head. 'They wanted her to move in with them. It's too much trouble for them to come down here to see her.'

'That's not very likely is it, Phyllis moving?' Swift asked.

'She'll not move there.' Ella smiled to herself. 'She went up for Easter to stay and couldn't wait to get back.'

'How did he seem, Gareth, when he read it?'

'He'd been laughing about something Dylan had done, but he didn't even finish telling me the tale. He read the letter and said he had to go out.'

'You don't know where?'

Ella pulled a large white handkerchief from the sleeve of her cardigan and dabbed her eyes. She shook her head.

'And otherwise, things were normal?'

'Better than normal. He was really positive, looking forward to the future for the first time in God knows how long.' Ella stifled a sob and blew her nose.

'Thank you,' said Swift. He patted her hand gingerly, as though it would burn him. 'You've been very helpful.' He stood up and looked at the cards on the mantelpiece. 'Is Sarah in the bungalow?'

'She'll be here now in a minute. I've sent Seren to fetch them. I thought I'd do a bit of lunch, see if I can get her to eat something.'

'I'd like a quick word with her, if that's all right.'

'You have your job to do, Craig. But be gentle with her, will you. She's not up to much at the moment.' Ella got to her feet and straightened up slowly, pushing the handkerchief back up her sleeve.

'We just need to check a few things, that's all. I'm so sorry about all this.'

'I know you are, Craig *bach*. Come into the kitchen.'

Swift sat at the table while Julie marvelled again at the view from the kitchen window. It was hard to believe that it was only twenty-four hours since she had been introduced to this barely tamed wilderness. Already it was beginning to look less desolate. Way down in the valley she could just make out a tiny figure.

'Is that your Milos?' she asked Ella.

Ella wiped her hands on her apron and picked up a pair of glasses from the window ledge. 'Where?'

'Down there, just above the trees,' said Julie, conscious of the fact that she had no idea what type of trees they were.

'I can see him. No. Not Milos.' Ella took off her glasses, opened a drawer and pulled out a pair of binoculars. 'So I can check the lambs,' she said, in answer to Julie's glance. She put the binoculars to her eyes and turned the focus. 'Now what's he doing back?'

'You've seen him before?' asked Julie.

'Yesterday,' said Ella, following the figure as he picked his way over the rough ground. Suddenly he stopped, and there was a small flash of light. 'Well, why would he do that? Do you think he's from the newspapers?'

Swift was beside Ella immediately, taking the binoculars from her. 'Photographs. The cheeky bugger's taking photographs.'

'Where did you see him yesterday?' Julie asked.

'He was up here by the gate when we left for the funeral. Sarah said he looked as though he was watching the house, but then she's a bit keen on the Agatha Christies, bless her.'

Swift handed Ella the binoculars and sat back down at the table. 'Did he have a camera with him then?'

'Not that I noticed. He was just standing there, looking at the house.'

'And he was on his own?'

Ella nodded. 'And I couldn't see a car either.'

'He'd gone when you got back?' Julie asked.

'Well you were here when we got back weren't you? You didn't see him did you?'

Julie blushed. 'Well, no. He wasn't here when we arrived.'

The sound of a small child making car noises stopped their conversation. Dylan had a small tractor in one hand and the soft toy they'd seen in the photograph in his father's office in the other. Seren followed him into the kitchen. Sarah was close behind her.

'Make sure you wash your hands after faffing with that dog,' Sarah said.

'Sarah.' Swift stood once more, scraping the chair on the flagged floor. 'How are you doing?'

'I don't know.' She waved for him to re-take his seat and pulled out a chair opposite him and sat down. 'I keep expecting him to come through the door. I just can't…'

'Seren, take your brother into the parlour. You can set the table in there today.' Ella shepherded the children from the kitchen and, after a quick stir of the contents of a pan on the Rayburn, she followed them from the room.

'I'm so sorry,' said Swift. 'If there's anything we can do, anything you need, just ask.'

'Just find out what happened.' Sarah pleated the edge of the tablecloth in her fingers. 'We need to know why.' She looked up at Swift. 'The kids need to understand. I don't want this thing to keep on going.'

'Suicide you mean?' asked Julie.

Sarah whipped round to face her. 'Yes, suicide. We've had more than our fair share of shit to deal with here, I suppose you've heard.'

'Sarah…' said Swift.

'Sorry. It's just that we thought everything was finally back on track. Gareth was his old self again. She closed her eyes and a single tear rolled slowly down her nose and dripped onto the plastic tablecloth.

'We'll leave you to it, Sarah. Maybe when you feel a bit better, in a day or two, we could have a chat about anything you remember that might help.'

'No. I'm fine.' Her breath caught in her throat, but she wiped her eye with the heel of her hand. 'What do you want to know?'

'Are you sure?'

'Let's get it over with.'

'Well, can you think of anything that might have been worrying him? A case maybe, something to do with the farm?'

Sarah stared at him, and looked down at her hands. 'He never talked about his cases. It's difficult when you know everyone, he said it was like betraying confidences.'

'Did he trust you?' Julie asked.

'Does she have to be here?'

'She's… we're just trying to get a few things straight. Carry on, *cariad*,' said Swift.

'Yes. He trusted me. He didn't want to put me in a difficult position. He thought it would be best if I didn't know who was beating his wife or who was screwing someone else's.'

'And there was nothing like that in your relationship?' Julie asked.

'What are you saying? You think Gareth beat me? Is that what happens where you're from?'

'It was more the other possibility which concerned me. Your relationship was solid, Mrs Watkin?'

'Where the bloody hell did you find this one, Craig? Yes, Sergeant, as a rock. You should be concentrating on what happened out there, on the hill. There's nothing for you here.'

'Sorry.' Julie pulled out the chair next to Swift. 'We just need to know how things were. To make sense of it all, for you as well as for us.'

'Ella mentioned a letter,' said Swift. 'Did he mention receiving anything in the post which upset him?'

'No, nothing.' Sarah's response was immediate and defiant.

'OK,' said Swift. If you think of anything that would help us, just ring me. Any time.'

Sarah nodded. 'We were really OK you know. Even after everything.'

'I know.'

'And you can't think of anyone who would want to harm Gareth?' Julie spoke quietly.

'You can't think anyone we know could have done this to him. Why would Gareth have any enemies?'

'It could have been something connected with his work maybe, or someone in the family? What about the man who was standing by the gate yesterday when you left for the funeral? Did you recognise him?' Julie asked.

Sarah shook her head and turned away from Julie. 'When can we have him back, Craig?' she asked. 'To bury him.'

Swift pictured the small graveyard at the bottom of the hill, imagined the plot next to Gareth's father, red soil under the shadow of the ancient yew waiting for the coffin. 'It'll be a little while yet. Until we're sure what happened.'

Down in the little ravine the bike had gone, but the tapes still surrounded the spot where Gareth Watkin had breathed his last.

'You were a bit hard on her there, Sergeant.'

'Yes, Sir. Sorry. There's just something not quite right about her.'

'How do you think she should be? The poor woman's just lost her husband.'

'But there's definitely something she's not telling us. Don't you think you might be just a bit...' Julie stopped, turned her head away to look out of the side window.

'A bit what, Sergeant?'

'Well, maybe just a bit close to it all, Sir. To them.'

'Are you saying I can't be trusted to be objective because I know them?' Colour began to rise in Swift's face.

'No, Sir. But we can't always see it ourselves, can we?' She turned back to face him. This wasn't the best way to ease yourself into a new job, was it?

Swift scratched his ear and looked past her towards the spot where the grass was flattened and bloodied. 'I know. Maybe you're right.'

'Sir?'

'It can be a balance between keeping the locals happy so they don't close ranks, and being objective.' Swift opened his window and the wind wafted into the car. 'Maybe your city hard case approach and my country bumpkin outlook might work well together, do you think?'

Julie hooked a stray strand of hair behind her ear. 'Was I a bit heavy-handed?'

Swift let off the handbrake. 'Let's get back to the station shall we?'

CHAPTER FOURTEEN

Rhys was sticking Velcro onto the back of photographs. He had written up the whiteboard in meticulous capital letters, which were connected by lines and arrows in various colours. He flipped a photograph of the sightless corpse of Gareth Watkin and stuck it in the centre of the board.

'Haven't we got one of him when he was alive?' asked Julie.

'We usually put the body on the board,' said Rhys. 'Well, a picture of it anyway.'

'Yeah, but that's just a bit…'

'To be fair, Rhys, I'd prefer not to have that looking at me every time I walk in.' Swift picked up a photograph from the desk. It showed Watkin in a dark suit and tie and a crisp, white shirt. He was smiling. 'What about this one?'

'OK, Guv.' Rhys ripped the photo from the board. 'The biker wasn't much help.' He stuck a fresh piece of Velcro onto the new photograph and turned it over to study it. 'He says he did see someone standing over the body, but that he can't be sure when it was.'

'Oh come on,' said Julie. 'He must know what he saw.'

'In and out of consciousness he was.' Rhys carefully stuck the new photo down. 'Says it was the shot that caused him to lose concentration, lose control of the bike.' He stood back to survey the board and lifted the top left hand corner of the picture a couple of millimetres.

'Did he just hear the one shot?' said Julie.

'He can only *remember* hearing one shot. I don't know which one he heard. He says he wouldn't know the difference between the sound of a shotgun or a pistol.'

'Can he describe the figure?' asked Swift.

'Male, Sir. That's about it.'

'Could he describe what he was wearing?' asked Julie.

'He just said dark clothes. To be fair, he's not really with it yet. Do you want me to go back this afternoon, Guv?'

'Leave it until tomorrow,' said Swift. 'Is he local?'

'Yep. Sennybridge. They don't think he'll be going home for a while yet though. The leg's badly smashed, they're going to have another go at pinning it.'

'Well let's leave him for now. What have we got then?' Swift examined the lines and arrows on the board.

Rhys took the top off a fat felt marker and pointed at the board. 'Right. Gareth Watkin, 43, local solicitor. Found with a gunshot wound.'

'Two gunshot wounds,' said Swift. 'We've got a bullet from a handgun which looks as though it killed him, and then a shotgun blast once he was dead.'

'Why would you want to shoot a corpse?' Rhys paused, pen in hand, unsure which colour to use.

'To obliterate the first shot,' said Julie. 'To disguise it.'

'But who'd…'

'That's already sorted,' said Swift. 'Milos Watkin's admitted to the shotgun.'

'His own brother? But why?'

'Milos thought Gareth had shot himself. The family's a bit sensitive about suicide,' said Swift. 'The question is, *did* Gareth shoot himself? Milos says there was a suicide note of sorts, saying that his cancer had come back.'

'But according to Greenhalgh and his GP he was clear,' added Julie.

'Hold on,' said Rhys, juggling pen lids. 'Have we got the note?'

'No. Could have been on his laptop. It's gone off to IT to see if they can find anything.' Julie examined the board.

'So there's a possibility he could have been murdered then?' Rhys uncapped a red felt tip.

'Ballistics have got both guns from Penrhiw, Milos's shotgun and the father's old army pistol, which was the one Milos thought Gareth had used to top himself,' said Julie. 'And there's someone who may or may not be suspicious floating about up there near the farm.'

'I've asked the lads in Garth to keep an eye on the farm,' said Swift.

'Brilliant,' Julie said. Out of the corner of her eye, she was suddenly aware of Morgan Evans rolling his eyes at Rhys. Evans pushed past her and handed a wad of paper to Swift. 'The ballistics report's back on the bullet from the handgun, Guv.'

'What's the conclusion,' asked Swift, not attempting to read the report.

'The bullet's Polish apparently. Ancient. Probably left over from the last war.'

'Polish?' said Julie. 'Do we know whether old man Watkin was in the war?'

'Probably not,' said Swift. 'Farming was a reserved occupation.'

'Has anyone actually checked that the ammunition for the father's pistol is the same as the bullet they dug out of Watkin's brain? Julie glanced at Morgan Evans as she spoke.

'Good point, Sergeant Kite.' Swift patted her on the shoulder with the ballistics report. 'Morgan, why don't you go and check that one out.'

Morgan Evans nodded. 'There's something else in the report that might be useful.'

'Well spit it out,' said Rhys.

'There was only one set of prints on the father's pistol.' Evans smirked. 'And they belong to Milos Watkin.'

'So,' began Julie, 'it looks as though we've got our murderer.'

Swift had opened the report and was riffling through the pages. 'I can't believe Milos would do that. Why would he shoot his brother with a pistol and then try to destroy evidence of the pistol shot? Why not just shoot him with the shotgun?'

'Maybe we should have charged him, Sir,' Julie ventured.

'Yes, thank you, Sergeant. It had crossed my mind.' Swift turned to the back page of the report.

'Oh well done, Evans. Half a story as per. The report says "The fingerprints on the pistol are consistent with its being handled, but there is no evidence of it being fired in the recent past. Also, there are no fingerprints on the trigger. It seems likely that the object was wiped clean or polished before being placed in the drawer where it was found."'

'Well at least we know Gareth Watkin didn't shoot himself, Sir. He couldn't have wiped the gun and put it back in the drawer, could he?' Rhys picked up the red marker pen. 'And why would Milos have wiped the gun and then picked it up again?'

'Get out to the farm now, Evans. See if Milos can shed any light on that one.'

'Shouldn't I just bring Watkin back with me?' Morgan Evans twirled his car keys round his index finger. 'So we can charge him.'

'No. Not yet,' said Swift, turning away and walking to his office.

CHAPTER FIFTEEN

Eileen Price watched the man walk slowly past her bungalow. He went as far as the lamp-post opposite the house where… Eileen knew who lived there; the short, grey-haired lady with the bright pink shopping trolley. With a son who worked in town. In a bank. Mrs… Oh for goodness' sake, she could remember it yesterday.

Then the man walked back, never taking his eyes off the bungalow. He stood, staring for long enough to make Eileen feel uncomfortable, and he sat on the low brick wall, just looking at the house. Looking at her. Where was Gordon? Where did he say he was going? She went into the kitchen and poured herself a cup of tea from the flask Gordon had left on the table, spilling some of the stewed liquid onto the polished table. If she waited here until she had finished her tea he might have gone.

When she eventually went back into the sitting room, the man began walking up the path. Not up the curve of the gravel drive, but straight up to the front door along the crazy paving path with neat flowerbeds to either side. He didn't look at her, just kept his eyes fixed on the front door. She had seen him somewhere before, she was certain of it, but he looked different somehow.

The front door bell shrilled. Eileen ducked behind the gather of curtain beside the window. The bell rang again, longer this time, summoning her out into the hallway. Through the patterned glass she could see his shape, small and slim, leaning against the wall of the porch. He bent to the letterbox and peered inside.

'Mrs Price, are you there?'

She took a step further towards the front door.

'I need to speak to Gordon. It's quite important.'

'He's not here. I don't know when he'll be back.'

'Could I come in and wait for him?'

He sounded pleasant enough. Eileen glanced at the plastic pouch, which was blu-tacked onto the wall by the front door.

'I'm not allowed to let anyone in,' she told him.

'We're old friends,' the man said. 'We've not seen each other for a great many years. I have a message for him.'

'I'm not... I can't...' Eileen was properly flustered now. Gordon would be cross if she let just anybody in, but if he was a friend...

'Just give him this then, would you.' The letterbox rattled and an envelope fluttered onto the doormat. 'Tell him I'll be back.'

Eileen watched the dark shape stand up, turn round and slowly recede as the man walked back down the path.

It was over two hours before Gordon got home, but when he opened the front door, Eileen was still standing in the hall with the envelope in her hand.

'He said he was a friend,' she chanted. 'He's left you a message and says he'll be back.' She smiled at him; relieved to have delivered her message before her memory swallowed it up and left it somewhere she could no longer access.

'Who was it?' asked Gordon, gently taking the envelope from her grip.

'He didn't say. I didn't let him in.'

'Well done, love. Let's go and sit down and I'll open this.' He steered his wife into the living room and sat her down in the armchair facing the television. He switched on the set and then stood with his back to the coal-effect fire and ripped the envelope open. Inside was a type-written note.

Price, I'm back and I'm watching over you – and your lovely wife.

'What does he say?' asked Eileen, not taking her eyes off the cartoon characters cavorting across the screen.

'It's nothing, love.' Gordon stuffed it into his trouser pocket. 'I'll go and get tea on shall I?'

Eileen nodded, giggling with the goggle-eyed fish on the screen.

Gordon closed the kitchen door behind him. Who the hell was it? He reached for the phone.

Brian Hughes was talking to someone on the phone as Julie walked through reception.

'When you say threatening, what exactly do you mean?' Brian raised his eyebrows and then a hand. Julie waved and held the door open for a young woman with a pushchair. A sturdy toddler tagged behind her, a blue plastic tractor clasped to his chest.

'Hello,' the woman said. 'Are you settling in?'

'Oh, yes I think so,' said Julie.

'It must be difficult moving somewhere new.' The woman ruffled the toddler's hair. 'Not that it'll ever happen to me.' She smiled at the little boy. 'Farmers aren't we, Robbie? Mind,' she added, 'nobody ever moves from here, farmers or not.' Brian put the phone down and the woman stepped up to the counter.

Julie walked out into the sunshine and across the car park. Why hadn't she thought of that before? What must it be like to know that you'll live in the same place all your life, for the kids to know what they'll do when they leave school before they even start school? She pointed the Fiesta towards the road that would lead her out onto the Epynt and down to Garth.

As she passed the farm her thoughts turned to Evans. He'd be in there now, throwing his weight about. What was his problem? There was obviously something she was doing that was really annoying him. She slowed down and paused at the end of the track down to Penrhiw. And there was something else that wasn't quite right here either. But what the hell was it?

Just before the road began to snake around the side of the hill and start its descent to Garth, Julie's mobile rang. She pulled over, onto a gravelled viewing area and picked up the call.

'Oh, so you're back in the land of the living at last.' Just for a second, the sound of Helen's cheery Manchester accent made Julie feel homesick.

'Not so's you'd notice,' she said. 'And this is the first time today I've had a mobile signal.'

'Up to your neck in sheep rustlers?'

'Funnily enough, no I'm not, although I can't be certain about the rest of the coppers I'm working with. You won't believe it, but I walked straight into a possible murder on my first day.' Julie opened the window and turned the engine off.

'I thought you told me it was one of the safest places in Britain.'

'It is, but that's only because there's nobody here.'

'So where are you?'

'I'm stuck up on a mountain in the middle of nowhere. There's nothing but grass and trees as far as you can see.'

'Sounds perfect to me. I'm stuck on John Dalton Street in a traffic jam. Listen.' Helen must have opened her window. Suddenly a chorus of car horns and expletives filled the Fiesta. Julie laughed.

'Yeah, OK, well there are some things I can live without. Listen to this...' she held her arm out of the car window.

'What am I listening to?'

'A Tuesday afternoon in Powys.'

'Now that sounds terrifying.' Helen laughed. 'Seriously though, how's it going? Do you think you're going to like it?'

'Well.' Julie ran her fingers slowly round the steering wheel. 'Most of them are fine. The DI's lovely, and the others are too, it's just...'

'Go on.'

'Well I don't know if it's because I'm just new, but one of the lads, a DC, seems to be out to prove something.'

'Bit of a closet misogynist do you think?'

'No, I don't think it's that. I'm probably imagining things, but... oh I don't know.'

'It'll take a while to get used to those stripes you know.'

'Yeah, I know.' Julie sighed. 'They all seem to know each other too. They're either related or they went to school together.'

'Now that *does* sound terrifying.'

'I just wonder if it makes them less objective.'

'Hmm. It might be worth keeping that to yourself for a bit. See how the land really lies eh? Listen, I've got to go, we're on the move. I'm off to sort out Peter Stringer and his charming missus. Bet you're sorry you're not here.'

'I wish I knew,' said Julie to herself after Helen had cut the connection. She got out of the car and leaned against the bonnet, gazing out over the unrelenting undulations of the Welsh countryside. Overhead a buzzard circled, on the lookout for a fallen lamb or worse. Suddenly Detective Sergeant Kite found herself yearning for the familiar, reassuringly busy streets of Manchester.

CHAPTER SIXTEEN
Wednesday, 27th April

Julie was awake before the alarm. She lay in bed, watching the room slowly fill with pale light. Surely Swift would have enough to charge Milos Watkin, so why was he letting Milos think he'd got away with it? And what the hell was Evans' problem with her?

She got up and walked to the window. The branches of the tree in the small garden shuddered in the breeze. Down on the lane someone was sitting on a quad bike and gazing up at the cottage. When he saw movement at the window, he kicked the quad into life and sped away. The black and white collie on the back jiggled its weight like a tightrope walker finding his balance.

Who was the man in black, hanging around near Penrhiw Farm?

'Can't sleep?' Adam propped himself up on one elbow.

'There's too much whizzing round in my head.'

'It's a lot to take in, new people, new place. You'll be fine, just give it time.'

'You sound like Helen.' Julie perched on the window seat and yawned.

'The wicked witch of the north has been in touch then?' He patted the pillow next to him. 'Come back to bed.'

'No. I'm going to get up. I want to go for a walk up the lane, see what's up there. I've hardly seen the place in daylight yet.'

'Well wake me up when you've got the coffee on,' said Adam, pulling the duvet over his head.

Julie stepped onto the lane, a narrow strip of tarmac no wider than the cottage's drive. To the left was the awkward gate with the horseshoe catch. Beyond that, where the lane snaked round to the right and along the valley to the main road, a steep hill with a pointed top soared into the pale blue sky. Its steep sides were a blur of fern punctuated by grazing sheep. She turned right, up a short rise through trees where grass grew in the centre of the tarmac. There was a scream, and a flash of blue and beige arced through the trees.

'Bloody birds,' she muttered. 'It's like a Hitchcock movie.'

Beyond the trees the land flattened, before plunging into hills once more. This little bowl of small green fields housed sheep, and young cattle with beige and brown coats. By a five-barred gate next to the lane, a large black and white horse stood resting a hind leg. His bottom lip drooped and moved gently as he breathed. Julie laughed and the horse opened his eyes.

'I thought you were a cow,' she said to the horse. 'But then I'm not well-versed in rural affairs.' She reached out a hand and carefully stroked his nose. The horse snorted and Julie jumped backwards.

'He'll not hurt you.' A man with a black and white collie stood behind her.

'Didn't I see you on a quad bike, outside the cottage?'

'They said you were a policewoman. You don't miss much then.'

'Officer,' said Julie. 'Police officer.'

'I saw you by Penrhiw yesterday.'

'You don't miss much either.'

'So you'll be finding out who killed Gareth Watkin?'

Julie squirmed under the direct gaze.

'You think someone killed him?'

'Don't you?'

'Our investigations are ongoing, Mr…?'

'It'll be someone from off you're looking for.'

'Off?'

'Someone who's not from here.' He pushed his cap further up his forehead, revealing the same pale, unweathered forehead as the man who had been complaining about his son in the police station when she arrived. Could that be less than three days ago?

'They have different rules there.'

'Meaning what?'

'We look after our own.' He said something Julie didn't understand to the dog, which skulked back beside him.

'So I'd have to live here for thirty years before I was accepted?'

'That depends.' The man bared his teeth in a smile. 'We might take to you a bit sooner.' He walked away down the lane, but as she watched him he turned round. 'The horse's name's Cam. He could do with a bit of company.'

Adam was in the kitchen when she got back. He had laid the table, found the cafetière, unearthed the toaster and was slicing thick chunks of granary bread.

'Well? What do you think?' He dropped four rounds of bread into the toaster. 'Isn't it amazing?'

'It's empty.'

'Oh come on, Jules. You have to admit it's stunning.' He slung the tea-towel over his forearm and pulled out a chair. 'If Madam would care to take a seat.'

'There's nothing here. I didn't see one other house while I was out.'

'There are other houses.' Adam poured water onto the coffee and transferred the cafetière to the table. 'Menna says they tend to build under the hill, out of the wind, so you can't always see them from the road.'

'I met one of the locals, bloke with a collie.'

'That'll be Joe. He's the landlord.'

'Of the pub?'

'No, our landlord. He owns this place.'

'Ah, hence the interest then.' Julie poured them both a coffee. 'So where does he live?'

92

'Give it a rest, Julie. It's like being interrogated.' Adam took the toast from the toaster and juggled it to the plates on the table.

'Occupational hazard,' said Julie, scraping butter onto her knife. 'Speaking of which, why do you have to go back to Manchester?'

Adam walked over to the sink and kept his back to her. 'I told you, there's still some stuff I need to pick up from school. Notes and stuff. I'd forgotten they were there.'

'And you have to go up there, do you? Couldn't someone post them to you?'

Adam whipped round to face her. 'Is this the way it's going to be from now on? I've said I'm sorry. I've said it won't happen again. If that's not enough, then…'

'Then what?'

Adam threw the tea-towel onto the back of a chair. 'If you can't trust me, then we may as well just call it a day.' He didn't wait for an answer, but slammed the kitchen door hard on his way out. Moments later she heard the click of cleat on pedal and he was gone.

'Yes, Sir, I know it's early, but there's something I need to check.'

'Well be careful.' Swift still sounded doubtful.

'I'll be the soul of discretion, I promise. Do you know if Evans brought the ammunition for old man Watkin's gun back from Penrhiw when he went to speak to Milos?'

'Not that I know of. I think Sarah was out when he went up there. Have you found something'

'Not yet, Sir, it's just a bit of a hunch.'

Tread carefully with Sarah, Sergeant.'

'OK, Sir. See you later.'

'Kite.'

'Sir.'

There was a pause, before Swift said, 'See you later.'

Sarah Watkin held the door open but stood blocking Julie's view into the bungalow.

'You again. Can't you leave us alone? Milos said we had one of yours round last night.'

'Sorry. I think we got off on the wrong foot.' Julie smiled. 'Put it down to me being from off.'

A chink of a smile smoothed the hard edges of Sarah's expression. 'Who's told you that?'

'My landlord, Joe someone.'

'Ah, you've met Joe then.' Sarah stepped aside. 'You'd better come in, but I have to take the kids to school in ten minutes.'

'It won't take that long.'

Inside, the bungalow was as modern as anything Julie had seen in the centre of town. The sitting room had two cream leather sofas and smoked glass and chrome tables sat on polished oak flooring. One wall was lined from floor to ceiling with books and on the opposite wall was a top of the range stereo system, its screen glowing blue, even in the bright sunlight.

'Wow. This isn't like the farmhouse.'

'Thank God,' said Sarah. 'It was like living in a mausoleum.'

'You lived over there?'

Sarah nodded. 'Before this place was built. We were all in there together.'

'That must have been cosy.'

'Cosy isn't the word I'd have used. And they've changed nothing since Gareth's father died, left it all exactly how he liked it.'

'That's a bit... well, you know.'

'Creepy, Sergeant? Yes I do know. Now, what can I do for you?'

'Ammunition. For his father's handgun. Did Gareth keep it here?'

'If it's about the licence, I told the officer who was here on Monday.'

'No, it's nothing to do with the licence. I had a thought about the ammunition, that's all, and whether anyone had used the gun since… well, since Gareth's father.'

Sarah walked across the hallway and into what must have been Gareth's office. There was a leather-topped desk and a swivel chair, two wooden filing cabinets and shelves full of law books and files. She reached up to a high shelf, retrieved a small key, and unlocked the bottom left-hand desk drawer.

Julie raised her eyebrows at the illegality of the arrangements for keeping the gun safe, but said nothing.

Sarah didn't miss the gesture. She sighed. 'It's not a real gun though, is it? It's just a relic. A reminder of the bloody past. It was in here, away from the kids. And you're right, nobody's used it since it came back from your lot in 2001. Milos dealt with all that.' She opened the drawer and Julie heard the breath catch in her throat. A photograph of a smiling Gareth Watkin beamed up at them. Sarah picked it up and stared at it.

'May I?' Julie took the photograph from her and studied it. She saw a dark-haired man with deep, dark eyes and a genuine smile. He was holding a collie puppy towards the camera. Behind him were tents and sheep pens.

'Local show.' Sarah wiped a tear from her cheek with the back of her hand. 'He loved that dog.'

'Have you still got the dog?'

Sarah nodded. 'It's the red bitch that follows Seren everywhere now. Milos couldn't get her to work for him. He's not the most subtle of dog-handlers.'

Julie put the photograph back on the desk. 'Was Gareth like his brother?'

Sarah turned on her with a mirthless laugh. 'God, no, chalk and cheese, Sergeant.' From the back of the drawer she took a small cardboard box, brown and foxed with age. 'Gareth couldn't bring himself to get rid of the ammunition, or the gun.'

'Mam,' Seren clattered into the study. She had plaited half of her hair in a lumpy plait but the other side was still loose, and she carried a ribbon in her hand. 'I can't get it to stay in.'

'I'm sorry,' Sarah took the ribbon from her daughter. 'I really have to get them to school.'

'No, that's fine.' Julie began backing out of the room. 'I'll see myself out. Can I keep this for now?'

'Take it, I don't want anything to do with it, or the gun.'

Julie drove slowly into the yard and past the farmhouse. As she reached the slope of the drive she looked in her rear view mirror. Milos was standing by the barn, arms folded, watching her.

CHAPTER SEVENTEEN

Julie sat on one of the hard chairs outside the Chapel of Rest and opposite Kay Greenhalgh's office. She could hear the pathologist's infectious laugh and wondered whether bereaved relatives had heard it too, or whether members of the Pathology Department had a sixth sense which prevented frivolity when there were people waiting to identify the remains of loved ones. What must Sarah Watkin have felt as she sat here, waiting for that door to open? What would she feel like if it was Adam in there, carefully shrouded to prevent a stray glimpse of incision scars and stitches.

'Sergeant Kite, what can I do for you?'

'I'm just on my way back to the nick and—'

Greenhalgh laughed again. 'I don't think I've ever heard Craig Swift refer to his office as "the nick", not in all the years I've known him.'

'I'm beginning to think they speak a different language here,' said Julie. 'And I don't just mean Welsh.'

'Quite a lot of them don't speak Welsh locally, but I think I know what you mean. It took me a long time to realise it really is a different country.' Greenhalgh held the door open. 'Come in, what have you got for me?'

Julie put the battered box down on the pathologist's desk.

'Wow, 3/6d – what's that in new money?'

'I'm going to send them to ballistics, but I wondered whether you could say if these are like the one you found in Gareth Watkin's head.' Julie shook the box and four bullets tumbled onto the desk.

'Well it was pretty badly damaged.' Kay pushed her hand into a latex glove and picked up one of the bullets from the desk. 'And I'm no expert, but I'd say these are far too fat. Entirely the wrong shape.'

'Brilliant.'

'That's the right answer then?'

'I think it just might be.' Julie gathered the bullets and put them back in the box. 'Although it does raise a whole lot more questions.'

'Ah, police work. What would we do without it?'

'Sleep through the night?'

Greenhalgh laughed. 'Have you got time for a coffee, Sergeant Kite?'

'It's Julie, and I could murder a coffee. Black please.'

'Just as well, we've no milk, as usual. Take a seat.' Greenhalgh gestured to the visitors' chairs by her desk. 'How are you getting on?'

'At work? OK, I think. It's been a bit of a baptism of fire, no chance to get to know people, but it's good to be busy.'

'So what brings you to Wales?'

Julie took the proffered mug and sipped the hot liquid carefully. 'A combination of things really, my husband's been desperate to move out to the country and then he was offered a job he really liked the look of at the High School.'

'What does he teach?'

'History. Personally I think he was born too late. He'd have loved to have been around when Lloyd George was Prime Minister.'

'He'll have a whole new curriculum to learn now then?'

Julie nodded. 'I think he's bought every book on Welsh history ever written, he's having a whale of a time reading about princes and drowned valleys.'

'How about you?'

'I'm not sure yet. So much of the job is the same as it was in

Manchester, and yet it's so different.' She cradled her mug in both hands and watched the steam rising from the dark liquid. 'And I'm more than a bit of a townie. I think I might be missing the noise and the pollution.' She looked up at Doctor Greenhalgh, who was smiling.

'God, do I know that feeling – mind you, I'm not sure I could go back now. Call me Kay, by the way.'

'How long have you been here?'

'For ever. I moved over here for the job not long after I qualified. You get used to it, and it's fantastic for walking. Like the Dales without all the people. People here still believe in the old values – community and family.'

Julie set the mug down on the edge of Kay's desk. 'Did you have any trouble fitting in?'

'Not really. It's like anywhere else. Well anywhere rural at any rate. You're a bit of an oddity for a while, until they get used to you.'

'I'm definitely feeling like an oddity.' Julie sighed.

Greenhalgh nodded. 'Like a penguin in a flock of sheep?'

Julie laughed. 'You're not wrong.'

'Give it time. I know you'll love it.'

Morgan Evans was standing by the whiteboard in the open plan office when Julie arrived back at the station.

'Nice of you to join us, Sergeant,' he said. 'As I was saying, from my visit to Penrhiw Farm yesterday evening, I now have definite confirmation from Milos that the pistol found in the bungalow is the one that belonged to Gareth's father.' He tapped the photograph of Milos which had appeared beside his brother. 'I'd bet my Scarlets season ticket that Milos shot his brother with it, wiped the gun and then returned it to the drawer at Gareth's bungalow, forgetting about the prints as he filed it away.'

'But surely the prints could have been there for years. Maybe even from the last time we looked at it after the father died?' Julie feigned wide-eyed innocence. Evans, who had opened his mouth to retaliate, paused.

'And we already know that ballistics said the pistol hadn't been fired recently,' Rhys said.

'They said they *thought* it hadn't been fired,' Evans snapped. 'It could have been cleaned. Someone who knows about guns could have sorted that out.'

'It hadn't been fired,' said Julie, walking from the door to the whiteboard. 'And there's no way it killed Gareth Watkin.'

'So how can you be so sure?' Evans' chin jutted forward, making him look like a defiant toddler.

'Because,' said Julie, holding up one of the squat, fat bullets from the drawer at Penrhiw Bungalow, these are the bullets for Gareth's father's gun. And this,' she held a colour photograph of a badly-damaged bullet against the whiteboard, 'is the bullet which killed Gareth.'

'Ah,' said Swift. 'So the father's gun wasn't involved at all.'

'That's it, Sir,' said Julie. 'And we don't know whether Milos or someone else brought the other pistol with them to shoot Gareth.'

Swift sighed. 'So we're back to square one then.'

'Shall I go and bring him in now?'

'Yes, Sergeant,' said Swift, watching the sneer slide from Evans' face. 'Take Rhys with you.'

CHAPTER EIGHTEEN

'Promise me you won't open this door.' Gordon Price stood between his wife and the television set, but she appeared not to notice. She continued to gaze at the corner of the screen, which was still just visible behind him.

'Eileen, love,' Gordon crouched down by the arm of her chair. 'Did you hear me?'

She nodded, without looking at him.

'It's really important. I won't be long, but I have to go out. You mustn't let anyone in.'

She laughed at the cartoon, which flitted across the screen, then her focus snapped onto him and she clung to his arm. 'Where are you going?' Her face was pale, her eyes wide as she realised what he was saying.

'It doesn't matter, just don't open the door. All right?'

'I'll come with you.'

'No, love. You stay here. I promise you I'll be as quick as I can.' He patted her hand. 'I'll bring you back a nice éclair. How about that.'

'Elephant's foot,' she said, smiling at him.

'Whatever you like.' Gordon released her hand from his arm and crossed to the door. By the time he left the room she was laughing at the cartoon again. Please God, just let her remember.

*

Eileen was still watching television when Gordon got back. He unloaded the shopping, and took it into the kitchen. Just by the back door was a small puddle of blood and tufts of fur. That blasted cat had brought something in again. He looked around for the tell-tale signs of tiny kidneys or feet and wiped up the mess with kitchen roll, washed his hands and filled the kettle.

'What do you fancy for lunch, Eileen love? I got some of that boiled ham you like.'

Eileen looked up at him as though he were a stranger; she frowned as though she was trying to place him.

'Eileen, love.' He knelt beside her chair and covered her hand with his. 'What do you fancy to eat?'

'Did you get my cream cake?'

'I did.' How on earth did she recall that when she had trouble remembering what he looked like? He'd only been gone an hour.

'I'll have that then.'

'Would you like a nice sandwich first? You can have the cake for afters.'

She clutched at his hand. 'Bobby's poorly.'

'Bobby? On the television?'

'Our Bobcat. The man said he'd been naughty.' Her eyes filled with tears and she began to weep like a small child, hiccoughing gulps of air.

'What man?'

Eileen rocked slowly in her chair.

'Eileen, what man?

She pushed his hand away. 'You're being mean now.'

'Was there a man here? Today?'

She nodded. 'Where's my cake?'

Gordon glanced round the room and ran into the hall. No cat. He checked the study, went back into the kitchen and even the downstairs cloakroom. She must have been dreaming. Or it was something on the television. He smiled and turned back towards the living room. Bless her. She really did watch too much television. What had she been doing now? He walked back into the kitchen and reached into the bread bin. Then he saw it. At the far end, on the floor underneath the table was a pool of blood. Small paw prints led out into the hall.

Gordon felt his knees begin to buckle. She couldn't have done anything to the cat, could she? He checked the top of the cupboard. The knives were all still there, out of her reach. So where was the poor cat? It could be bleeding to death somewhere.

He unfastened the child gate at the second attempt and ran up the stairs. He could feel his heart hammering against his ribcage. Downstairs the television was still booming and Eileen laughed. He caught sight of himself in the mirror on the landing; his face was haggard and deeply lined. God, how long could they go on like this? He glanced into each room. Nothing. His breathing began to slow. He pushed open the door of the last room at the end of the landing. There, in the middle of their bed, was the little cat, lying on a deep scarlet stain soaked into the white cotton bedspread. Dear God, had Eileen done this?

He scooped the cat carefully into his arms and walked slowly down the stairs. Had someone else been here?

'But it's just a bloody cat.' DC Morgan Evans slammed the car door shut. 'Why is he sending CID out to an attempted moggy murder?' He pulled the seatbelt from its mooring and clattered it into position. 'It's not even dead.'

'He must think it's important.' Julie Kite slid into the passenger seat and fastened her seatbelt.

'I'm surprised he's sending you.'

'And why would that be, DC Evans?'

'It doesn't need a DS does it? Does he think you need to hold my hand?'

'What *is* your problem, Morgan?' She turned to face him but he looked away, twisted the key in the ignition and revved the engine.

'I don't know what you're talking about.'

'And that's because I'm not from here is it? You don't understand the accent?'

'So you've got a chip on your shoulder, have you? Think we're all Welsh nationalists?'

'No, Morgan, I haven't. Like it or not we have to work together, so let's try a modicum of civility.'

He shook his head and slammed the car into gear. 'Or what? You'll go running to Swift?'

'What have I done to deserve all this?'

'Forget it.' Morgan switched the radio on to Radio Cymru and drove out of the car park faster than was sensible.

Neither of them noticed the man, dressed in black and sitting on the low wall by the entrance, who waved slowly as their car pulled into the traffic.

Gordon was waiting for them.

'I have to explain about my wife,' he said, before they had even set foot into the hallway. 'She gets confused.'

Julie read the notices in their plastic covers pinned to the wall by the front door. *Do Not Open the Door* said one. *Gordon's mobile number* said another. As they were ushered into the hall she spotted the stair gate.

'Alzheimer's is it, Mr Price?'

Gordon nodded. 'Pre-senile dementia. She's had it for years, it started off quite mild really, but just lately things have been getting much worse. Some days she's off the scale.'

'My grandfather had Alzheimer's. You must find it difficult.'

'So where's this cat then?' Morgan pushed past her and towards the kitchen door.

'Could you keep your voice down? I don't want to upset Eileen.' Gordon pulled the living room door properly shut and led them into the kitchen. 'The cat's still at the vets. They say it's touch and go.' He shook his head. 'I took the bedding off, just in case Eileen... it's outside on the patio. In the bin.'

Morgan sauntered outside. They heard the lid of the bin hit the ground.

Gordon watched Evans wrestling the bedding from the dustbin. He reached up on top of the tall fridge. 'This arrived yesterday, when I was out. I don't know who it's from.' He handed Julie the note, which he had wrapped in a plastic ziplock bag. 'I did touch it, but I was careful, so if there are any prints…'

'You sound as though you know what you're doing, Mr Price.' Julie put the bag on the draining board to get a better look.

'Ex-job,' said Price, walking over to join her. 'I took early retirement to care for Eileen.'

Outside, Morgan Evans was peering into a large plant pot. It wouldn't have hurt him to tell her that Gordon had been a copper, would it?

'So you think there might be a connection between the note and what happened today?' Julie put the note into her bag.

'I've never believed in coincidence, Sergeant.'

'Nor me. Have you any idea who could be doing this?'

'I'll be honest with you. When I got home, I thought it could have been Eileen who did it.'

'You think she tried to kill the cat?'

'You get to the point where you don't know them anymore. She doesn't recognise me half the time and I don't know what she's capable of.' He sat down at the table. 'It was only when I reread that note that I realised it wasn't necessarily her who injured the cat.'

'I'm guessing she can't use the computer?'

Gordon shook his head. 'She can't manage the stairs now either, not on her own. Heights bother her. I have to go with her if she wants to go upstairs. The computer's up there in the spare bedroom.'

'Out of her reach?'

Gordon nodded. 'It's not like it sounds.'

'I know what you mean. So you know it wasn't her.'

'Absolutely certain.'

'Then who do you think it was?'

'I've no idea.' Gordon shook his head. The television had been turned up in the sitting room.

'She was frightened by the man yesterday. I don't know what he said, she doesn't remember, but thank God she didn't open the door. He shoved the note through the letterbox. I phoned the station, but they said without a description there wasn't much they could do. Brian Hughes said it would go on the file in case anything turned up.'

'Who do you think it is?'

Gordon shrugged. 'You make a few enemies in this game.'

'Tell me about it,' said Julie, glancing at Evans.

Evans stood up and saw Julie watching him. He pushed the bedding back into the bin, removed the bin liner and knotted the top, before bringing it back inside.

Gordon intercepted him. 'I'm not being funny mate, but could you park that outside? It's just…'

'Yeah right. Can I talk to your wife now?'

Gordon looked from one to the other. 'If you don't mind, I'd like the Sergeant to speak to her. Her being a woman and all.'

'Perfect. I'll just wait in the car shall I?'

'That's very kind of you,' Gordon said, holding the front door open for him. 'She gets a bit flustered, especially after the visitor the other day.'

'Visitor?' Evans turned to look at him.

'Shall we go and speak to your wife, Sir.' Julie smiled and gestured for him to lead the way. To Evans she said, 'Why don't you put the bag in the car and have a quick look round upstairs, just in case Mr Price has overlooked something?' Evans stared at her, pressed his lips together and flounced out onto the path, swinging the bag.

Gordon switched off the television. It took a moment or two for Eileen to notice, but once she had, she looked straight through Julie as though she wasn't even there.

'Eileen, love, this is Julie. She's come to ask you some questions about the man you saw. All right?'

Eileen nodded. 'Are you from the police?' she asked.

'I am.' Julie knelt down beside the chair. 'I just wondered if you could help me.'

Eileen smiled. 'Gordon's a policeman.'

'Not any more, love.'

'Could you answer a couple of little questions?' Julie spoke quietly.

'I'll try,' Eileen said.

'Gordon tells me you had a visitor yesterday. While he was out. The man put a note through the door.'

'I... it's hard to remember sometimes.'

'I know it is.' Julie patted her hand. 'But anything you can remember will really help me. Did he say anything?'

Eileen stared at the blank television screen and narrowed her eyes in a frown. 'I think he might have.'

'Did you recognise the voice?'

'No. I don't think so.' She looked down at Julie. 'It was a funny accent, not from round here. But it reminded me of someone. He wanted to come in, but I wouldn't let him.' She smiled then. 'Gordon says I mustn't let anyone in.'

'Did you let him in today?'

Eileen shook her head. 'No. Definitely not.'

Gordon sighed and shrugged.

'But I did see him outside the door. The glass makes people funny shapes, like those mirrors. He was standing outside.'

'He was outside the front door today?' asked Gordon.

'I think it was today. You weren't here.'

'Could you tell what he looked like?' Julie glanced at Gordon. He obviously hadn't heard this before.

'He wasn't very tall. Not as tall as my Gordon.' She stopped to smile at him. 'I thought he was from the school.'

'What made you think that, Mrs Price?'

'His clothes. They were black, like the uniform they wear.'

'Could it have been one of the kids from the High School?' Julie asked.

Gordon shook his head. 'They changed the uniform years ago. It's not been black for a long time.'

Julie tried again. 'Did he get into the house without you letting him in?'

Eileen frowned again. Evans was making his way up the path and back into the house. 'That's him.'

'That's not him, love. That's the other policeman.' Gordon sat on the arm of her chair. 'He's helping this lady.'

Julie raised an eyebrow, but said nothing. They heard Evans run upstairs and walk across the landing.

'He was up there. I heard him.' Eileen's eyes traced Evans' footsteps as he went into the master bedroom.

'But you didn't let him in?'

'No!' Eileen almost screamed the word at Julie. 'No, no, no.'

'It's all right love.' Gordon wrapped his wife in a hug. 'Don't you worry.'

'Sorry.' Julie stood up. 'I didn't mean to upset her.'

'You're only doing your job.'

'Is there anyone at all you can think of who might be capable of this, Mr Price?'

'I really don't know.'

'No altercations with the neighbours who might not like…' She looked down at Eileen and mouthed 'cats' silently.

Gordon shook his head.

'Well I don't need to tell you to be careful. If there's anything at all you can remember, please phone and ask for me.'

'I will, Sergeant. And thank you for taking the time with Eileen.' When they were back in the hall he said, 'She used to be sharp as a tack, really capable, but these days…' He stood up. 'I'll show you out.'

'I don't suppose you knew a Gareth Watkin, did you, Sir?'

'Why do you ask?'

'Probably nothing. Just a thought.'

'I knew him years ago, when he was duty solicitor.' Gordon

opened the front door as Evans bounded down the stairs. 'When you say knew, do you mean…'

'He's dead, Sir.' Evans peeled off his blue latex gloves. 'Died on Monday. In suspicious circumstances.'

CHAPTER NINETEEN

'I thought you believed me.' Milos glared across the table at Swift.

'And I thought you were telling me the truth,' said Swift. 'You've left me no option but to bring you in.'

Milos slouched in his chair. 'There is such a thing as loyalty.'

'Works both ways, Milos.'

'I've told you everything I know.'

'And I just want to get things absolutely straight.'

'Are you charging me?'

'I could charge you with obstruction right now.'

'But you won't.'

Rhys Williams shuffled uncomfortably. 'Sir.'

'Persuade me I shouldn't, Milos.' Swift folded his arms and stared at Watkin.

'I've done nothing wrong.'

'Apart from shooting your brother in the head with a shotgun you mean?'

'You know why I did that.'

'What about this suicide note you say you found.'

Milos rocked backwards on his chair until it was on two legs and he was leaning against the wall. 'I told you.' He reminded Swift of how his son had been as a teenager, truculent and surly. 'I ripped it up. I didn't want Sarah or the kids seeing it.'

'And have you still got the bits? Did you throw them away?'

Milos shrugged. 'They could still be in my coat.' He thrust his hand into his pocket and pulled out a length of baler twine, a padlock and key and a large oil-stained handkerchief. As he shook the handkerchief, small squares of paper fluttered onto the table.

'Is this it?' asked Swift. Milos nodded. Swift scooped the pieces together with the aid of a pen from his jacket pocket and stared hard at Milos. 'Tell me again. What did it say? Exactly.'

'Sir.' Williams shoved a post-it note under Swift's nose. *Shouldn't he have a solicitor present?* Swift read the note and screwed it into a tiny yellow ball.

'Go on, Milos, I'm waiting.'

'It just said *It's back.*'

'And that's all?' Swift prodded the pieces with the end of his pen, pushing them into some sort of order.

'He always said he couldn't do it to the wife and kids again if it came back. He swore he wouldn't put Sarah through it all over again.'

'This note.' Williams looked over at the jigsaw of paper. 'It was typewritten?'

'It was. I told her that on Tuesday, that nosy bloody woman of yours.'

Rhys Williams cleared his throat. 'And would Gareth have typed a note to members of the family, rather than handwriting it?' Williams looked at Swift. 'Wouldn't that be a bit unusual? I mean, if it was a proper letter then maybe, but a note?'

'Answer him, Milos.'

Milos let the chair drop back onto all fours and stared at Rhys. 'You might have a point there. He used to have these little cards, thick cream-coloured cards. Poncy little things really, but he liked to fill them with that unreadable writing of his.' Milos rubbed his eye. 'Always in black ink from his gold fountain pen. Made Mam laugh it did.'

'So he'd be unlikely to have typed a note like that.' Swift picked up the screwed-up ball of post-it note and weighed it in his hand. 'Did Gareth use the computer at the bungalow?'

'Not that I know of. Sarah's is used for the farm accounts and her own e-mails. The kids play their games on it too I think, but

111

you'd have to ask Sarah to be sure. But there's nothing on it, I told you, I checked.'

'You've got a key for the bungalow then, have you?' said Swift. Milos blushed and looked down at the table.

'It's just for emergencies,' he said.

'Was it in Welsh or English, the note?' asked Rhys, straining to see the faint print over Swift's shoulder.

'Welsh,' replied Milos.

'Was that normal?' asked Swift. 'Did you always speak Welsh with Gareth?'

'We all do at home. *Iaith yr aelwyd.*' Milos picked at his fingernail and brushed the resulting detritus from the table. 'Father was from up there on the Epynt, a first language Welsh speaker. It was important to Mam to make sure we kept his language going at Penrhiw.'

'So Ella learned Welsh from scratch as a second language?' Swift raised an eyebrow.

'Third language.' Milos looked up at Swift.

'Of course. Does she still speak... her own language with her sister?'

Milos shook his head. 'Lady Catherine refuses to speak anything but English in that plummy posh accent of hers. She never even tried to learn Welsh. Dic wanted her to, probably so she could look the part at chapel, but she wouldn't. It didn't fit the new character she'd invented for herself.'

'So you're not keen on Catherine?' Swift asked.

Milos shrugged. 'She's harmless enough.'

'So you're fairly certain that Gareth would write the note, his last communication with his family, in Welsh.' Rhys frowned.

'I hadn't really thought about it,' said Milos. 'It never crossed my mind. You know how it is. You just switch between the two without thinking about it. And I had more on my mind just then than checking it for linguistic ability.'

'Good point.' Swift nodded. 'But it's fair to say that if Gareth typed this note, which in itself would be unusual, you'd have expected it to be in Welsh?'

'I suppose so, yes.'

'*Mae nôl*. Is that all it said?' Rhys was still frowning. 'So it could have meant *it* or *he* or even *she's* back at a push?'

'It could I suppose.' Milos stared at him. 'But what sort of sense would that make?'

'What indeed?' said Swift. 'Thank you for clearing that up.'

Milos pushed his chair back and went to stand up.

'Now there's just the small matter of the pistol that killed him.'

'I've told you.' Milos sat back down. 'I found father's pistol beside Gareth. I thought I'd lobbed it. When I saw him lying there my first thought was that I had to get it away from him, but then I must have picked it up and taken it home, because it was there, at the bungalow when they came for it. I honestly don't remember.'

'But there's a different gun involved here, Milos.' Swift removed a photograph from the folder in front of him. 'This is the bullet which killed your brother. And this...' he pulled a bullet from the box retrieved from Penrhiw Bungalow and held it up in front of Milos. 'This is the size of bullet which fits your father's gun.'

'But...' Milos picked up the photograph. 'You've lost me now. Are you saying it wasn't Dad's gun I found next to his... next to him?'

'That's exactly what I'm saying. Can you shed any light on that?'

'Of course I can't. Where would the other gun have come from?'

'So if we search Penrhiw we won't find another hand gun, the one you say you threw away?'

'What the hell would I want with a pistol?'

'So why did you keep your father's gun after he died?'

'That was different.'

'How was that different, Mr Watkin?' Rhys picked up the photograph.

'I have no use for it. It just got kept somehow.'

'And your father didn't have any other hand guns?'

'No.'

'You seem very definite on that one, Milos,' said Swift.

'There are only shotguns at Penrhiw.'

'Right, thank you, Milos. You can go.' Swift closed his notebook and stood up.

'But Sir, do you think…' Rhys's objection petered out when Swift turned to look at him.

'Get onto IT would you, Constable, ask them to check Sarah's laptop.'

'Right, Sir.' Rhys hovered for a second, before leaving the two older men alone.

'Is that everything, Milos? No more surprises?'

Milos stayed in his chair, staring at the table between them.

'I get the feeling you're being more lenient than you could be.'

'Just don't let me down, Milos.'

'You don't think I killed him, do you?' Milos looked up slowly, until he was holding Swift with his stare.

'No I don't. And I do understand why you did what you did.' Swift sat down again. 'But I wish you hadn't.'

Milos nodded. 'Stupid. If I hadn't had the shotgun in the Land Rover…'

'He didn't mention anything to you about feeling depressed, any worries he might have had?'

'Nothing. I can't think of anything that would have made him do this. I just thought he was sick again.'

'So do you really did think he'd killed himself, that it was your father's gun in his hand?'

Milos frowned. 'Are you really saying he might have been – that he didn't commit suicide, you're not just winding me up?'

'I think there's a very real possibility he might have been murdered, yes.'

'Oh shit, Craig, what the hell have I done?'

*

Julie stopped the car in the gravelled pull-off where she knew she'd get a signal. Fat fluffy clouds scudded across the spring sky leaving shadows on the green landscape beneath. From here the view was almost surreal. Tiny white farms studded the landscape and narrow lanes bordered by neatly trimmed hedges wandered the hills, joining up the hamlets and villages. She pulled out her phone and checked for messages. Then she dialled Adam's number.

'Hi. You've reached the voicemail of Adam Kite. Leave your number and ...'

She cut the connection and dialled Helen instead.

'Hi, how are you doing?' Julie could hear the smile in Helen's voice.

'It's gone mad all of a sudden. I think we've a nutter on the loose as well as a potential murderer.'

'Connected?'

'No. At least there's nothing to suggest it yet. What are you up to?'

'Just sorting out the paperwork on Cheetham Hill. Then we're off to the pub after work. Frank's had a result on the Levison case.'

'That's fantastic. Buy him a pint for me.'

'What's the social life like there, or don't you know yet?'

'So far it's run to two coffees and a piece of bara brith.'

'Bara what?'

'Don't worry. I'm just being miserable. That DC's still being a pain in the arse.'

'Why don't you ask him what his problem is?'

'Because I'm not totally convinced I'm not being completely paranoid, and I can do without causing rows at the office this early in my brilliant career as a sergeant.'

Helen laughed. 'Anyway, what's with this nutter of yours?'

'Oh nothing much. Frightening demented old ladies. And killing cats. Well one cat and only attempted moggycide to be precise.'

'Nice. Why have you got lumbered with that?'

'I've no idea. The poor woman's got Alzheimer's and she's so confused it's difficult to know what to believe, but it appears that this bloke turned up and frightened her, left a note which may or may not be threatening and now their cat's been hurt.'

'Lovely. And more the sort of thing you'll have to get used to?'

'I do hope not.'

'Have you picked up your cat yet?'

'I thought I'd better make sure we were unpacked first.'

'What you mean is you've not told Adam yet?'

'I'm going to tell him tonight.'

'Where does he think Sid is?'

'With you. He was almost grateful. Said he didn't have you down as a cat lady.'

'Ha. I'd have loved to see that. Is he behaving?'

'I think so, I phoned the cattery this morning and they said he's fine.'

'Not the cat, Adam.'

'Ah. Not sure.'

'Go on.'

'It's probably nothing. We've already had a row about my suspicious mind.'

'That goes with the job. What's up?'

'He was on the phone when I got in last night. It sounded as though he was arranging to meet someone.'

'Well that could be innocent enough.'

'He says he's got to go back to Manchester next weekend, something to do with collecting stuff from school.'

'That could be true too.'

'I know. He's probably right. Maybe I'm obsessing about it.'

'But?'

'But it sounded as though he changed the subject when I came in.'

'Ah. And given his track record…'

'You've caught up.'

There was a pause on the end of the line. In the background Julie could hear the squeal of tram wheels.

'I hate to say this.' There was hesitation in Helen's voice now. 'But maybe you just have to give him a chance to get things sorted out. Look Jules, nobody was more surprised than I was when he said he wanted to move to Wales. He's made a big commitment by moving you both over there.'

'And you think he might be telling the truth?'

'I'm just saying he could be, and I suppose it's just going to take a while for things to get back to normal.'

'I'm not sure we ever did normal.'

'Well I think you have to give it a go. Anyway, you need to concentrate on making your presence felt on this enquiry.'

'Yeah. I know. You're right.' Julie watched two kites as they hung in the air, riding the thermals. Suddenly one plummeted into the reeds while the other hovered above.

'Well I'm afraid I must leave you and get back to the multifarious joys of B Division. Good luck with the cat discussion.'

'I don't suppose we'll even see him much with all this wildlife to go at.'

'Makes a change from Adam doing the hunting then.'

'Very funny. On that note, DC Mitchell, I'm going home to look after my devoted husband.'

CHAPTER TWENTY
Friday, 29th April

Ella Watkin stood looking out of the kitchen window over the moorland beyond. It seemed strange not to see Gareth in his running gear, bobbing along the tracks, waving just in case she was there, standing in the window. You shouldn't outlive your children. Especially not Gareth. She stopped the next half-formed thought before it lodged itself. She turned away from the window. Everything looked exactly the same as it had before. The clock still ticked, the kettle still steamed slowly on the Rayburn. How could life just carry on as though nothing had changed?

Dylan's little wooden farmyard was on the table. She'd been with Gareth when he had bought it at the Royal Welsh Show. It had been a glorious July day and he'd been so pleased with the ideal present for his little boy. Every third person in the gigantic crowd had seemed to know him. It had taken them an age to get anywhere; even in the sheds people had stopped to shake his hand and share a smile. She would never be able to face the showground again.

The front gate clanged. Ella pasted on a smile and went to greet her visitor.

'Ella. How are you coping?' Catherine placed one highly-polished pointed shoe on the threshold and went to climb the step. Ella didn't move and Catherine had to take a step backwards.

'You've taken your time coming back.' Ella folded her arms and leaned on the warm stone of the doorframe, looking down at her sister. 'You must have been busy with more important things.'

Catherine pouted. 'I didn't want to interfere. It must be difficult for you with the police involved.'

'After all, it's unlike you to interfere isn't it? You were on the phone often enough when you wanted to slag Gareth off. You just never stop with the superior act, do you?'

'And you wonder why I don't come more often, when this is the sort of reception I get.'

'It's not about you though, is it? Just for once, Catherine, it's about someone else. It's about Gareth.'

'Are you going to let me in, or do you want to discuss your son's death on the doorstep?'

Ella raised her hand and Catherine flinched, but Ella just pushed the door open, turned away and walked off down the hall. Catherine trotted after her, her kitten heels clicking on the stone floor. 'I hope you realise it was just a small misunderstanding in the office the other day. I suppose Gareth told you what it was all about and blew it out of all proportion?'

'I don't want to know. It doesn't matter now.' Ella pulled out a chair and sat at the kitchen table. 'Nothing matters now.'

Catherine sat opposite and put her handbag down on the little wooden farmyard. 'I hope you don't blame me for what happened to Gareth.'

'No, I don't blame you, Catherine. But I do blame you for making his life at work very unhappy.'

Catherine's eyes narrowed. 'What do you mean? He knew I only have the best interests of the partnership at heart.'

'So you say.' Ella stared hard at her sister. 'At least the police have stopped hounding Milos for the time being.'

'Dear God.' Catherine crossed herself elaborately. 'But why would they think Milos would want to murder Gareth? That's ridiculous.' She gazed past Ella, towards the window. 'Have they thought about…'

'About what?'

'Well, the animal who murdered that little girl above

Llanfihangel, the case Gareth almost compromised with his slap-dash way of going about things. He's just been released from prison, far earlier than he should have been apparently. I heard from one of my contacts in Manchester this morning. He brought a successful appeal based on a technicality. He threatened retribution on a grand scale when he was sentenced, didn't he? And what with Gareth having messed up so spectacularly at the time…' Catherine brought her focus back and smiled sympathetically at Ella, 'Well, you never know, do you?' She sat back in her chair.

'Is that what you came to say, Catherine? Is that the sum total of your condolences?' Ella stood up and walked to the kitchen door. 'Have you mentioned any of this to the police?'

Catherine remained where she was. 'I thought, given that it might be detrimental to Gareth's memory, I would inform you first.' She tucked a stray hair behind her ear and smiled. 'After all, it might be his fault that this maniac is free to roam the streets.'

Ella flung the door open, but the gesture was lessened as it caught on the uneven stone floor and stuck fast. 'I think you'd better leave.'

Catherine feigned total innocence as she rose from the table and carefully replaced the chair. 'But of course I'm sorry about what happened to Gareth, why wouldn't I be? Why do you always take things the wrong way, Ella?'

'Sorry? Why are you sorry? Because his death blows a hole right through your cosy retirement plans for Dic? Because you won't be able to plot and scheme against my son any longer?'

'No, Ella. I'm sorry that Gareth's dead. I'm sorry we don't seem to be able to have a sensible conversation these days, and I only came to see if there was anything I could do to help.'

'Oh,' said Ella. 'Right.' She moved away from the door and transferred the kettle to the fast hob.

CHAPTER TWENTY-ONE

'Come on, people, we're getting nowhere with this one.' Swift scanned the room. 'Anything new?'

'What do we think about Sarah?' Julie asked in the silence that followed Swift's question.

Morgan Evans' lip curled into a sneer. 'What's your problem?' He looked at Swift for affirmation.

Swift ignored him. 'Go on,' he said to Julie.

'She's too angry.' Julie frowned.

'But that's often the case after a suicide in my experience.' Evans stood up and walked across to the board. He tapped the photograph of Gareth Watkin. 'He's left her with two kids, a Neanderthal brother-in-law and a domineering old biddy.'

Julie shook her head. 'Yeah, but in *my* experience, the anger comes later. She's too controlled.'

'She's always been reserved though.' Swift moved away from the board and sat on Rhys's desk, leaving Evans by himself. 'Even when her mother died she was stoic about it. No tears.'

'Formidable lady,' Rhys said. 'I wouldn't want to cross her.'

'I think I've already done that.' Julie grinned at him.

'There's a surprise,' muttered Evans.

Julie opened her mouth to speak, but Swift cut across her. 'Any thoughts on the third gun?'

'You mean the first gun, Sir?' Goronwy said. 'Chronologically speaking.'

'Yes, very good.' Swift walked back to the board and uncapped a red marker. In the section where Rhys had detailed the firearms in tidy green capitals he scrawled 'Handgun, Eastern European, possibly Polish?'

'And we've no idea where it came from?' asked Goronwy.

'No. And no idea at all where it is now,' Swift replied.

'And we're sure it wasn't suicide?' Goronwy strolled over to the board and examined the entries. 'Actually, we've got bugger all haven't we?'

'Apart from the odd hunch,' said Julie.

'So I suppose by that you mean we're back to your hobby horse, Sarah Watkin.' Evans shook his head. 'You don't even know the woman. She's very well thought of by the locals, does loads of charity work.'

'She could be Mother Teresa for all I care,' said Julie. 'But she definitely knows more than she's letting on.'

Swift put down his pen. 'What about the business with Gordon's cat? Do we think there's a connection?'

'It's out of danger,' laughed Evans. 'Off the kittycal list.'

'Why is that so hilarious?' Julie glared at him. 'The vet says it could have been kicked.'

'Or clipped by a car,' said Evans. 'My money's on that option. Their road's a bit of a rat-run.'

'What about the note the Prices received?' asked Swift. 'You said it was threatening, Kite?'

'Could have been, Sir.'

'I don't get that. All it meant was that they should talk, surely. Or that the sender of the note was looking after them.' Evans reached for the file. 'It's even got his initials on the back. LM, look. Hardly anonymous is it?'

Julie frowned. She had missed the initials. 'But "*I'm watching over you…*" sounds well dodgy to me. And do we know who LM could be?' She addressed the room in general, but nobody answered her.

'OK,' said Swift. 'We'll leave that one to Gordon. He knows what to do if anything else happens. Right. What's the plan for today?'

122

'I want to follow up on Watkin's car, Sir.' Julie said.

'What about it?' said Evans.

Julie walked to the board and pointed to the photograph of the place where Gareth Watkin died. It had been taken looking down on the spot and showed the silver motor bike, the ambulance and the pathologist's black Alfa Romeo.

'It's not there,' said Julie. 'So he's unlikely to have driven himself there, and it's too far to walk from Penrhiw if he'd taken it back there first.'

'Good call, Sergeant,' said Swift.

'Williams, get back to the hospital and see if the motorcyclist can remember any more.' He slid down from the desk. 'And Evans, a word in my office please.'

From the police station, Julie took the main road that skirted Epynt Mountain, as Rhys called it. Even here, on the main A470, the traffic was slow with stock wagons and Land Rovers. As she turned left at Llyswen a uniformed PC with a hand-held radar gun waved at her as she passed. How on earth did he recognise her in her little blue Fiesta?

The road was a succession of mini-switchbacks and sweeping bends, rushing alongside the River Wye like the water tumbling over rocks and roots. She stopped at the junction in Builth where she had crossed the bridge on Tuesday morning, on her way to her new job. It seemed like weeks ago now. Ahead of her the gable end of a shop had been painted with a gigantic mural. At the top was the head of a bemused-looking king, and underneath a winter scene with people running through leafless trees. She smiled. A bit like Mid Wales Police, scurrying about and getting nowhere. There had to be a story behind it. She would ask Rhys when she got back to the office. No doubt he'd be able to shed light on it, and a couple of other things too.

*

The manager at the Metropole Hotel was extremely helpful. Yes, the car park had CCTV and yes, they kept DVDs for a week. It took him less than ten minutes to set Julie up with his desk, the correct DVDs for Tuesday morning and a cup of strong black coffee.

'Just come and find me if you need anything else,' he'd said.

Julie pressed play and settled back in the plush leather chair. She dialled Swift's number on her mobile.

'Kite, where are you?'

'Metropole in Llandrindod Wells, Sir.'

Swift laughed at her pronunciation. 'We'll have to get you on a Welsh course, even if it just helps with the place names. Rhys says the biker's being released from hospital later today, but he can't remember any more than he's already told us. I want to organise a line-up with Milos for this afternoon, see if it'll jog the lad's memory.'

'So Milos is back in the frame?'

'No, not yet, I want to try to work out whether the biker saw Milos or whoever got there before him, if we believe Milos's timings. I'll get Evans to pick Milos up. He can check on your BMW while he's up there.'

'Sir.' Julie stopped the DVD. 'I've got Gareth's car coming into the car park at 09.20 on Tuesday.'

'Right. It'll be interesting to see what happens next. See you later.'

On the screen, the BMW parked, but Gareth didn't get out. Julie fast-forwarded. At 09.28 a silver, soft-topped Mercedes pulled up next to him. She could see Gareth's door start to open, but then a laundry lorry pulled up between Gareth's car and the camera. Julie watched the lorry driver clamber out of his cab and bring down the tail-lift. The silver Mercedes reversed out of the parking space. When the lorry finally pulled away, the black BMW was still there, but it was empty.

It was 10.45 before the Mercedes returned. Gareth Watkin climbed out of the passenger side and leaned in through the driver's

124

window. He watched the Merc disappear before taking his keys from his pocket and unlocking his car. Suddenly a figure in black darted across the car park. Julie froze the frame. Whoever it was, they were shorter than Watkin, but the raised fist connected with the right side of Watkin's head. Another blow landed in his stomach and he doubled over. But he didn't fight back – why not? The assailant pushed Watkin towards the passenger side of the BMW and Watkin opened the door and got in. The figure in black climbed into the driver's seat and the car sped out of the car park. The time was 10.47. Who the hell was it?

Julie replayed the DVD to see where the assailant had come from. Maybe she could find his car, get a lead on who he was, but he had run into the frame from outside the camera's field of vision. What about the weirdo up on the hill by Penrhiw? Could it be him? She rewound the DVD five or six times. Why did Gareth just stand there and let them bully him? It had to be someone he knew. Otherwise he would have fought back, surely. She took the DVD from the machine and went in search of the manager. He was helping an elderly couple with directions to the red kite feeding station in Rhayader. He smiled as she leaned on the counter, but he wouldn't be distracted from the task in hand. Julie drummed her fingers on the edge of the mahogany.

'So it's up this road, the A483,' he pointed to the map once more. 'Then at Crossgates you turn left at the roundabout.' The old man followed the route with a crooked finger. 'Follow that road all the way into Rhayader and turn left here, by the clock. Gigrin Farm is just along on the left. You'll see the sign.'

The old couple thanked him, and he came out from behind the desk to open the front door for them. Julie could feel her blood pressure rising.

'Now then,' he said, strolling back to the desk. 'How did you get on?'

'Have you got another camera in the car park? Anything covering the area nearer the entrance?'

CHAPTER TWENTY-TWO

The cat was still woozy. The plastic lampshade collar unbalanced him and Eileen watched him as he tottered across the carpet before settling on the rug in front of the fire.

'Bobby is going to get better?' Eileen looked up at Gordon, her eyes as wide and innocent as a child's.

'He'll be fine now, Eileen love. We've just got to keep him warm and quiet.'

Eileen stared at Gordon's face. 'There's something I need to tell you about what happened, but it just won't… I can't remember.'

'I know. It's OK. It'll all be all right now.'

The doorbell made Eileen jump. The cat raised its head slightly from the rug, but lay back down as though the movement had taken the last ounce of its strength. Gordon moved over to the window and stood looking out, hidden by the drape of the curtain. There was a figure on the doorstep, but close in to the wall, so it was impossible to see who it was.

'Gordon?' Eileen looked at him over the back of her chair, her pale, frowning face reminding him just how frightened she must be.

'Don't worry, love, I'll just go and see who it is.' He put his hands on her shoulders, pushing her gently back into the chair and he put the television remote into her hand. 'Why don't you see if you can find me some sport?' Eileen smiled, happy to have been given a task, and began to press the buttons, slowly and deliberately.

The outline of a man was distorted by the patterned glass in the front door. He had to be six feet tall. Gordon glanced at the cricket bat between the umbrellas in the coat stand, but opened the door empty-handed.

'I wonder if you've ever thought about what will happen to you once you've died?' The man on the doorstep wore a three-piece suit, and by his side was a child of about six years old, dressed in grey trousers, a white shirt and a tiny blue blazer with brass buttons.

'What the hell are you talking about?' Gordon's face contorted as he thrust it towards the man on the step.

'Do you think that everything ends with death?' The man seemed unperturbed and reached slowly into a brown leather satchel and retrieved two pamphlets. 'There is a different way,' he said, smiling.

'How could you use a child for this?' Gordon reached up and grasped one of the man's lapels. 'Have you no shame at all?'

'And do you not think it important that we should spread the word as widely as we possibly can?' The man was still smiling his smug smile.

'Get away from me and my wife. Leave us alone.' Gordon spoke in an urgent whisper, and had pulled the man's face down towards him. The child stood with his back to them, looking out across the street.

'So much anger,' said the man.

'Mr Bristow, has he hurt you?' Two women came running across the road and onto the crazy paving path. They too carried brown leather satchels and they wore floral dresses and pastel-coloured jackets as though they were going to church. As they reached the doorstep one of the women held out her hand and led the child away while the other tried to push herself between Gordon and his visitor. 'How dare you assault Mr Bristow? I'll report you to the police if you don't let him go.'

Gordon released his grip, Mr Bristow patted his lapels back into shape and, in one smooth movement handed one of the documents to Gordon. *The Watchtower* it said on the front – *How can God help you?*

*

Julie fought to keep all traces of a smile out of her voice. She knew that Gordon was extremely worried, but the thought of him, of all people, accosting a Jehovah's Witness on his own doorstep just appealed to her sense of humour. Now he was even more worried, about what might happen if they reported him. She stopped smiling.

'I've not heard of anyone phoning it in, Mr Price. I'm sure they must be used to irate residents. You didn't actually hit him did you?'

'Of course not, what sort of person do you think I am?'

'No, sorry. And how's Mrs Price?'

There was a silence at the end of the line. 'You know how it is, Sergeant.'

'I do. Have you had any more thoughts about the note?'

'None. It's probably just a wind-up. I've been trying to think about old cases, but nobody has come to me. There was one madman who stands out. He threatened everyone connected with his conviction with a particularly nasty death, said he would remember every single one of us, but it can't be him. He'll still be safely locked away for years yet.'

'Well, keep me posted.'

'I will. Could you let me know, Sergeant, if anyone puts in a complaint about me?'

Julie reassured him once more and cut the connection. She walked into reception and waved at Brian Hughes. In reply, he flourished a white postcard. He read it again before handing it to her.

'Now normally, I'd just bin it as the work of a crackpot, but given the goings on with Gordon Price and his visitors, I wondered if there could be a connection.'

Judge not, and ye shall not be judged: condemn not, and ye shall not be condemned: forgive, and ye shall be forgiven. Luke 6:37

Lord, how oft shall my brother sin against me, and I forgive him?
Matthew 18:21

She read the card twice and frowned. 'How did it get here?'

'Someone left it on the counter, yesterday afternoon.'

'Do we know who it was? Was it anything to do with Jehovahs?'

Brian shook his head. 'Morgan Evans was down here when it was left. He said it was a man on his own. They always hunt in pairs the Jehovah people, don't they?'

'But what did he say to Evans?'

'You'll have to ask him. I don't think he was taking much notice.'

Only Rhys Williams was in the office when she walked in.

'Where is everyone?'

'The boss has got them all fussing over this line-up.'

'He's OK Swift, isn't he? A decent bloke to work with?'

'Yeah, he's pretty sound.'

'Not sure I'd say the same about Evans though.' Julie watched Rhys squirm as he tried to find a diplomatic reply. 'Don't worry, Rhys, it's my problem.' She slung her jacket over the back of her chair. 'Did he say anything about the man who dropped this off?' She waved the card. 'Some sort of religious type apparently.'

'Let's have a look.' He took the card from her, read it and shrugged. 'Somebody's obviously having trouble with his neighbours or maybe he's just got the family from hell.'

Julie grimaced. 'There's got to be more to it than that. Why would he just leave this and not report anything?' She pulled her purse from her bag. 'I need caffeine, lots of it.'

He grinned. 'White, with loads of sugar, ta.'

The canteen was quiet. Nerys was wiping down tables, singing to herself.

'Are you doing coffee?'

'I am, I couldn't let you have that stuff that comes out of those while I'm still here.' Nerys grimaced at the machines. 'How are you settling in?'

'OK.' Julie picked through the bowl of packets by the till, searching out the brown sugar.

'It must be very different to what you're used to?'

'You can say that again. Can I have two coffees please.'

'Anything to eat?'

'I'd better not.'

'I've just made Welsh cakes.'

'I'm going to have to stop coming in here.'

'There's nothing of you, lovely. Here, on the house.' Nerys handed Julie a plate with four Welsh cakes on it.

'Thanks, I'll share them with Rhys.'

'He's a nice lad, even though he is married to my cousin.'

'Nicer than some of the others.' Julie put two saucers on the tray.

'Ah, so I'd guess you're having a bit of trouble with Morgan Evans are you?' Nerys handed over the two cups and took Julie's £5 note.

'Has he said something about me then?'

'Ignore him, *bach*, he's just a bit impatient to be Chief Constable is our Morgan.'

Julie laughed. 'I thought it was because he's not that keen on incomers.' She took her change. 'Or women?'

'Nothing so complicated,' said Nerys. He had his eye on your job, but he failed his Sergeants' Exam.'

'Oh God, that doesn't make me feel any better.'

'Don't worry about it. He'll get used to the idea.' Nerys wiped the counter. 'Just give him a bit of time. He's not a bad lad once you get to know him.'

Rhys had been accurate in his assumptions. Swift was indeed flapping about the line-up.

'Milos, if you scowl like that you'll not do yourself any favours in there. I'm doing this to try to help you.'

Milos scowled harder still.

'You can decide where you want to stand. Just tell the constable.'

Milos slouched into the centre of the line-up and held the card with the number five on it. There were eight others in the line-up, a couple as tall as Milos, and three who were much shorter and slighter. Morgan Evans wheeled the motorcyclist in. His leg was encased in a huge plaster with what looked like a Meccano frame running the length of his lower leg.

'Are you sure you're feeling up to this?' Swift eyed his witness with concern.

'I'm grand. Much better than I was a couple of days since anyway, and a damned sight better than my bike.'

'Well, whenever you're ready, just tell me if you can see the man you saw out there on the Epynt on Monday morning.'

'I didn't see much, I couldn't see his face at all.'

'So what did you see?'

The biker closed his eyes. 'He was bending over something on the ground. Well, the body, as it turns out, but I couldn't see that from where I was. It was just a shape in the grass.'

'Could you tell how tall he was?'

'Not sure.'

Swift pressed the button on the microphone next to him. 'Get them to turn to the left and bend down.' The nine men shuffled into position. Two of them were attempting not to smile at the request. 'Like that?'

'Er, I can't be certain. They're all taller than I thought.'

'But you were maybe what, twenty yards away?'

'Dunno. I really wasn't with it, and there's a ruddy great crack in my visor. Something like that maybe. Sorry.'

'Are there any you would discount for any reason?'

'Look, this might not be reliable. I was very hazy.'

'Just give it your best shot.'

'Well number nine's not right. Too much hair.'

'So he had short hair?'

'Maybe. And five and six are much too tall.' He tried to straighten up in the wheelchair and winced. 'Sorry, I've not been much use.'

'Don't worry,' said Swift. 'You've been a great help. If anything comes back to you please let us know.'

Julie looked up as Swift walked back into the office. He looked tired. 'You OK, Sir?'

'Nothing conclusive from the line-up,' said Swift. 'Other than the biker must have seen the killer rather than Milos.'

Julie smiled. 'Well that's positive at least.'

'He can't remember anything much. Smaller than Milos, he says, and with short hair. That's about it.'

'So it could have been a woman?'

'Yes, Sergeant, I suppose it could have been a woman.' Swift took off his glasses and rubbed his eyes. 'What about this CCTV footage from the Met?'

Julie flourished the remote control and the DVD whirred into life. Swift watched Watkins' car arrive and the Mercedes arrive and leave. 'There could be an innocent explanation, a business meeting, getting a lift somewhere?'

'Maybe. But what about this bit?' She watched Swift's face as he watched the confrontation and the BMW driving away.

'Bloody hell. Can we see where he ran from?'

'No, I checked. There is a camera overlooking the far side of the car park, but nothing ties up. He could have run in off the road, not be parked there at all.'

'Still, have you checked the vehicles against hotel records?'

'Yep. The Manager said that locals use the car park to nip to the lake or round to the shops. Most of the cars check out against hotel residents or local addresses.'

'Most?'

'There were a couple of hire cars, I'm waiting for confirmation of hirer details. The hotel's checked the guest list and they're all accounted for.'

Swift nodded. 'Is the Merc local?'

Julie picked up her notebook from the desk. 'I wondered if it could be Catherine's, but nothing so straightforward. It's registered to a local company.' She flicked through the pages. 'Southam Associates?'

Swift shrugged. 'I've not heard of them, do we know where they are?'

'They're out towards Hay-on-Wye apparently.' Julie went back a page in her notes. 'The company's owned by a Jessica Southam.'

'What do they do?'

'I'm not sure. Some sort of financial services. I've had a quick look at the website, but I'm not really any the wiser. I'll get onto it now and see if I can find out a bit more about her.'

'So it was probably a business meeting then?'

'Not necessarily, Sir.' Julie smiled, but Swift did not acknowledge the comment.

'I don't suppose there's CCTV on the street?'

Julie shook her head. 'There is a camera on the front of the hotel, but I've checked the tapes and there's nothing useful.' She rewound the DVD to the point where Watkins was assaulted in the car park. 'It's a really poor quality recording, and I did think at first that it could have been the oddball we saw out on the hill by the farm, but given Gareth doesn't put up any resistance, maybe it could be Sarah.'

Swift closed his eyes. 'Run it once more.' He watched the punches, watched Gareth meekly climbing into the passenger seat of his car. 'OK, OK. I'll get Evans to bring her in and I'll get a warrant. We'll just have to take the bungalow and the farmhouse apart. That third gun's got to be in there somewhere, it's not out on the hill.'

CHAPTER TWENTY-THREE

Gordon Price was in the front garden, weeding tiny strands of grass from between the spring bulbs. Another couple of weeks and Eileen could sit out here in the sun. He'd have to dust off the garden furniture, and maybe they could manage a little trip out to the garden centre and she could choose new cushions. Mind, it would be busy this weekend. They could go in the week when it was a bit quieter and Eileen wouldn't get so flustered.

'Sergeant Price. How lovely to see you again after all this time.'

Gordon stopped weeding as a shadow darkened the soil in front of him. 'What a pretty garden you have. It's been such a long time since I've been able to enjoy the spring sunshine.'

Gordon looked up slowly, taking in the pointed black shoes, black trousers and jumper, and the prison pallor under the short dark hair. But it was the small, pointed teeth he remembered most. He shivered, despite the warmth in the late afternoon sunshine. Stephen bloody Collins. But how the hell did he get out? Gordon reached into his pocket for his mobile phone.

'I wouldn't bother. I have every right to be here.' Collins bared his sharp little rat-teeth in a smile. 'The parole board felt I had atoned for my sins. They realised that I had learned my lesson and readily agreed to my release on licence.'

'I'd have thrown away the key.'

'Now, now, Mr Price, that's not a terribly Christian sentiment.'

'After what you did? I'd have brought back the death penalty for what you did to that little girl.' Gordon shuddered as the image of the broken little body flashed into his mind. 'I'd have pushed you through the trapdoor myself you evil bastard.' He lunged forward, soil-covered trowel still in his hand and held it in Collins' face. 'You don't deserve to be alive after what you did.' Collins shook his head and ignored the threat, ignored the sandy soil as it dropped onto his polished shoes.

'I have managed to put all that behind me, Sergeant Price. I understand the reasons, the traumas of my childhood which led me to that unfortunate situation and now I need you to understand that I bear you absolutely no malice.' Collins folded his hands in front of him like a minister about to deliver a sermon. 'I appreciate that you were simply following flawed procedure when you arrested me. I had hoped to offer an olive branch to poor Mr Watkin too, but alas, it was too late for him to be saved.'

Gordon brought the trowel ever closer to Collins' cheek. 'You need to leave now. Get off my property and don't ever think of coming back, otherwise…'

'Otherwise what, Sergeant. Surely you abhor violence? I have waited such a long time to see you, I really think it would be polite of you to hear me out, especially now that poor Mr Watkin is no longer with us. I wanted to tell him that I also bear him no malice, despite his pitifully unconvincing performance as duty solicitor that night. Nobody else knows what I went through, but the two of you were there.' He grasped Gordon's wrist and forced the trowel away from his face. 'I was treated like an animal, Sergeant. Worse than an animal.' He smiled slowly. 'Here, kitty.'

'So it was you who hurt the cat, you bastard.'

Collins shrugged and flicked a lump of soil from his sleeve. 'A righteous man regardeth the life of his beast: but the tender mercies of the wicked are cruel.'

'I'm phoning the police.' Gordon glanced across at the house. Eileen was standing in the front window. She waved when she saw him looking. He waved back with a smile, not letting her see his agitation.

'Perhaps your lovely wife would be more receptive to what I have to say, more forgiving. Shall we ask her?' Collins turned to walk towards the house and Gordon leaped over the flowerbed and lunged at him.

'I don't think you heard me, Collins. Get off my property.' Between every word Gordon jabbed Collins in the shoulder, but Collins showed no sign of noticing. He was almost at the open front door now and Gordon pushed himself between Collins and the step. Collins reached into his pocket and Gordon ducked away from him, but it wasn't a weapon which Collins withdrew. It was a small, black bible with scraps of paper marking certain pages.

'*Repent, then, and turn to God, so that your sins may be wiped out, that times of refreshing may come from the Lord.* Matthew, Chapter Six, verse 14.'

'You're sick, Collins. Get away from us.' Gordon pushed him again and Collins staggered backwards onto the flowerbed, but once he had recovered his balance he smiled benignly and riffled through the bible.

'*For if you forgive men when they sin against you, your heavenly Father will also forgive you. But if you do not forgive men their sins, your Father will not forgive your sins,* Acts 3, verse 19.' He closed the Bible and slipped it back into his pocket. 'I should very much like to meet your wife.' He pushed his way over the threshold and into the hall. 'She's in here, is she?'

Gordon felt his fingers close around the trowel as Collins looked past him, into the house. 'I'm warning you one last time.'

Collins bared his teeth again and shook his head. 'So much anger, Sergeant Price, where does it all come from?' He turned his back on Gordon and reached for the living room door handle, pushing his way in. Eileen flew across the room towards him, hurling herself at him and catching him off balance.

'Don't you dare hit my Gordon.'

There was a splintering sound as Collins pitched forward and his head hit the door. He slid to the carpet, leaving spatters and smears of blood on the woodwork. The door swung back on its hinges as he crumpled and it tilted him as he hit the carpet, leaving one open but unseeing eye visible. Eileen screamed and kicked out at the door again and again, trying to close it, but Collins was wedged in the doorway. Gordon retched, unable to take his eyes off Collins. He slammed the front door closed behind him, suddenly aware of how much would be visible from the road.

'It'll be all right Eileen. We can sort this out.' He reached for the phone and had punched in two nines before sinking to his knees. Eileen had retreated to the far end of the living room and she sobbed, rocking gently as she knelt by the cat.

'What have I done?' she repeated over and over like a mantra. Gordon dropped the phone and ran to her, held her in his arms, rocking with her.

'We'll sort it out,' he said as he stroked her hair. 'Everything will be fine. Trust me.'

CHAPTER TWENTY-FOUR

Sarah watched Morgan Evans drive into the yard, saw Milos climb out of the passenger seat and heard him slam the car door, hard. When were they going to leave him alone? Moving away from the window, she picked up her car keys from the kitchen table. She'd leave now and take the eggs down to the shop on the way to school. There was a solid thump on the window. Why did he still not use the doorbell? But at least she'd managed to stop him walking straight into her house.

'Come in, Milos, tell me all about it.' The figure on the step had his back to the door, but Milos definitely hadn't been wearing a dark grey suit and tan brogues when he got out of the car. 'Oh. I thought…'

Evans turned to face her but didn't look at her. 'Mrs Sarah Watkin, I would like you to accompany me to the police station.'

'Morgan, don't be daft now, I'm not in the mood for jokes.'

'It's not a joke, Mrs Watkin.' He looked at a point just past her left shoulder.

'Morgan? What the hell is going on?' Sarah frowned. 'I need to collect the children from school, I can't come with you now.'

'I'm just following orders. Can't Milos do the school run?'

Sarah stared at him. 'I'll have to phone the school, tell the secretary I won't be there. Why can't I just pick them up first?'

'I'm sorry, Sarah, but you can't, you're to come with me now.'

She was already on the phone before he had finished speaking. 'Mam, can you pick up the kids? I'll phone the school now, tell them.' She glanced at Evans as she spoke. 'It's something to do

138

with the police. Nothing to worry about, they just want to ask me a few more questions.' There was a pause as she listened. 'I don't know how long. Could they have tea at yours just in case? I'll see you in a bit.'

She put the phone down and lifted the receiver again immediately. While she waited for the school to answer she turned her back on Evans. 'Sorry, Hazel, I know it's ridiculously short notice, but Mam will pick up the kids now, if that's OK.' She pulled a scarf from the coat-stand by the door, and picked up her bag. 'No it's fine, it's nothing to worry about. I'll see you tomorrow.'

Sarah followed Evans to the car. He opened the rear door on the driver's side, but she ignored it and went round to the front passenger door. 'I'm not one of your criminals, Morgan.' He hesitated, but closed the rear door and climbed into the driver's seat.

'What's it all about then?' she demanded, as he turned the car round.

'DI Swift asked me to collect you. He said to tell you that they're going to need to search the bungalow too. Uniform are on their way with a warrant.'

'For God's sake, what is this? Milo is off the hook so it has to be me now, is that it?'

Evans shrugged. 'It's not my idea, Sarah.'

When they reached the interview room, Swift and Julie Kite were waiting for them.

'Thank you, DC Evans, we'll take it from here.' Swift shepherded Sarah round the table so that she was facing the door.

'Do I need my solicitor?' asked Sarah. 'Oh no, sorry, he's not available is he?'

Swift switched on the tape, waited for it to bleep and looked squarely at Sarah. 'You can, of course, have a solicitor present, that is your right. You do not have to say anything. But it may harm your defence if you do not mention when questioned something which you later rely on in court. Anything you do say may be given in evidence. You should know that we have applied for, and been granted, a search warrant to search the property known as Penrhiw Bungalow.'

'Craig, what the hell is going on? Am I under arrest?'

'Interview commenced at…' he looked at the clock, '3.15pm on Friday, 29th April. Those present DI Swift, DS Kite and Sarah Watkin.'

'Where were you on Monday morning, Sarah?' asked Julie.

'You know where I was. I was at Annie Lewis's funeral in Builth.'

'What time did the funeral start?' Swift was checking a newspaper cutting in the folder on the desk in front of him.

'Half past one. We were in the church by quarter past. There are a couple of hundred people who can vouch for me.' Sarah looked hard at Julie. 'Annie was very popular. Check the undertaker's lists if you don't believe me.'

'So you'd have to leave Penrhiw at what, about twenty past twelve?'

'Something like that.'

'Where were you in the morning?' Swift turned over several pages of hand-written notes.

'I took Dylan to school, then I called in at the shop on my way past.'

'So you were home about…' Julie flipped pages of her notebook.

'I didn't get back until about twelve. I had things to do.'

'Things?' asked Julie.

Sarah sighed. 'I had an appointment in Llandrindod.'

Swift and Kite exchanged glances. 'Where was this appointment?' Julie said.

'Is this really relevant?' Sarah directed the question at Swift.

'Is is. We need to know where you were between ten thirty and about eleven forty-five.'

Sarah leaned back in her chair and looked at the ceiling.

'Sarah, where were you at 10.30am on Tuesday?' Swift sounded terse now.

Sarah Watkin leaned down beside her chair and picked up her handbag. She unzipped a pocket on the front of the bag and pulled out a white appointment card. She put the bag down and threw the card across the table. I was here, all right?'

Julie picked up the card and turned it over. 'Marriage guidance?'

'They call it Relate these days.'

'But what…'

'You wanted to know where I was. Phone them. They will confirm I was there from 10.30 until just after ten past eleven. Then I went to the shop in Llanwrtyd and because I was running late I had to rush straight back to Penrhiw to make lunch for Seren, then I picked up Ella and we went to Annie's funeral.'

'And why were you there, Sarah?' Swift picked up the card. His voice had lost its hard edge.

'Why does anyone go?'

'Was the marriage in trouble?' Swift sounded like an old friend now.

Sarah didn't look at either of them, but picked up her bag and rummaged for tissues. 'I wanted to know what my options were. Just in case.'

'And was there a particular reason for that?'

'No, Sergeant, it was just on a whim. Bored housewives, you know how hysterical they get.'

'Did it have anything to do with Jessica Southam?'

Sarah gave a mirthless laugh. 'Gareth's liaison with that awful woman was purely business-related, Sergeant.'

'But then why did you need marriage guidance?'

Sarah looked from Julie to Swift and sighed. 'Nobody knows about this. We weren't seeing eye to eye on something important.'

'And did this thing make you angry enough to want to kill him?' Julie asked.

'Never!' Sarah jumped to her feet and the plastic chair smacked hard against the wall. 'He was the father of my children. He always will be.' Sarah's face crumpled and she began sobbing, gasping for raw, ragged gulps of air. Swift signed off for the tape and switched off the machine.

'I'm sorry.' Julie picked up the chair. 'We have to ask these questions if we're to find out who killed your husband.'

Sarah let herself be guided back into the chair. Still sobbing she rested her head on the desk, her arms blotting out her accusers.

'I think I'll just... coffees...' said Swift, closing the interview room door quietly behind him.

'Sarah. Look at me.' Julie put her hand on Sarah's shoulder, but it was shrugged away. 'All I want to do is find out who did this to your family.'

'Why did he bring me in?' Sarah nodded towards the closed door where Swift had exited. 'Does he really think I could have killed Gareth?'

Julie picked up the folder from the desk. 'Can I run you back to Penrhiw?'

CHAPTER TWENTY-FIVE

Adam's bike was propped against the wall by the kitchen door when Julie got back to the cottage. There was no sign of the chains and padlocks he had insisted on at home. She smiled and lifted the shopping out of the back seat of the car. In Manchester the road bike and the mountain bike had lived indoors in the hallway, snagging tights and making squeezing past with shopping bags a nightmare. Maybe there was something to be said for living in the arse-end of nowhere after all. She plonked the bags on the kitchen table and reached for the kettle.

'Hello, I'm home,' she shouted.

'Coming.' There was a scuffling and Adam opened the door to the living room about six inches. His head appeared first, then the rest of him slid through the narrow gap he'd left himself.

'Coffee?' Julie stopped, teaspoon poised over the jar. 'What are you doing?'

'Nothing. Coffee would be great. You're early.'

'We've come to a bit of a lull in proceedings. It looks as though I'll get my day off tomorrow after all. I think the DI's being kind, with the move and everything.' She poured milk into one of the mugs. 'Adam, I'm sorry about the other day. I shouldn't have… It's just force of habit.'

'What you mean is you've been doubting me for so long it's become second nature?'

'No. I mean…'

Adam smiled the lopsided smile she loved. 'I know what you mean. It goes with the job.' He took the milk from her and put it in the fridge. 'And I've been a total shit in the not too distant past.'

'Well, when you put it like that, I can't argue.' She handed him a mug. 'But I've got a confession to make.'

'Tell me more. Have you been cavorting in the stationery cupboard with the DI?'

'Not in my wildest dreams. Or Swift's for that matter, he's a very happily married man.'

'So am I, Jules, and I'm sorry.'

'Yeah well, just wait until I tell you…' She cupped both hands round her coffee mug and stared into the steaming liquid. 'You know I said I'd found a home for Sid?'

'With the formidable DC Mitchell. I still can't quite believe that somehow.'

'Well…'

'Well?'

'The thing is…'

'Is that my mobile? Hang on a tick.' Adam darted for the sitting room door. Julie took a step towards it, but forced herself to turn back. She wouldn't eavesdrop on his calls. When he returned, she was standing by the sink, looking out of the window. 'You were saying?'

She turned round, determined not to ask who had been on the phone. In Adam's arms was a small ginger cat.

Julie, inexplicably, burst into tears. Adam bundled the cat into her arms and kissed the top of her head.

'Well if I'd known you'd be that upset to get him back I wouldn't have spent half the day tracking him down.'

The cat purred as Julie stroked under its chin. 'I thought you'd be annoyed that I'd brought him.'

Adam shook his head. 'I never thought it was fair keeping him in that flat, too scared to let him out because of the road, but now that we're here,' he shrugged.

'How did you know?'

'Your Mum let it slip at your leaving do.'

'And you let me worry about it all this time?'

'Well you should have been honest with me.' Adam stroked the cat's head.

'How did you find him?'

'I heard you talking to the cattery people this morning. All I had to do was ask Menna about local places not too far from your route. Knowing what you're like with maps.'

'We'll make a detective of you yet.' Julie grinned and put the cat down on the floor. 'I think he'll be happy here.'

'Seriously though, Jules. We need to start again. Put the past behind us.'

'I know. I've spent the afternoon with a woman who's going to have to come to terms with a very different future for herself and her kids.'

'Is this anything to do with the murder up the road?'

Julie nodded. 'And I've been a real cow to her.'

'Situation normal there then.' Adam ducked away as Julie punched his arm.

'I just can't read the people like I could in Manchester. It's like walking a route you know really well, but in the pitch dark. There are so many things to trip over.'

'It'll just take time. Anyway, you just have to get the job done. Can't afford to be too soft can you?'

'Have I mentioned that before?'

'Once or twice.'

'It just that I worry about what sort of person it's turning me into. I can't help being suspicious of everyone and everything.'

Adam said nothing. Between them they found a home for the shopping and cooked dinner. Sid followed them from cupboard to cupboard and sat under their feet as they cooked. Julie was washing the dishes when Adam's mobile phone really did ring.

'… Great, no, that's even better. I'll see you tomorrow then, round about lunchtime OK?' He put his phone down and wrapped his arms round Julie's waist as she heaved a pan out of the soapy water.

'How do you fancy coming to Manchester tomorrow? That business with the paperwork, Fran's managed to get it sorted out sooner than she thought. If you've got a day off?'

'God that's tempting, but…'

'But you can't leave the jurisdiction of Mid Wales Police?'

'Something like that. Sorry. Maybe we can go back home for the weekend once this is sorted out?'

'No worries,' Adam said, picking up the tea towel from the back of a chair. 'Do you mind if I stay over and come back on Sunday?'

CHAPTER TWENTY-SIX

Eileen stood and watched as Gordon dragged the man across the hallway and through the little door that led to the garage. It was handy, having an inside door, she thought. It meant you could get to the freezer and the tumble drier without going outside. Much nicer when it was raining. The heels of the man's shoes left tracks in the carpet. She'd have to get the hoover out. Wherever it was.

Then there was the blood. The man must have cut himself badly to bleed like that, dark red, almost black. It was all over the door and on the carpet. Could you use bleach on a wool carpet? She heard the car door being opened, the way it grated against the brickwork, then lots of bumping noises as Gordon helped the man to get into the car. He looked quite out of breath when he came back into the hall.

'Get your shoes on, love, we're going for a little ride in the car.' Gordon washed his hands at the sink in the kitchen. He used nearly a whole bottle of liquid soap, scrubbing and scrubbing. What had he been doing to get so dirty?

'Are we taking the man with us?'

'Don't worry about that now, love, just get your shoes and your coat.'

'Which coat shall I take? Are we going shopping?'

'Just for a ride in the car. Here.' Gordon reached into the hall cupboard and handed her the pale lilac anorak. Was that her coat? Gordon pushed her arms into the sleeves. He seemed cross. Had she done something wrong? 'Just get in the car for me, Eileen,' he said, sliding the chain across on the front door and checking the snick was up.

It was a bit of a squeeze getting into the car. Gordon usually drove it out of the garage so she could open the door properly, but even so, there seemed to be less room than ever.

Mrs…Beswick, see, she knew she'd remember, Mrs Beswick was in her front garden. She waved as they drove past but Gordon didn't notice her. Eileen waved though. She always waved.

'I should have fed Bobby.'

'What?' Gordon's eyes bulged as he turned to look at her. He looked like that fish on the television.

'Bobby needs his tablets regularly. The vet said. You told me.'

'Not now, Eileen.' Gordon looked in his rear-view mirror. Mrs Beswick was still watching the car.

'Where are we going? Will we be back in time to feed him?'

'We won't be long.'

'How long?' Gordon didn't answer her. 'How long, Gordon?'

'Not long.'

'But where are we going?' She could see that vein on the side of this head, like a pale blue earthworm wriggling its way down his temple.

'Just for a little ride in the car, love. You like that don't you?'

Eileen nodded. 'Can we go to the Elan Valley? I'd like to look at the water.'

Gordon's grip loosened a little on the steering wheel and he glanced at his wife with a little smile.

'Yes.' he said. 'That's a grand idea.'

Eileen turned in her seat to share her good fortune with the man in the back, but he wasn't there. She smiled anyway, at Gordon's praise, and settled back in her seat. She liked the Elan Valley. They used to drive up there on a Sunday when the kids were small. Vicky had that little pink bike with fat, white wheels and wobbly stabilisers. John had liked to stride out with his dad, the two of them up ahead, Gordon pointing out birds and trees, taking him to visit the little church. Where had it all gone? Where had all the time disappeared to?

There were still a few cars at the Visitors' Centre, but dusk was creeping down the valley. Soon it would be too dark to be out there on the hills. You might never be found if you ventured off the tracks. Eileen shivered at the thought of being lost up there, in the black peat and the weather-faded reeds.

'Cold?' Gordon turned up the heater controls. 'You'll warm up once we get you inside.' Eileen frowned. He was wearing gloves. He never wore gloves, not to drive in. He glanced at her again. He always seemed worried about her these days, always watching her. Poor Gordon. She'd always thought that being a policeman must be a horrible job. He'd seen things people shouldn't have to see, not even someone as brave as Gordon, terrible things. He should leave and find a nice job in an office. Eileen began to rock gently, the seat belt rubbing rhythmically against her coat as she moved. He indicated and pulled off the road.

'You just have to wait here, in the café, for a little while. Do you think you can do that for me?'

Alone now, Gordon drove past the great stone wall at the bottom of Caban Coch Reservoir. It was a calm evening, there was no water blowing over the top or cascading down the wall and the surface of the water beyond was a mirror reflecting stands of pine, the charcoal trunks of spruce wearing a faint smudge of green. The verdigris dome of the Foel Tower stood out still, even in the fading light, against the muted greens and browns. The valley looked like an old black and white postcard with the colours painted in. He knew Eileen still had one of those postcards. He had sent it when he went on his very first training course in London. It showed Trafalgar Square and all the double-decker buses had been picked out in red. The water in the fountains was a pale blue. *Miss you* he'd written. It was the first time they had been separated since they met.

Gordon turned the car towards the long stone bridge that separated Caban Coch from Garreg-Ddu Reservoir. Straight ahead, the little church gazed out over the water. He'd always felt there was something terribly sad about Nantgwyllt with its drowned chapel and the big house where Shelley used to come with his poor wife. They were all eventually lost to still, dark water. He slowed the car, checked in the rear-view mirror and pulled off the road onto a track through the trees. The surface of the water was silver against the black trunks.

She hadn't been out anywhere like this for so long. All her days seemed to merge into one somehow. Through the window, Eileen watched a squirrel scurry up the trunk of a pine tree. Maybe she should have asked if they could go somewhere where there were more people. Into Brecon maybe, where she could sit and watch them, while Gordon went to get his paper, and get her a cream cake from Greggs. There were one or two families here, the children clutching little paper bags as they left the shop, but otherwise she was alone and the centre looked as though it was about to close. What would she do if they made her leave? Where was Gordon?

He wasn't gone long. It must have been a very short walk. Not like the ones they used to do, whole days out there in the countryside. But she was worried about him. His breath came in short gasps, he was so pale. When Eileen reached up to touch his face, his skin felt clammy. He sat next to her at the table and closed his eyes.

'Do you think they'll have any of that nice coffee cake?'

It was several seconds before Gordon opened his eyes, and Eileen was petulant. 'It'll have all gone by the time we get to the counter. We need to go now.' Eileen's voice rose to a wail and Gordon closed his eyes again immediately. 'Now,' she said. 'We need to go now.'

Gordon scanned the café and the little shop beyond, but nobody was taking any notice, nobody seemed to have heard Eileen. She was picking at an old napkin that had been left on the table, shredding it slowly and carefully, and dropping the bits onto the floor. He put his hands over hers and gave them a squeeze.

'Once we get home,' he said 'you can have whatever you like.'

A car scrunched to a halt outside the window. The driver flashed – two quick bursts of light – and then he began to turn the car round. Gordon took the napkin from Eileen's fingers.

'That's us,' he said. 'Let's go home.'

CHAPTER TWENTY-SEVEN
Saturday, 30th April

When Adam had left, Julie tidied the kitchen, went upstairs and looked at the cardboard boxes still sitting in the spare bedroom. Not today. She'd allow herself a proper day off today. Maybe tomorrow. Sid wound himself round her legs and purred.

'As for you,' she bent down and rubbed his head, 'you need to learn about cat flaps.'

She was on her knees on the kitchen floor. 'See, just push it with your nose.' She plonked the cat in front of the flap and pushed it open with her finger. 'Nothing to it. Just reverse the process when you want to come in.' Sid looked at her, blinked, yawned and stayed where he was. 'Look, if you just push it with your head.' Julie got close up to the curved plastic door and turned round to look at him. 'I hope you're not still sulking about the cattery?' As she turned back she was aware of a shape outside the door. Slowly the owner of two wellingtoned feet bent down until her face was almost on a level with Julie's.

'Morning. I just wondered if you wanted some eggs?'

'Ah.' Julie stood up and opened the door. Menna stood on the path with two egg boxes in her hand. 'I was just trying to show the cat how to use the cat flap.'

'Ours live in the shed,' said Menna, handing over the eggs. 'Never come in the house. Dogs neither.'

'He's never been outside. I think the thought of all that space terrifies him.'

'What about you? Terrify you too does it?'

'A bit.' Julie grinned. 'I can't get used to the quiet. And the dark.'

'You will. I'm the other way round. I can never sleep when we go away. Everywhere else is just too noisy. How are you getting on?'

'Work's been busy. I've not really had time to go exploring.'

'Joe said he saw you talking to his horse. Do you ride?'

'No, not since I was about ten. I've always fancied learning to ride properly, I even applied for the Mounted Section once, but they didn't like the look of me.'

'Well if you fancy it you could always come out with me. Joe's horse is a sensible, ploddy old thing. You'd be safe enough.'

'I'll have to have a think about that one, but thanks.'

'It would be nice to have a bit of female company for a change.' Menna looked round the kitchen. 'At least they decorated before they flitted.'

'Who?'

'The last tenants. They only lasted three months. He had some grand plan about renting a bit of land and being self-sufficient.'

'What went wrong?'

'The winter. I think she thought it would be like Gardeners' World, all walled gardens, fruit trees and marrows and terracotta pots on sunny little patios.'

'What happened?'

'They were snowed in for a month and scarpered back to Cheltenham. I told Gwyn they wouldn't last. Let me know about the riding.' Menna glanced at the cat. 'Just chuck it out and it'll find its way back in if it's hungry.'

'What do I owe you?'

'Don't worry, we're drowning in eggs.' Menna took the Land Rover keys out of her pocket. 'Oh, I almost forgot. This was stuck in the gate. I don't suppose it's anything.' She handed Julie a stiff white card.

Is it lawful on the Sabbath days to do good, or to do evil? To save life, or to destroy it? Luke 6:9

153

Again, the devil taketh him up into an exceeding high mountain.
Matthew 4:8

Julie closed the door and turned the catch on the cat flap. 'I wonder,' she said to the cat, 'what the hell's going on here?'

From up on the hill, the cottage looked like a dolls' house, dwarfed by the steep-sided valley. She could see Cam just along the lane, and cows, like little figures on a fuzzy-felt board. Directly beneath her a collection of low farm buildings huddled in the lee of the hill. That must be Menna's. She could hear the whine of a quad bike drifting up the valley. For the first time she began to realise the significance of each person, each farmstead in this remote landscape. How many people had lived on her street in Manchester? How many of them had she met or would even recognise if she met them in the pub or the supermarket? The quad bike rounded the crest of the hill. She could see the collie clinging onto the back, the dark-clad figure of Joe, hunched over the handlebars like a kid on a BMX, as though that would make the bike go faster.

As she watched Joe, she thought how conspicuous she must be here, how conspicuous any newcomer must be. Surely someone must know if the man who had visited the Prices was the same man she and Swift had seen on the Epynt, watching Penrhiw? Maybe he was the one who left her the message at the cottage. She shivered, despite the warmth of the sun. So what about the people handing out *The Watchtower*? Were they real Jehovah's Witnesses, or were they part of this too? Maybe it was all linked. There could easily be a connection between a police officer and a duty solicitor, couldn't there? She followed the quad's descent. But who would know? How could she check it? Ella obviously hadn't recognised him and poor Eileen... well. Maybe she could start with some background on the con Gordon Price had mentioned, the one who had threatened everyone in court when he was sent down. It was all she had, but at least it was a start.

She set off down the hill. She needed to think about something else before she drove herself mad. But what would she do with herself all day? It couldn't hurt to go and have a word with Gordon Price could it? Unless – maybe Adam was right. Maybe she was just a little bit obsessed with the job. Still, it would give her a head start on Monday morning. And she could try and find Merthyr and have a look at the shops while she was over there. Just a couple of questions, that's all it needed, tacked onto a shopping trip.

CHAPTER TWENTY-EIGHT

Julie parked the car in front of the Price's house and switched off the engine. This was obviously the more affluent end of town, all neat gardens and net curtains; daffodils nodding in the freshly-turned earth of regimented flowerbeds. She walked up the crazy-paving path to the front door and pressed the bell. There was movement on the other side of the patterned glass, but not towards her. She rang the bell again and bent to peer through the letterbox. An acrid, eye-watering smell struck her immediately and she let the letterbox drop. Had Eileen had an accident with the bleach bottle? There was a rattle of chain and two bolts were drawn back.

'Sorry, Sergeant, Eileen was just … What can I do for you?'

Gordon Price had opened the door just wide enough for her to see his face. He looked tired, with grey circles under his eyes and paler than he had been when she last saw him. Alzheimer's had done that to her mother, all those years trying to care for her grandfather had chewed her up and spat her out, finally left her guilt-ridden that she'd had to admit she needed help.

'Can I come in? I don't really want to discuss this on the doorstep.' She stepped onto the threshold but Gordon didn't open the door any wider.

'Eileen's not feeling very well, Sergeant. I don't really want to upset her.' She felt the pressure of the door against her foot, and tried to see past him into the hallway. He shifted slightly and blocked her view. 'What can I help you with?'

Julie dug out her notebook from her bag. 'It's about the man Eileen saw, the one dressed in black who left you the note.'

Gordon Price shrugged. 'I'm not sure I can tell you any more. She's having a bad week. She probably imagined the whole thing, got him confused with someone on the television.'

'Still, the note was real enough wasn't it, Mr Price? I just want to be sure I'm not missing anything. What about Gareth Watkin? Was there anything that might have happened when he was duty solicitor and you were there at the same time, arresting officer maybe?'

'There must have been a few nutters over the years. We worked together quite a lot at one time, but he was taken off the rota for some reason.'

'But was there anything memorable from that time? Anyone you can remember who was particularly obnoxious, threatening.'

Gordon shook his head. 'You know what it's like, Sergeant. You have to grow a bit of a hard shell, let it pass you by. You don't notice after a while, do you? If Eileen tells me anything else I'll let you know.' He turned away. 'I must go, Sergeant. Enjoy your weekend.'

Julie removed her foot from the door and it closed in her face. She stepped backwards off the low step and looked up at the house. There was something else worrying Gordon. Poor man. Forty years from now, would Adam end up looking after her like that? She zipped her notebook back into her bag. Only if she let him. As she turned, something caught her eye. In the window, Eileen was waving.

The satnav chugged through the route to Merthyr. Why did it take so long? In Manchester it had worked out where you were going before you managed to fasten your seatbelt. Not that she had needed it very often; only on the rare occasion that they made it as far as Stockport or Hazel Grove. She used to think Offerton was the back of beyond.

'At the end of the road turn left.'

*

She sat in a café and watched Merthyr go by. Nowhere near the scale of Manchester, but, it was hectic with shoppers. The inevitable bank holiday weekend rain had arrived, and people scurried across the road into the shelter of shops. There were raincoats and umbrellas weaving between youngsters in tee shirts and flip-flops. So coats were as uncool here as in Manchester. She dialled Helen's number. Straight to voicemail.

'Anyone sitting here, lovely?' A young woman with a baby in her arms squeezed into the chair opposite.

'No, you're fine.'

'You're not from round here are you? London is it?'

'Manchester.'

'We went to Manchester last Christmas. That lovely market with all the German sausages and gingerbread and stuff.' She jiggled the baby in her lap. 'We're staying closer to home at the moment though, with this one, aren't we *cariad*?' She smiled at the little girl, then up at a man balancing a tray across the handles of a brand new pushchair. He put the tray down and held out his arms.

'Should I put her in her chair, just while you have your coffee?'

The woman hesitated but then handed the little girl to her father.

'I'm hopeless I am. I just want to *cwtch* her all the time.' She grinned at Julie. 'You got kids?'

Julie shook her head.

'Best thing we ever did.' She watched the man buckling the baby into her chair. 'I'd do anything for her.'

'She's beautiful,' said Julie. Her phone jiggled across the table. 'Nice to meet you,' she said, and left them fussing over the baby.

'What's up?' Helen sounded amused. 'You missing him already?'

'No,' Julie answered, too quickly. 'Are you working?'

'Nope. I'm in the Arndale, trying to find something to wear for Alison's hen night. You going to be able to get back for it?'

'Not the way things are going.' Julie stood out of the rain in the doorway of the café.

'Pity. It'll be a great night, she wants to go to the Rev.'

The Revolucion De Cuba: fifty different types of rum, and salsa lessons. It seemed about as far from Merthyr as it was possible to get. 'I'm not sure Wales is ready for that sort of thing.'

'How daft are you? There's one in Cardiff.'

'Are you sure?'

'It's not a million miles away is it? You should be down there tonight, while the cat's away.' Helen laughed at her own joke. 'Talking of cats, how's Sid getting on?'

'I can't get him to go through the cat flap. No, that's not strictly true, I can't even get him to venture off the lino and onto the doorstep.'

'Ah. It'll take a while, he's just not used to all that space. Have you ventured off the lino yet?'

The rain seemed to have stopped and Julie strode out, into the mêlée of people in the street. 'I've got as far as Merthyr Tydfil, although I'm not sure what the name means yet.'

'What it means?'

'All the place names here tell you something about the place itself. Rhys told me.'

'And who's Rhys?' There was a smile in Helen's voice.

'Just a DC.'

'Oh yes.'

'Helen, you're obsessed.'

'Yeah, I know. Sounds like you're settling in though.'

'It's different.'

'Well it was always going to be. There's nowhere quite like Manchester. How's the prat who was giving you grief?'

'Still being a prat, but at least I know why now. The woman in the canteen told me. He's just failed his sergeants' exams.'

'Ah, and you've got the job he thought he should have.'

'You should be a detective.'

*

159

Craig Swift followed his wife dutifully round John Lewis. He exchanged a conspiratorial nod with an old boy who sat surrounded by carrier bags next to the escalator. Swift sighed. There was still something not right about Penrhiw, but what the hell was it? He believed Milos. OK, so he did have what Kite referred to as something dark and brooding about him – Gwen had always called him Heathcliff. But was he a killer? Craig couldn't see it. And then there was Sarah. After she'd lived through the aftermath of Gareth's surgery and the chemo, the endless visits to hospitals miles and miles away and then his long, slow recovery, could she really have pulled the trigger on her children's father?'

'What do you think about this. Too flowery?' Gwen held up a duvet cover in its plastic shell. 'They do matching curtains.'

'Where's it for?'

'Spare bedroom. I want to get Rob in to give it a coat of paint.' Gwen watched him. 'I thought I'd do the ceiling black with silver stars, and paint the walls puce,' she said.

'Fine,' said Swift.

'Craig…' She put the duvet cover back on the shelf and linked her arm through his. 'It's poor Gareth is it?'

'I can't help thinking I've missed something.'

'How's the new sergeant getting on?'

'She's going to be good, once she gets used to the way things are done round here. She's keen mind, and seems really bright.' Swift grinned. 'I think it's given them all a bit of a shaking. Rhys has taken her under his wing.'

'He's a lovely lad.'

'He'll do. He's got no ambition whatsoever, other than his rugby, but he's pleasant enough.'

'Why don't you buy me a coffee and a large piece of gateau in Druckers. Then you can drop me off at home and go into the station for an hour, see if you can get things a bit clearer.'

'You don't mind?'

'Not if it helps you sleep tonight. I can do Cardiff any time.'

CHAPTER TWENTY-NINE

Julie flicked through the photographs which had been left on her desk. These were the as yet unidentified cars which had been parked in the car park at the Metropole Hotel at the time of the last sighting of Gareth Watkin. There was a blue Peugeot 205, a bright yellow hatchback, an old soft-topped Land Rover and a grey people carrier with the registration number MM06 AJK. She knew that index number from somewhere. MM for Manchester and Merseyside and AJK were almost Adam's initials. Where had she seen it? She sat down and switched on her computer.

The car had been stolen from Manchester's Heaton Park on Saturday morning. Julie stared at the screen. Had she seen it up there then, in Manchester? But where? She picked up the phone and dialled, heard it ringing at the other end and pictured the office, with its view over the city towards Salford and the red brick ventilation tower of Strangeways Prison. After the riots in 1990 it had been renamed HM Prison Manchester, as though a new name could sweep away the past, the riots and the history, the execution shed and one hundred hangings. Julie had been four at the time of the riots, but she had never referred to it as anything but Strangeways. It seemed to suit the place.

'CID.'

'Frank, how's life in God's own city?'

'Much the same as it was at the end of last week. How are you doing?'

'Grand, thanks. It's quiet though. I can't sleep.'

'Sergeant Kite. Have you got used to it yet?'

'The stripes or the place? I think they'll both take a while to be honest.'

'What can I do for you, sweetheart?'

'There was a car stolen from Heaton Park last Saturday morning. Don't suppose you could find out if anyone's dealing with it?'

'Go on.'

'It's a dark grey Vauxhall Zafira, index Mike Mike zero six alpha Juliet kilo. It's turned up here and it might be connected to a case. I could do with knowing if there's any CCTV covering where it was nicked from.'

'What else would I do with a Saturday afternoon? Give us your mobile number and I'll call you back if I get hold of anything.'

'Thanks, Frank, I owe you one.'

Julie put the phone down and tapped the screen with the end of her biro. 'I know you're something to do with this.'

'Can't stay away, Sergeant?' Swift threw his coat over Rhys's chair and sat down.

'No, Sir. There's something bugging me.'

'Me too. You first.'

'Well,' Julie walked over to the board. Rhys had rubbed out Swift's observations and replaced them with his neat capitals. 'There's still something odd going on at that farm, something Sarah's not telling us.'

Swift granted her a small nod.

'Although I think you're right that there's no liaison between her and Milos.'

'I never thought there was.'

'No, Sir. And then there's this business with the cat, and Gordon Price's visitor.'

'Gordon Price? How's he connected with Penrhiw?'

'I don't know that he is, but I went round this morning, just to see if there was anything else he could tell me, and Price was acting very strangely.'

'Strangely? Elaborate.'

'He looked tired. I suppose that's par for the course, but there was something else. It was as though he was frightened of something. He refused to let me in.'

'It's not been easy for him, with his wife the way she is.'

'No, Sir, but it just feels as though there's more to it. Maybe whoever shot Gareth Watkin is also putting the frighteners on Gordon and his wife.'

'Is that it?'

'Yes. Well. This is probably nothing, but these photographs were on my desk, follow up from the CCTV footage from the Metropole. This people carrier, it was nicked from Manchester last Saturday.'

'As you say, probably nothing.'

'But I've seen it somewhere before, somewhere other than the car park at the Met, and recently. But I can't remember where.' She stared at the board and sighed. 'What about you?'

'About the same really. As you say, there's something not quite right with Penrhiw, but I can't make out what it is, and without more information there's nothing more we can do.'

'Sir.' Goronwy was holding out the phone. 'Someone's been found in a car in the Elan Valley.'

'And what's that got to do with us?' Swift took the phone from him. 'Yes?' They watched him as he listened. Swift replaced the receiver and reached for his coat. 'With me, Sergeant.'

The site had been taped off by the time Kite and Swift got to the reservoir. There was very little to see in the dense woodland. A blue-suited SOCO was taking a photograph of tyre tracks and two more were balanced on the steep slope above the water. The car was parked sideways to the track, deep into the trees. As they got out of Swift's Volvo they could see that Morgan Evans was directing operations.

'Ah, Sir. All under control here. The guy who reported it said he thought the casualty had been beaten up, but to me it looks as though he must have got out of the car and had a fall – maybe on that slope over there – but managed to get himself back here.'

'Do we know who he is?' Swift got as close to the police tapes as he could without needing a paper suit.

'Not yet. No wallet, just these.' Evans wafted a plastic evidence bag under Swift's nose. 'Oh, and this.' Another bag contained a small black bible. 'Bit of a way out for God-botherers, Sir.'

Swift ignored him, but Julie reached for the bags. The first contained a set of car keys. She smoothed the plastic. No key fob, but the black plastic on the key carried the unmistakable griffin of the Vauxhall logo. She walked round the back of the car and checked the registration. MM06 AJK. Coincidence? She hated coincidence, but then in a city of two and a half million people like Manchester the odds had always been longer. How many people were there in Powys, or even in Wales for that matter? She turned towards Swift and pointed to the number plate. Swift whistled.

'Morgan, do we know anything at all about the driver?'

'No idea, Sir. There was nothing to identify him in the car either according to the SOCOs.'

Julie looked out across the water. On the opposite bank, people were walking and cycling. High above the path one or two cars squeezed past each other on the narrow road. This side of the reservoir seemed much less accessible, not part of the tourist trail.

'Who found him?' Her question was directed at Evans. He addressed Swift with his answer after checking his notes.

'It was a bird watcher, over at the top end of Caban Coch. Had his binoculars out looking for the lesser spotted heron or something.' He smiled to himself. 'He reckons there's something special nesting over here, thought whoever it was might be after the eggs. He caught a glimpse of the car through the trees and came over to take a look. Just as well he did.'

Swift nodded. 'Come on, Kite. Hospital visiting I think.'

'Shall I come with you, Sir?' Evans went to duck under the tapes.

'Just let me know if they find anything, Constable. Was there anything in the boot?'

'Not that we've come across.'

'It might be worth getting a boat into the water, just to see if there's any sign of anything having happened down there on the bank.

'Yes, Sir.' Evans smiled again. 'Leave it to me.'

At least Julie knew her way to the hospital by now. Six days and she was beginning to feel as though she had been here for weeks. The patient was in ICU, plugged into various machines. He was ghostly, almost indistinguishable from the crisp white pillowcase. Black hair peeped out from a heavy bandage which swathed his head and his eyelids looked sunken, pale grey. His lips, over pointed little teeth, were edged in purple. Nurses strode silently and purposefully and machines sighed and blinked. The registrar stood with them as they watched him, seeking inspiration, but he soon ushered them out onto the corridor.

'So what are his chances?' Swift looked back through the glass.

'Honestly? I don't know. We've got the hypothermia under control, but...'

'Hypothermia?' Julie asked.

'Judging by his body temperature when he was brought in he must have been there overnight.'

'Is it cold enough for hypothermia at this time of year?' Swift brought his attention back to the doctor.

'If you're injured and underdressed it is.'

'We'll need his clothes,' said Julie.

'I sent them down to Dr Greenhalgh.'

'So you think there's a possibility he won't make it?'

The doctor shrugged. 'I've no idea. At the moment I'd say sixty-forty against, maybe more. He lost a lot of blood and even if he does come round... Well we'll just have to wait and see, but the chances are he could have some brain damage.'

*

Kay Greenhalgh answered the knock on her door.

'My, you've been busy this week.'

'You too. Don't you ever go home?' Swift gestured for Julie to go before him, into the doctor's office.

'About as often as you do by the looks of things.'

'What can you tell us about the guy in ICU?'

'He was lucky.'

'Lucky?' Swift raised an eyebrow. 'How?'

'They said upstairs he's lost a hell of a lot of blood. It's a wonder he was found in time, especially given where he was.' Kay Greenhalgh took the three photographs Swift held out and laid them on her desk. It's an impressive head injury.' One of the photographs showed the side of the patient's head, his hair matted with blood.

'And would you say this was done while he was out of the vehicle, can you tell?' Julie picked up another of the photographs which showed the vehicle's interior. Greenhalgh took it from her and studied it.

'There's hardly any blood in the vehicle and certainly not enough for the head injury to have been sustained in situ. There's no spatter pattern, nothing to indicate he hit his head on anything in there.'

'Any idea how he might have got the injury?' Swift perched on the edge of Greenhalgh's desk.

'Well,' she reached up to the shelves above her desk and brought down a small plastic pot. In the bottom of the pot were minute slivers of wood. 'These were embedded in his scalp. They dug them out in A&E, they thought I might like them.'

'Tree or baseball bat?' asked Julie.

Kay Greenhalgh shook her head. 'I don't think so. There was a trace of white gloss paint in the hair, and there were tiny amounts of soil and compost too. Not the sort of soil you'd find by the side of the reservoir, this had potash in it.'

'What's your best guess?' said Swift.

'Well, the wound is consistent with being made by the edge of a door or window. Not the weapon of choice for your usual mugger.'

'And not the most obvious weapon to hand by the side of a reservoir,' said Swift.

'Quite,' said Greenhalgh, handing the photographs back to him.

'Anything interesting about the clothes?' asked Julie.

'Not particularly. All well-worn though.' Greenhalgh lifted a clear plastic bag onto her desk. Swift and Julie exchanged glances. They were black. Black shoes, trousers and thin jumper.'

'There were gloves and a hat in his trouser pocket.'

'What about his shoes?'

'Now you're talking, this guy has taste. Black leather, Italian I'd say, very stylish, and with leather soles too.' She handed the bag to Julie. 'And the only soil on them was the same as I found on the clothes, which would suggest…'

'That he hadn't got out of the car where it was found,' said Julie. 'So it's even more unlikely that he was injured by the side of the reservoir.' 'Who the hell is he?' said Swift.

'That,' said Kay Greenhalgh, 'is your department.'

CHAPTER THIRTY

It was gone seven when Frank called her back. She had opened a tin of baked beans and was standing in the kitchen of the cottage, eating them cold, straight from the can when the phone rang.

'You're in luck, Julie love. No cameras in the right place in the car park of course, but the ANPR picked him up on Bury Old Road and again towards Langley.'

'So if he was heading for the M60 he must know the area. Were there any clear shots of his face?'

'I've not found anything on CCTV yet, but I'll keep looking. The owner of the vehicle saw the car drive away, but he didn't see the driver.'

'How did that happen?'

'He left the keys in the ignition.'

'Oh, very clever.'

'Small child desperate for the toilet, apparently. The father wanted to save his upholstery.'

'And it would have been our fault if he hadn't got it back. You're a star, Frank Parkinson.'

'Anything for you.'

'Yeah, I know. Seriously: thanks. I owe you a pint.'

'Did you say *if* he hadn't got it back?'

'We're good down here, Frank. We've found it. With a male occupant, badly injured.'

'So it's been in a smash?'

'Nope, the car's in perfect nick, apart from the odd blood stain.'

'I think the owner might have preferred the alternative type of stain…' Frank was chuckling to himself as the phone went down.

Julie picked up the can and stabbed at what was left in the bottom with her fork. So the car's stolen in Manchester, by someone who knows the area, and it turns up in the middle of rural Wales. Who the hell is he? She filtered the tomato sauce, searching for any last fragments of bean. Gordon Price and his wife have been bothered by someone with a 'strange accent' according to Eileen. Could that be a northern accent? Cheek. So just supposing the car thief is the man in black who left the note for Gordon. What was the connection between the two places?

She lobbed the empty can into the bin. God, she'd been thick. The Zafira had been parked on Maes y Derw, near the Price's house. Not today though – Wednesday maybe? And he could definitely have been the mystery rambler on the Epynt, watching Penrhiw. She picked up her mobile.

'Morgan? Julie Kite.' There was a pause at the other end of the phone. 'Did you get anywhere with the boat?'

'No. We persuaded the water company to get their inflatable out, but there's nothing down there.'

'Could you do me a favour?' She didn't wait for his response. 'Could you go round to Gordon Price's. Just check that Price's car's still there, and tell me what colour the doors of his house are painted.'

'You're joking?'

'Nope.'

'Any doors in particular?'

'The downstairs ones will do, internal and external. And check if there's any obvious damage to the ones leading off the hall.'

'Does it have to be now?'

'You got something planned?'

'Well no, but…'

'Yeah, OK. Tomorrow will do.'

'Thanks.'

'Oh and Morgan,' she could hear the sigh at the other end of the phone.

'Yeah?

'Have a nice evening.'

She grinned and cut the call off while he was still struggling for a suitable response. This guy in the Vauxhall had to be the link, they key to the whole thing. So why was she convinced that the person she saw on the CCTV with Gareth Watkin was a woman? She reached into a cupboard for a tin of cat food and pulled the ring. Sid weaved round her legs, purring and miaowing and she finally freed the lid. The ring-pull was still on her finger and as she looked down at it she smiled. The person in black who had assaulted Gareth Watkin wore jewellery. It was a bad recording, but something had glittered in the sunshine, third finger, left hand. So was it a diamond?

'Are you starving that cat again?' Adam grinned. 'It's not done anything for your nerves, this move to the country then?'

'God, Adam, you made me jump. I didn't hear you come in.'

'Great to see you, too.' Adam folded her into a hug.

'What are you doing back? I thought you were staying over.'

He took the lid from her and put it in the bin. 'It didn't take as long as I thought. I wanted to get back to you.'

Or had things not quite gone to plan up in Manchester? 'What about the stuff you had to collect?'

'Got it all. Fran had got it all sorted by the time I got there. But I brought you a little present back with me.' He grinned and held out his hand to her. 'Come and see.'

Julie put the cat bowl down on the floor and followed Adam out onto the drive. Propped against his car was a brand new bike. Hanging from one of the handlebars was a cycling helmet.

'But you've got two bikes already.'

'Happy Anniversary.' Adam watched her face. 'It's a hybrid, so you can use it on the road or on the Forestry tracks. We can go and explore.'

'But…' Julie rested a hand on the narrow saddle, 'I've not been on a bike for years.'

'You never forget, so they say.'

'I did though, didn't I? I forgot all about our anniversary. I'm so sorry, Adam, what with the job and the move…'

Adam laughed at her expression. 'Don't worry, you've a couple of days yet before you're in arrears, and you can take me out for a meal to celebrate. Fresh start, eh Jules?'

'So when you were on the phone… the other night, you were …'

'Trying to get this organised. Helen was helping me. You don't think I'd have chosen a pink helmet do you?'

'And I thought…'

'I know you did. I'm sorry. I should have told you, but I wanted it to be a surprise. Moving here's given us a second chance hasn't it, we can put the past behind us now, move on.'

'I'm not sure I'll be moving on for a day or two – I can't even remember how to change gear, and what about those pedals.'

'Ah, madam will require cycling shoes.' Adam pulled a box out from the car. 'These have been road-tested by DC Mitchell.'

'So that's why she …'

'What?'

Julie shook her head. 'You two. I thought you hated each other.'

'Let's just say we've reached a truce. And tomorrow the two of us can go exploring. You'll love it, Jules, the scenery's as good as the Peak District, but right on the doorstep. I've got a route all planned and you can buy me lunch. I've found a little pub right on the edge of the Tywi Forest.'

He was like a puppy, trying to please her. Maybe Helen was right. He *had* given up a lot to start again in Wales. 'Thank you,' she said. 'It's a great idea. But we'll need an early night beforehand, don't you think, make sure we're rested?'

CHAPTER THIRTY-ONE

Monday, 2nd May

Julie was in the office early, re-checking the photos from the Metropole. She fast-forwarded through the DVD, watched the cars arriving and leaving, watched Gareth Watkin being bullied into the passenger seat of his own car. The picture quality was poor, even after IT's interventions, and Watkin's assailant never looked directly at the camera. Julie froze the picture. Watkin wasn't putting up any sort of a struggle. After the punch landed he didn't react. She rewound. He definitely knew his attacker, just the way he stood made her think he hadn't felt threatened. She pressed pause. It was more of a slap than a punch, an open-handed slap to the side of the head. She watched as Gareth Watkin climbed awkwardly into the passenger seat of his own car, the last sighting of him alive.

The still photographs at the end of the DVD were time stamped. The Vauxhall had arrived just after Gareth's car and was still there when he was driven away. The picture quality was better on these photographs and she leaned forward for a closer look. The sun visor was down, but there was someone sitting in the driver's seat the whole time.

'Morning, Sarge.' Morgan Evans was standing over her, twirling his car keys. Carefully, Julie sat back in her chair and winced quietly. 'You OK?'

'Blasted bike riding. Reminds me why I stopped doing it. So was Gordon's car in his garage?'

'Yep. Nothing out of the ordinary either, it looks spotless.'

'What about the doors? What colour paintwork does Gordon favour?'

'Everything's white gloss, pretty bog standard, nothing out of the ordinary.'

'No handy blood stains then?' Julie smiled.

'Blood stains, Sarge?'

'The bloke in the Zafira had been assaulted *before* he was put in the car.'

'But you can't think Gordon Price had anything to do with the assault?'

'I don't like coincidences, Morgan. And there are too many coincidences piling up now, even for a place this small.'

'Did you ask him about the bleach?'

'Bleach?'

'Don't tell me you didn't smell it?'

Swift swept into the room with Rhys in his wake. 'Right then, boys and girls, what have we got?'

'I think Gareth Watkin's murder and this assault are definitely connected.' Julie walked over to the board. 'I'd say the man in black we saw on the Epynt is the same person who called on Gordon Price and frightened his wife, and is now in ICU.'

'That's a bit tenuous, isn't it?' Goronwy said.

'Go on.' Swift perched on the edge of a desk, his coat still over his arm.

'The car he was found in is a dark grey Vauxhall Zafira, registration MM06 AJK. This vehicle was stolen from Heaton Park in Manchester last Saturday. This same car was on the car park at the Metropole Hotel in Llandrindod Wells on the morning that Gareth Watkin was murdered. It was also parked near Gordon Price's house on Wednesday morning, on the day their cat was injured. And,' she fished the card Menna had found out of her handbag, 'there's this.'

Swift read the card and handed it to Rhys, who stuck it on the board.

'Where did you find this?' Swift asked.

'It found me. It was wedged in the gate at home.'

'That's a bit worrying, if whoever this guy is knows where you live.'

'I had thought of that one, Sir. But I think he's trying to show us how clever he is rather than anything more threatening.'

'All the same. I think you might be lucky that he wasn't planning anything evil on the Sabbath.' Swift re-read the card. 'Be careful, Sergeant.' He looked over the top of his glasses at her and back to the note on the board. 'Where's the note that was handed in to Reception?'

Julie rummaged in her bag and handed over the card she had collected from Brian Hughes. Swift sighed. 'Better late than never, Sergeant. So what's the significance of Luke and Matthew do we think?'

'He just likes the New Testament maybe?' Rhys pinned the second note on the board, lined up exactly with the first.

'Or it's just in alphabetical order?' Morgan Evans shrugged.

'So you're saying the two cases are definitely connected and Gordon Price is involved with the assault, Sergeant?' Swift had put his coat down and was standing in front of the board, studying the notes as though seeking divine inspiration.

'Well, maybe. I'm saying that it's possible that this unidentified bloke in ICU could well be the one who threatened Eileen Price and posted the note through the door.'

'But Sergeant Price is one of us.' Rhys shook his head. 'He would never be involved in anything like this.'

'Not even if his wife was threatened?' Julie turned a hard stare in Rhys's direction. 'And this same bloke could be the one who was hanging around Penrhiw when the women left for the funeral on the day Gareth Watkin died.'

'But all we've got is the car. We didn't see the Vauxhall on the Epynt, the man was on foot both times you saw him.' Swift walked over to the board. 'So this car, which was stolen two hundred miles away is the only concrete piece of evidence we have.'

'Yes, Sir.'

'And the fact that our casualty possibly drove it from Manchester.'

Julie's phone began to ring and she went to pick it up. It was Frank.

'Hello my lovely.'

'Sergeant Parkinson.'

'You got company?'

'I have, yes.'

'Well I've got some good news and some bad news.'

'What's the good news?'

'I was at a bit of a loose end yesterday, so I followed up on your Zafira. It was picked up on a speed camera on the M6 just north of Lymm, Saturday afternoon a week ago.'

'So that confirms he could have been down here by Monday evening.'

'Better than that.' There was a pause. Julie knew Frank Parkinson was smiling. 'I know who the driver was.'

'God, Frank, you're not winding me up?'

'Nope. That's the bad news. It's Stephen Collins.' From the tone of his voice, Frank was waiting for her response.

'Who?'

'You must remember Collins, the sad bastard who murdered little Janey Wilson. Took her from outside her parent's house in Crumpsall, 1989.'

'Frank I was three years old in 1989.'

'You must have heard of him. Vicious bastard. She was only five years older than you were then. He picked her up from the front garden of the Wilsons' house in Harpurhey. When they found her…'

'Go on.'

'Let's just say it wasn't just me who would have volunteered to put him out of his misery.'

Julie shuddered. 'Thanks, Frank. I now owe you at least a few pints when I get back up there.'

'Pleasure my love. They caught him down where you are somewhere. God knows where though. I don't speak the lingo.'

'I'm not sure I speak it either.' She looked round at the still unfamiliar surroundings and reached for a pen.

'Don't be too hard on yourself. It's always awkward going to a new nick. Even if you'd moved to Preston you'd have to learn the ropes. Give it time.'

'I know. I always was impatient.' Julie laughed. 'Just spell the place for me. I'll look efficient if I don't have to pronounce it.'

It took several attempts to get the letters and spaces in the right order. Julie re-wrote it neatly and mouthed the name under her breath. *Llanfihangel Nant Pabuan.*

'So is there anything else I can help you with?'

'No, that's brilliant. I owe you one. Another one'

Frank yawned. 'Anyway, you look after yourself. If you need anything you know where I am.'

'Cheers, Frank.' Julie cut the connection. She knew exactly where Frank was, could picture him at his desk by the window. She walked back over to the board and waited for Swift to finish speaking.

'Does anyone remember the Stephen Collins case? 1989. Murder of a five year-old girl. She was found here.' Julie folded the paper and pinned it to the board.

'Dear God.' Swift sat down heavily on the desk. 'That was just after I was promoted to CID. It was a horrible case. He kept her underground in some sort of pit inside a barn, up near where you're living, Sergeant. He was finally arrested running around the Brecon Beacons somewhere.'

'And was this Collins a deeply religious type?' Julie tapped her front teeth with the pen.

'Not that you'd notice.' Swift shuddered. 'Nobody who did what he did to that little girl could be accused of being a God-fearing type.'

There was a moment's silence, until Julie asked, 'I don't suppose you can remember who the investigating officer was?'

Julie examined the flowerbed by the front door, noting that there was a slight kink in the row of regimented bedding plants, as Swift leaned on the bell. There was a light on in the sitting room, but the curtains were drawn against the daylight. Julie could imagine them both, sitting there either side of the fire, with the ailing cat on the rug between them. This was the moment their lives could change for ever. No wonder Gordon wasn't in a hurry to answer the door. Swift rang again, and this time he kept his thumb on the bell push. When this failed to bring out his suspect he bent to the letterbox.

'Gordon, it's Craig Swift. I need a word. Now.' He signalled for Julie to go round to the back of the house, but before she could move, the door opened. Swift inserted his foot into the gap. 'We need to talk to you.'

Again, Price tried to keep them on the step, but the DI was having none of it. He pushed past, and Price blinked in the daylight like an animal caught in a headlamp.

'You can't just barge in here, you're not my superior these days, Craig.'

'I think you'll find I can, Gordon.' Swift waved a folded sheet of paper. 'I have a warrant. What can you tell me about Stephen Collins?'

'What? But why Collins? There's a blast from the past. What I can tell you is that he was one of the most evil bastards I ever came across in all my years on the force.'

'How did you come across him, Mr Price?' Julie bent down and felt the carpet. It was still slightly damp, and the smell of bleach was unmistakeable. So much for Evans' powers of observation.

'I was the arresting officer, Sergeant. I was the person who took that scum off the streets. You'll be too young to remember Janey

177

Wilson, but what that… what he did to her is still there when I close my eyes. I'll never forget what I saw when we broke into that barn.'

'That's not for now, Gordon.' Swift's voice was gentler now. 'But I think Collins was here. I think he talked to Eileen. I think he left you a note saying he wanted to talk to you, and I think he came back here yesterday.'

'He should still be banged up. From what I heard he wasn't exactly a model prisoner. I can't see them letting him out early.'

'He was released last Friday.' Julie kept her voice neutral, tried not to show any sympathy for this beleaguered man. 'We have reason to believe—'

'What is this, Craig?' Gordon grabbed his old boss by the shoulders. 'What's going on?'

'A man answering Collins' description was found earlier today.' Julie continued as though he hadn't spoken. 'He had been subject to a serious assault. We'd like you to come down to the station to answer a few questions.'

'What questions? Am I actually being accused of something here? For God's sake, Craig, you know me. What am I supposed to have done?'

'The man had been seriously assaulted, Mr Price.'

For a second she thought Gordon was going to collapse. His knees gave way and he stumbled forwards.

'Is there anyone who can look after Eileen?' Swift's voice was soft, almost confidential. 'Or would you be happy for PC Davies to sit with her?'

'I can't tell you anything. I've done nothing wrong.' Gordon was pleading now, but Swift turned away, just as a white-suited SOCO officer stepped into the hallway.

'The carpet's been cleaned with bleach, just here.' Julie pointed at the faded carpet in the doorway and turned back to Gordon. 'Can we have your car keys, Mr Price?'

'My car keys, Sergeant? What are you expecting to find in my car?' He reached for his coat on the stand and retrieved a set of keys from the pocket. Julie passed them to the SOCO, who nodded, put them in her case and began to swab the carpet.

There was a tentative knock on the front door and it was pushed open slightly. 'Hi, I've got a confession to make,' said a man's voice from outside. He peeped round the door. 'But I can come back later. I should have realised that you'd be…' He backed away from the step and turned to walk back down the path.

'Oh yes?' Gordon folded his arms across his chest, his width filling the space left by the half-open door.

'I thought maybe I should tell you, to save any potential misunderstanding, just in case… But perhaps it would be better left until you're less…busy.'

'And perhaps it wouldn't.' Swift stepped outside the door, followed by Julie and Gordon Price. The man attempted a smile. 'I've been away with work, or I'd have told Mr Price sooner.' He looked away, across the road and then back at Gordon. 'I've only just moved in. Well, a fortnight ago. If I'd known the circumstances, I'd have explained to you, Mr Price, rather than bothering your wife. I didn't realise. It was only when I was telling my neighbour about it, she said I should talk to you.'

'Didn't realise?'

'That she…that I would upset Mrs Price so much. I did tell her I'd be willing to pay the vet's bill.'

'Start again,' said Swift, 'and explain exactly what you're talking about.'

The man looked from one to the other and addressed his reply to Swift. 'I live over there,' he nodded towards the houses across the road. 'I was backing out of my drive the other day.'

'What day was that, Mr…?' Julie wrote in her notebook.

'Atkinson, Tony Atkinson.' He closed his eyes. 'It must have been Wednesday. I was in a hurry. I was running late, on my way to see a client. I just hadn't left myself enough time.' He stopped talking and looked down at his feet.

'Go on.' Swift said.

'As I pulled away, this cat ran straight across the road in front of me. I knew I'd hit it and I did stop, tried to get hold of it, but it went for me and ran off.' He held up his hand. Three half-healed scratches ran the length of the back of it. 'I couldn't get anywhere near it. Mrs Beswick said it was your cat and that Mrs Price would be worried, so I came over to tell you. I told your wife, said how sorry I was, and that I would pay any vet's bills. She seemed fine about it. She said she'd tell you when you got home. When I left she was waving at me from the window. I didn't know that she would be confused... I mean I'm sorry if I upset her, but when I saw all this activity just now, I thought I'd better come and explain.' Atkinson's face flushed as his speech petered out. In contrast, Gordon Price's face was ashen.

'Thank you, Mr Atkinson. I'm sure Mr Price will be very relieved to have the story straight,' said Swift. 'It will be a great weight off his mind.'

CHAPTER THIRTY-TWO

Gordon Price was being helped into a patrol car when Julie heard a low wail from the sitting room. PC Davies was doing her best to calm Eileen, but she refused to be consoled. As Julie walked into the room, Eileen flung herself towards her.

'Tell this woman about my Gordon.'

'Let's just sit down shall we, Eileen.'

'She's come for Gordon.' The look she flashed the uniformed officer was pure venom.

'She's come to sit with you for a little while, that's all. Shall we put the television on, find something you like?' Eileen nodded and allowed herself to be led back to her chair. 'Shall I get you a nice cup of tea?' To the PC, Julie said 'I'd appreciate it if you'd stick the kettle on for her. Sorry, I know what you're thinking.'

PC Davies grinned. 'Want one yourself, Sarge?'

Julie nodded and flicked through the channels. There was a children's programme on S4C, all bright colours and exaggerated presenters. 'What about this one?'

'They talk in scribbles.' Eileen rocked gently in her chair. Julie could see where the idea had come from as she watched the excitable girl in dungarees talking to a life-sized squirrel.

'What about this?' A cartoon fish darted across the screen and stared out, goggle-eyed. Eileen giggled like a little girl.

'You're good with her.' PC Davies carried a tray to the low table. 'Sugar, Mrs Price?'

Eileen ignored her and chuckled at the antics of the goggle-eyed fish.

'Will you be OK?' Julie picked up a mug and crossed to the kitchen door, but immediately Eileen began the low, animal moan. 'Or maybe we should both stay?'

The PC let out a breath. 'You sure, Sarge?'

'Yeah. I'll just go and see if I can find their address book, see if there are any relatives or friends who could come over. God knows how long we'll be with Gordon. Just keep an eye on the tea, make sure she doesn't spill it on herself or we'll have all sorts of bother.'

Once the patrol car had taken Gordon away, Julie opened the curtains and turned out the light. She motioned for the PC to sit with Eileen and went through the kitchen into the hallway. The SOCO officer was still on her hands and knees.

'They've done a fantastic job at cleaning this up.' She passed an ultraviolet beam across the woollen tufts of the carpet. See here, just the smallest speck of blood. Nowhere near enough to get a sample without ripping the carpet out and taking it away.'

'Bugger.' Julie grimaced. 'OK,' she said. 'Do what you have to do.'

'It's a pity they didn't think about this though.' The SOCO's torch raked the bottom of the door. In the groove left by the door trim a tiny rill of blood remained, glowing bright in the beam. Carefully, she scraped a sample from the door and placed it inside a lidded plastic tube. The two women shared a look.

'I'll have a look in the garage and on the drive anyway, just in case I can establish whether the Vauxhall was here, but this should be enough. Just keep your fingers crossed.'

'I'm hoping it's not him to be honest.' Julie watched Eileen through the open door.

'I know, sorry. Sometimes I get carried away with the thrill of the chase.'

Julie nodded. 'Me too, but this is different. What would happen to her?' She gestured towards the sitting room. 'If anything happened to him, where would she go?'

'No family?'

'As far as I can tell, the only family they've got is that cat. Oh, and two kids who've buggered off to live on the other side of the world.'

'Well, we can't let that stop us doing a thorough job, eh, Sergeant?'

Gordon Price was shaking, and Swift wondered whether it was from fear or anger. In the strip lighting of the interview room his skin was the colour of parchment. Every line and wrinkle was magnified.

'I just don't believe this. How you could think I had anything to do with this… for God's sake, Craig. You've known me for over twenty years.'

'Please sit down, Mr Price.' Swift sat opposite Gordon, and Morgan Evans sat down next to Swift. 'Interview with Mr Gordon Price, Monday 2nd May. Those present DI Craig Swift, DC Morgan Evans and… for the tape please, Mr Price.'

'Gordon Price.'

'Also present Mr Mervyn Protheroe, Mr Price's solicitor.'

Swift recited the caution, which seemed to irritate Gordon still further, and then he settled himself in his chair and laced his fingers together. 'Where were you on Friday afternoon, Mr Price?'

'I was at home with Eileen.'

'Were you there all afternoon?'

Gordon nodded. 'I made us some lunch, and then we watched television. That is, Eileen watched her cartoons and I read my book.'

Evans flicked through his notebook. 'So you deny you were anywhere near the Elan Valley on Friday afternoon.'

'Of course I do.'

Evans stared hard at Gordon. 'You, of all people, know that it's only a matter of time before we come up with someone who saw you there. Why not save us all the time and bother.'

'You'll find, Constable, that once you reach a certain age you become invisible. Besides,' Gordon returned Evans' stare, 'the Elan

183

Valley's not exactly teeming with potential witnesses, even at this time of year.'

Swift stretched out in his chair. 'It must be very difficult for you, the way Eileen is.'

Gordon glared at Swift. 'What would you know about it? Yes, of course it's difficult. Have you any idea what it's like to see the woman you love disappearing before your eyes? Every day I lose a bit more of her.'

'I'm sorry,' said Swift. 'And you worry about keeping her safe?'

'Where's this going, Craig?'

'Would she be more forthcoming about where you were on Friday afternoon, do you think?'

'Don't you dare!' Gordon slammed both hands on the table and stood up, toppling his chair and causing Evans to flinch. 'Leave Eileen out of this. You know she's in no fit state to be questioned about anything.'

Swift got up slowly, walked round the table, replaced Gordon's chair and motioned for him to sit. 'So you must have been concerned when your recent visitor left a note with Eileen, containing what seemed like a threat?'

Gordon Price sat, as directed. 'I've told you before, I've no idea who that was.'

'What did it say…' Swift flicked through several sheets of paper in a beige folder and read the note aloud. 'It sounds to me as though he wasn't going to let it go, Gordon, as though he was intending on a second visit. Can you tell me anything about that?'

'I don't know anything about it. I just got the message when I got home. I didn't see him.'

'And the fact that he mentioned Eileen must have worried you.'

'Not particularly.'

'Would you say the note sounded threatening at all?' Swift referred to his own notes.'

'I suppose you could put that slant on it.' Gordon glared at Swift.

'But you put that slant on it yourself, Gordon, when you phoned the station and spoke to Sergeant Hughes. You said you had received a threatening note.' Swift looked up from the page. 'Those were your words, weren't they?'

Gordon glanced away but Swift continued to stare at him. 'I might have over-reacted. I worry about Eileen.'

'I know you do,' said Swift. 'Did you have any idea who might have written the note? Could it have been someone you'd come into contact with through work?'

'Come on, Craig. You know how it goes when you put on the uniform.'

'Is there anyone in particular you can think of?'

Gordon shook his head. 'I can't think of anyone.'

'What about Gareth Watkin. Can you think of an incident where the two of you worked on the same case?'

'There must have been dozens of times. Gareth was duty solicitor for a couple of years.'

'So you don't remember the two of you being threatened by a prisoner who said he would "make you both pay"? Gareth wasn't in court, but you'd been called to give evidence. It was at Manchester Crown Court, in November 1989. There can't have been many cases like that one, Gordon.'

Gordon Price closed his eyes tight and put his head in his hands. 'I still see that little girl. Every night when I close my eyes she's there. That broken little body, still clutching her blood-stained teddy bear.' His face was still hidden but Swift watched tears drip onto the grey plastic of the table. Morgan Evans cleared his throat.

'Shall I show him the photographs, Sir,' he whispered.

Swift shook his head. 'And you thought it might be him. Collins?' Gordon nodded, still not looking at Swift. 'Can you tell me why you thought it might be him?'

Gordon Price gave a feral sigh, and wiped his face with the back of his hand. 'He threatened Gareth Watkin at the time of the trial.

185

He said he'd stitched him up instead of looking after his interests like he should have done as duty solicitor. I can't remember all the detail. It was something to do with not documenting an expression of remorse, which would have affected the length of his sentence and whether he could apply for parole. It was all rubbish, of course, but Collins knew the system. And he threatened me. He accused me of using undue force when I arrested him. He said that because of my treatment of him he was too traumatised to defend himself properly when he was questioned.'

'Was there any truth in either of those allegations?'

'No!' Gordon was shouting now. 'He was a lying bastard scumbag trying to wriggle out of it.'

'Was?'

'Sorry?'

'You said he *was* a lying bastard scumbag.' Swift tapped his pen on the folder of notes.

Gordon's eyes opened wide.

Swift spoke more gently this time. 'Why would you say that?'

'I meant at the time. When I arrested him he was…' Gordon shrugged.

'I see. Didn't he also threaten Eileen? That must have made you angry.' Swift had to fight the sudden wave of sympathy he felt for Gordon. 'I know I would have been absolutely furious, if anyone had threatened my Gwen.'

Gordon looked down at the table and nodded. 'She said something about Collins to a journalist. She didn't know he was a journalist at the time. He'd followed her when she went shopping, stood behind her in the queue at the bread shop and started chatting. It ended up in the *Manchester Evening News*.'

'And Collins got a message to her.'

'I blame him for the way she is now. She changed after she got his disgusting letter, lost all her confidence. She wouldn't go out for months afterwards unless I was with her and she still has to have all the doors and windows locked, even when we're in the house.'

'That must have been horrible, Mr Price.' Evans's voice was soft.

'It was. It still is. You've seen how she is now.'

'So yesterday, when he turned up on your doorstep, you wanted your revenge.'

'Gordon, you don't have to answer.' The solicitor avoided Swift's gaze.

'Thanks, Mervyn, but I do. This has gone on for seventeen years. It's too late now.' He looked across at Swift. 'Yes,' he said. 'I wanted my revenge. For a lifetime of nightmares, for watching my wife disintegrate before my eyes, I wanted revenge. But I didn't do anything. I promise. He started reading the scriptures to me and told me I had to forgive him. He said he wanted to talk to my Eileen. I asked him to leave but he pushed past me into the house. I tried to stop him and he fell. He must have tripped over the step.'

'Gordon. I have to warn you…' The solicitor put his hand on Gordon's arm. 'We need to talk about this.'

Price shook his head. 'It's too late. I admit it, he was there, but I didn't kill him.'

Craig Swift considered his options and heard himself say 'He's not dead, Gordon. Not yet.'

Gordon stared at him, his face grey and his hand clutching at the edge of the table. His sobs were still audible over Swift's sign-off.

CHAPTER THIRTY-THREE

Julie looked back at the house. In the window Eileen was waving.

'What do you think will happen to them?'

Swift let out a long breath. 'That depends on whether Collins survives.'

'Is there any news from the hospital?'

'No change. I spoke to the doctor just now. He's no worse, which is a good sign apparently.' Swift drove past the place where Julie had remembered seeing the Zafira. 'It was a damned good spot of yours that, Sergeant. I don't think I would have noticed that it was the same car in the car park at the Met.'

'Just lucky. Maybe I wouldn't have noticed either if it hadn't been a Manchester plate. I was probably just feeling homesick.'

Swift indicated left, and pulled into a trickle of traffic on the A470, the main road from North to South Wales. 'Are you homesick?'

Julie stared out of the side window. The smattering of houses which made up the village where Gordon and Eileen lived had already given way to steep-sided hills, blurred with new bracken. 'It's different, Sir.'

'How are you getting on with the rest of the team?' Swift kept his voice neutral and his gaze on the road ahead.

'Fine, Sir. Rhys and Goronwy have been great. Nerys is lovely, and you're right about Brian Hughes. There's nothing he doesn't know, is there?'

'Not much. And Evans, are you OK with him?'

'Yeah.' Julie stared out of the side window. 'Where do you go for a night out round here?'

Swift let it go. 'Where do I go for night-life?'

'I don't mean clubbing, Sir,' Julie blushed. 'Where would you go for dinner?'

'Special occasion?'

'Wedding anniversary.'

'Congratulations. Well, there's the Red Lion and there are a few really nice places in Builth, and The Drovers in Llanwrtyd is always good. What does he think of the area, your husband?'

'Adam? He thinks he's died and gone to heaven. He's rabid about triathlons, says it's perfect training country, all the hills and no traffic.'

'You not interested in that sort of thing?'

Julie snorted. 'I'm a rubbish swimmer. I can't even run on the flat and if yesterday's bike ride is anything to go by I'm useless at that too.' She shifted carefully in her seat.

Swift laughed. 'Does he mind you working all the hours God sends?'

'No, Sir. I think it's suited him up to now. Given him time to pursue his other activities.' As Swift glanced across she blushed again, but he seemed not to notice.

'So where are we with Watkin's death do you think, Sir?'

'Well, with Collins' car in the car park at the Met and the connection between them, he has to be favourite for the shooting. The picture quality's so bad on the DVD from the hotel it could quite easily be him. Right sort of height, right clothes.'

'I still don't think it was him. There was no ring in his effects, and he's definitely not wearing one now.'

'But Sarah's alibi holds up. The marriage guidance people confirmed she was with them on that morning. She wouldn't have had time to get back to the Metropole. And I'm sure you noticed that Ella doesn't wear a wedding ring, if we're still working on your theory that he knew his assailant.' Swift slowed down. In front of them a small trailer loaded with sheep weaved its way towards Builth behind a battered Land Rover.

'So it's not just us working on the bank holiday then.'

'It's an every day of the year job, farming. The people who think it's a cushy lifestyle should go through the lambing season up here. They're dead on their feet by now.'

'I'd never been on a farm before. Penrhiw was the first.'

Swift shook his head. 'You must have been. You never went to a farm as a kid?'

'We went to a riding school once. My Dad thought it would be a good idea to introduce us to the great outdoors. Exmoor, I think, and I was about ten. It was a total disaster. My horse walked backwards over a Jack Russell and my sister fell off and broke her arm.'

Swift was laughing now. 'No wonder you were a bit apprehensive about Penrhiw then.'

'You must admit though, it is a bit sad. The house just the way the father left it and them living with all those memories every day. And Milos, he's well creepy.'

'He's lived all his life in that house, never known anything different. He doesn't get further than the local pub or the mart but he's happy with his lot.'

'I can't imagine knowing you'll never move from the place you were born, or spending your whole life in the same house. What keeps them going?'

'Hill farmers live on the very edge of what can be cultivated. It's a battle keeping it all usable. They do it to hand it on to the next generation, build on what their forebears have achieved.'

Julie gave a half nod in capitulation. 'Do you know anything about this Joe character, our landlord at the cottage?'

'Not much. He lost his wife a few years back. He's not the best at looking after himself, but he won't accept any help. No kids from what I gather, but loves his ponies.'

*

The hospital car park was full, but Swift edged into a 'Staff Only' slot. 'We won't be long. We might as well just have another look at him.'

'You'll get a ticket if you leave it there.'

Swift wheeled round to find Kay Greenhalgh grinning at him. 'If it wasn't such a bus you could have found a space over there. I was going to phone you. The Bible that your victim was carrying, there were a list of addresses inside the back cover, Penrhiw Farm was one, and the house at Maes y Derw was there too. I've sent it back upstairs, with the clothes.'

'Thanks, that's going to be useful,' Swift said.

'Just try not to find anything else for me. I'm off to Yorkshire for a couple of days.'

'It's all right for some,' Julie said

The registrar was adamant that there had been no change, but Swift insisted on looking for himself. Collins looked much as he had on Saturday. Maybe slightly less pale. The purple tinge was gone from his lips.

'I think he looks a bit better, Sir,' whispered Julie.

'Fingers crossed, Sergeant.' Swift looked across at the machinery and back to the slight figure in the bed. 'I never thought I'd be praying for this bastard to survive.' He scratched his ear. 'Have we had any thoughts about how Gordon Price got back from the Elan Valley without a car, if we still think he drove this one up there in the Zafira?'

'I can't see how else he could have done it given the Zafira was found up there.'

Swift sighed. 'Neither can I. But how did Gordon know that Collins had pitched up to his place in the Zafira?'

'Key fob in his pocket maybe? He'd spot an unusual vehicle on their road though, wouldn't he, with his experience?'

'So we've nothing new?'

'No, Sir. Nothing at all. Is it worth putting out an appeal, see if anyone gave him a lift back from where the Zafira was left?'

Swift shook his head. 'If I know Gordon he wouldn't have left it to chance. He wouldn't have left Eileen alone in the house if he didn't know how or when he was going to get back.'

'He could have taken her with him.'

'But then if they were both hitching a lift, he couldn't rely on her not to blab about what they'd been doing, could he?'

'Fair point.'

'No, Sergeant, he must have arranged for someone to collect him, or maybe both of them. Someone who wouldn't let on to us or to anyone else if Eileen let anything slip.'

'A friend, then?'

'I know what you're thinking, Julie, but it could have been anyone, not necessarily someone on the force.'

Swift's phone buzzed and the registrar pointed towards the sign above the double doors. Swift and Julie crept from ICU and they stood in the stairwell while he took his call. Slowly a grin spread across his face and he bounded down the wide stairs. 'Come on, Kite. We've got work to do.'

CHAPTER THIRTY-FOUR

The offices were plush, stainless steel and light oak with thick gunmetal grey carpets and potted plants trailing artfully. Swift showed his warrant card to the girl on the reception desk.

'Do you have an appointment,' she asked in the sing-song style of a much-repeated question.

'If you could just inform Ms Southam that Detective Inspector Swift and Detective Sergeant Kite of Mid Wales Police would like to talk to her.'

'She has a very full diary. You should have phoned in advance.'

Swift leaned towards her over the desk. 'Samantha,' he said, reading the security pass round her neck, 'please tell Ms Southam…'

'This way, is it?' Julie smiled at a dark-suited man who was holding the security door open for her.

'You can't!'

'I think you'll find we can,' said Swift.

Samantha scooted round the desk and through the open door ahead of Julie. The corridor was decorated in the same understated way as the reception area; several light oak doors with brushed steel handles were illuminated by subtle lighting. The nameplate on the door at the far end of the corridor read, 'Jessica Southam, FFA, Senior Partner.'

'FFA?' mouthed Julie. Swift shrugged. Samantha knocked gently, and slipped into the office, closing the door firmly behind her. Swift put his ear to the smooth oak. Ms Southam, it seemed from his expression, was not best pleased at being visited by the police.

'She will see you now.' Samantha, tight lipped and pink-faced, pushed between them.

'Jessica Southam?' Swift asked. The woman behind the desk was well-preserved, late thirties he guessed. She wore a pale grey wool suit with a cream silk blouse. As she stood up and held out her hand it was apparent that Jessica Southam was more than a little bit pregnant. 'DI Swift, Sergeant Kite, Mid-Wales Police.'

Jessica Southam gestured towards the visitors' chairs and sat back down, rather awkwardly.

'Your car, a silver Mercedes cabriolet was seen in the car park of the Metropole Hotel in Llandrindod Wells on Tuesday morning. Can you tell me about that?'

'And what business is it of yours, Inspector?'

'We are investigating the death of Gareth Watkin.'

Jessica's face betrayed no emotion. She hooked a stray strand of hair behind her ear and placed her hands together like a child about to say a prayer. She rested her chin on her thumbs, placing both index fingers against her lips, sealing them closed. The slender fingers were beautifully manicured, the nails gloss-black. 'I see.'

'We have reason to believe that Gareth Watkin got into your car that morning.'

'Whether or not Mr Watkin got into my car has nothing to do with your investigation, officer.'

'Could you tell me the nature of the relationship between yourself and Gareth Watkin?' Julie asked, attempting to read the large, leather-bound desk diary upside down. Southam snapped the diary shut. 'We were colleagues, Sergeant Kite. My consultancy works closely with Mr Watkin's firm.'

'What exactly is your line of work, Miss Southam?' Swift stressed the title.

Jessica Southam's gaze was icy. 'By profession, *Mr* Swift, I am an actuary.' She lingered on the word *profession* and offered Swift a small smile. 'My consultancy offers advice on acquisitions and mergers to the major players in industry. We also assist private individuals with pensions and investments, provided of course that they have sufficient assets to make investment worthwhile.'

'Were you assisting Gareth Watkin in any way at all?' Julie looked past her and out of the large picture window at the manicured lawns and carefully tended shrubs which surrounded the low building.

'I don't think I like your insinuation, Sergeant.'

'Let me make it less subtle then. Were you having an affair with him?'

'That has absolutely no bearing on Gareth's death.'

'On the contrary, Jessica, it could have everything to do with his death.' Swift stood up and leaned over the desk. 'Was Watkin the father of your child?'

Southam looked away. 'That,' she said, 'is categorically none of your business.'

'And would he have known if the baby was his?' Julie remained in her chair, stretching and relaxing into the soft leather.

'I couldn't possibly comment.' Jessica Southam smiled slowly.

'So what was the plan? Was he going to leave his wife and set up house with you? Were you going to play Happy Families and have Seren and Dylan to stay when he felt like it?' Colour was rising in Swift's face.

Southam attempted to make herself more comfortable in her chair, but succeeded only in twisting her jacket awkwardly around herself. 'Our relationship was purely a professional one, Inspector. We were looking forward to a closer working relationship.'

'I bet you were,' muttered Swift.

'Your attitude is totally unacceptable.'

'Oh is it?'

'Sir,' Julie said quietly. 'Ms Southam, could you tell me whether you have other offices.'

'We have offices in various select locations in Wales and the North West.'

'And where would they be?' Swift was barely civil, spitting the question at her.

'The larger offices are in Crickhowell, Knutsford and Chester.' Southam paused just long enough for maximum effect. 'I also have an apartment in Prestbury in Cheshire and a house in Bath.'

Julie spoke before Swift had the opportunity. 'How would you have communicated with Gareth Watkin? Would you have used e-mail?'

'Well how else, Sergeant? Carrier pigeon?'

'So you wouldn't have written him a letter, say within the last fortnight?'

'It's quite possible, Sergeant.'

'This is important, Jessica. Did you write to Gareth recently and post the letter in Stockport?'

'How the hell…' Jessica stared at Julie, as did Swift.

'Can you tell me what was in that letter and why you couldn't just e-mail him?'

'It was purely a work-related matter. It has no bearing at all on your investigation.'

'Please, Jessica. It may be totally irrelevant, but we need all the help we can get. Do you think Gareth killed himself?'

'Absolutely not. He was extremely positive about the future.'

'So that was in that letter?'

'It was nothing exciting. I just wanted to tell him that I'd had the paperwork drawn up forming the basis of a contract between Southam Associates and the new company which Gareth was setting up and that I wanted to arrange to meet him to get them signed.'

'New company?' asked Julie.

'I'm afraid I'm not at liberty to discuss the business relationship any further.' Jessica Southam stood up with a little difficulty and glared at Swift, who was reading a letter on the top of the pile in the curved wooden in-tray.

'And why couldn't you e-mail him or write to his office?' Swift was still belligerent, but Julie could see he realised that his earlier outburst had been unwarranted.

'Because Gareth was convinced that someone in his office was checking his e-mails and going through his post. We decided it would be simpler to write to him at the farm. We were careful. As far as I know, none of the others in the practice knew that he was intending to take over the account. If they'd known he was planning to establish a completely new business entity there would have been some rather vocal opposition. He was trying to avoid confrontation for as long as he could.'

'Do you know who was intercepting his correspondence?' asked Swift.

'I've no idea. Gareth was ridiculously loyal to the partnership. He felt guilty that I had asked to work only with him going forward, rather than staying with Dic Jones. Dic's a lovely man,' she looped her hair back behind her ear, 'but he's just not up to date enough for what we need now.'

'So where did you go after you left Gareth Watkin in the Metropole Hotel car park at 10.46 am on Tuesday?' said Julie.

'My, you have been busy. I came straight back here, Sergeant.' I had meetings here from 11.10 am until I left the office at 9.15 that evening.'

'We'll need the names of the people who were with you – attendees at the meetings and any staff who may have seen you during those hours.' Swift stood up and held out his hand, which Jessica Southam shook.

'Of course. Samantha will e-mail you a list by this evening. I had no reason to kill Gareth, Inspector. Quite the opposite in fact.'

Swift slammed the car door hard and snapped his seat belt home. 'People like her, they think all they have to do is click their over-privileged fingers.' He turned the key in the ignition.

'It takes two to tango though, Sir. Maybe Gareth simply saw it as a way of setting up on his own, or even to get out of Penrhiw Farm. Perhaps he wanted to run away from the futility of it all, the battle with the elements, the death and destruction.'

'Is that how you see it?'

'I don't know. It just seems…' Julie floundered for an appropriate word. 'Well, joyless somehow. There's such an inevitability about everything, the thought that no matter how hard you work, the farm will be exactly the same as it was a century ago.'

Swift turned to look at her. 'Unless something upsets the natural order of things?'

'Watkin's death you mean?'

'Or the fact that he didn't want to work the farm with his brother. That could have ruffled feathers.'

'So, we're back to the family, then.' Julie said slowly. 'Jealous of him maybe, or the fact that he had a cushy office job? Or perhaps he had told them about the new venture with Jessica Southam. Where would the new job have been based? Could he have told them he might be moving out? How would that have affected the farm finances I wonder? Would his work as a solicitor have been subsidising the lean times on the farm? Was that what Sarah's problem was, that sent her scuttling off to marriage guidance?'

Swift sounded weary. 'Back to square one then, Julie. Let's go home. Start again tomorrow. By the way,' he managed a small smile, 'you did well in there. It works well, the town mouse and the country mouse routine.'

'I'm not sure that story had an altogether happy ending, Sir.'

CHAPTER THIRTY-FIVE

Tuesday, 3rd May

It felt as though she had been in Wales forever. Julie said good morning to Brian Hughes on her way through reception and got the usual cheery reply. He had been good friends with Gordon Price hadn't he? They were both about the same age, maybe even joined the force at the same time. She sighed and pushed the buttons on the keypad to open the door. Why was she always so suspicious? She didn't even know these people. What were the chances of Brian having been the mystery driver who picked Gordon up from the Elan Valley? Just over a week ago, she'd been dropping Sid off at the cattery, not even sure of where the new house was. She had never set foot on the Epynt, never felt the claustrophobia of Penrhiw or seen the damage a red kite could do to a fresh corpse, and now she was inventing back stories to fill in the gaps.

Swift was already in his office, but it was still too early for the others. She knocked quietly on his door.

'Morning, Sir. Anything new since yesterday?'

'Nothing we didn't know already. Gordon Price's car was clean and so was his garage, and the Zafira's had a good going-over by the SOCOs. There's absolutely nothing out of the ordinary. There's lots of unidentified DNA, but there'll have been God knows how many people and kids in that car. My first guess is still that Gordon hit Collins, saw the damage then panicked and drove him to the first place he could think of. The problem with that theory is that there's only blood on the driver's seat, nowhere else in the vehicle. So where was Collins on the journey if he wasn't in the driver's seat?

'Good.' Julie offered a wan smile.

'I know what you mean. I was just about to phone the hospital again. Could you give them a ring, just see whether there's any change.'

Julie walked back to her desk, but before she could pick up the phone to dial, it rang.

'Morning, Sergeant.'

Julie recognised Greenhalgh's voice. 'Morning, I thought you were up north?'

'That was the plan. There was a fatal RTA on the Sennybridge Road. The news came in just as I was making my escape. Witnesses said they thought the driver was drunk, he drove straight into the armco. And despite being on call, Graham bloody Wilson had cleared off to Aberaeron for the day with his latest girlfriend, so it was down to yours truly.'

'And was he drunk?'

'No, the poor bugger seems to have had a hypo. Not enough food probably.'

'What a waste.'

'Anyway, that's not why I'm phoning. I've some interesting news for you. A&E dug a bullet out of an Army Cadet's leg late last night.'

'Dear God, don't tell me they let them loose with live ammunition.'

'Don't be soft. The Cardiff boys were camping on the Epynt over the weekend, Outward Bound type stuff, building campfires and whatnot. All very jolly and Ging Gang Goolie, until one of them found a pistol in a bog.'

'This bog, was it anywhere near Watkin's final resting place?'

'Yep. Just about within throwing distance if you're an Olympic discus thrower or possibly even a hulking great farmer.'

'So if the bullet matches…'

'I've passed it to ballistics, along with the gun, but from a first look, and from the remaining bullets, I'd say it's been fired from the same gun that killed Gareth Watkin.'

'Did the SOCOs find any fingerprints?' Julie held her breath as Greenhalgh riffled through the paperwork.

'Well the cadet didn't do us any favours there.'

'Or himself.'

'Quite. And his mates all had to have a look. They're bringing them over to you for fingerprinting and statements. Look out for a minibus arriving any minute.'

'How many are there?'

'Fifteen and the two minders.'

'Is the lad who shot himself still in hospital?'

'Yep, but he won't be here for long. His parents are coming to pick him up. Not much more than a flesh wound. He was lucky.'

'Dr Greenhalgh you're a star.'

Maybe she should have mentioned how many kids would need processing, but Swift hadn't asked and seemed happy enough for her to go to the hospital. He could always delegate. Evans would love it. Not.

The cadet had frightened himself. Even now he blinked back tears as he answered her questions.

'You're not in any trouble, Owen. Just tell me how you found the gun and what happened.'

'It was all Tommo's fault. We were larking about.' He sniffed and wiped his nose on the sleeve of his fatigues. 'He sort of pushed me into the boggy stuff and I lost my footing. As I tried to stand up I tripped over a rock in the water and it must have dislodged the gun. I never thought it was a real one.' His face crumpled. 'I'll never get into the army now will I?'

'I'm sure they'll realise it was an accident. It *was* an accident wasn't it?'

Owen nodded. 'I didn't mean to fire it, it just went off. And it really hurt.'

201

'You were lucky.' Julie reached a tissue from a box on the bedside table and handed it to him. 'You could have easily shot one of your mates.' Owen screwed up his face and squeezed his eyes tight shut. 'I'm guessing you'll be a bit more careful with firearms in the future.' She knew she was being unfair, the poor lad was probably still in shock, but she had seen the results of too many handgun incidents in her time. He looked bereft, a little boy in grown up clothes, sitting on the bed.

'Look, I'm sure they'll go easy on you. You were just in the wrong place at the wrong time.' Like Gareth Watkin, she wondered. 'Would you be able to show me exactly where you found the gun and where you and Tommo were scrapping? We can wait for your parents and go up there together.' He nodded. 'I've just got to go and see someone upstairs. Will you wait there until I get back?' Another nod.

Collins' skin had lost the grey, corpse-like pallor. The jumbo bandage had been replaced by a Melolin dressing, stuck onto shaved scalp, but he was still unconscious.

'Can you tell me how he's doing?'

The nurse nodded as Julie flashed her warrant card. She picked up a large bundle of notes and scanned the front page. 'He went down for a second scan first thing.' She flipped the pages over. 'He must have an incredibly thick skull.' She put the notes down and smiled at Collins. 'We'll have you out of here yet, lovely,' she said.

Julie recoiled at the sentiment. 'Do you really think there's a chance he'll pull through?'

'It's still too soon to say, but it's looking more promising. There's a lot less swelling than there was. Look, the consultant will be in later on. Shall I phone you if there's anything new?'

'Thanks.' Julie wrote her mobile number on the back of one of Swift's cards. 'This one's just got to survive.'

'It's upsetting to see them like this isn't it?' The nurse looked down at her charge. 'Fingers crossed eh.'

The cadet's parents were with him when she got back to the ward. The mother was tearful, her arm draped around her son's shoulder. The father was gruff.

'Silly little bugger,' he said, to himself as much as to anyone else, but Julie turned away discreetly as he sniffed quietly.

'They've said we can take him home.' Owen's mother squeezed his arm. 'But he says you need him to help you.' She managed a watery smile. 'He's a good boy. Anything he can do…'

'If you don't mind, I'd just like you to drive him back to where he found the gun, so that we can set up a search of the area where the cadets were. Will you be able to follow me?'

'Is he going to be in any trouble?' Owen's father already sounded defeated.

'I shouldn't think so. It was just an accident.'

'So you need to look for evidence to back that up?'

'Well, there's a little more to it than that I'm afraid.' Julie hesitated. They would have to know if the boy ended up giving evidence. 'We've been looking for the weapon in connection with another matter. Shall we just tell one of the nurses that we're leaving, and then we can get going.'

Julie watched the car drive away, winding up the steep hill. The boy's face still looked haunted as he looked out through the rear window. Two SOCOs were working within a taped-off area, maybe fifteen metres from where Gareth Watkin's body had been found exactly a week ago. They hadn't moved far in a week had they? Julie watched the men sifting meticulously through the reeds and grass. How the hell had they missed a handgun so close to the body? God this case was frustrating. Had Swift been too soft on Milos? Was he too keen to accept Sarah's innocence? But what evidence did they actually have? Had Collins driven Watkin out here and shot him, thrown the gun into the reeds and walked away? But then why was Collins still hanging around Penrhiw after Gareth Watkin was already dead if that was the case?

Ghoulish interest? Returning to the scene of the crime? Taunting them? She walked back to her car and drove to the spot where she knew she would get a mobile signal.

'Cheer me up.'

'I thought you'd be chuffed to bits.' Helen sounded crestfallen. 'Didn't you like the bike?'

'Sorry, Helen – the bike's fab. I can't sit down for more than twenty minutes at a time now, after an epic inaugural ride, but it was a lovely idea. I can't believe you knew what he was going to do and you didn't tell me. And there was me calling him all sorts.'

'I didn't want to spoil the surprise. It was me who suggested it might be a good idea for him not to stay over Saturday night. Honestly, Julie, he doesn't realise half the time what it looks like to you. Especially with you being the suspicious type.'

'Cheek.' Julie laughed. 'Mind, you're not wrong. We must be bloody awful to live with, especially in the middle of a case.'

'Speak for yourself, Mrs Kite. I'd be the model of wifely virtue.'

'I'm not sure I am. I've been so preoccupied with these cases. It's really difficult when you don't know the place. Everything takes me twice as long as it should. I know Adam wants to show me the area, but I just can't spare the time.'

'Are you making any progress with the cases?'

'Not really. We're going round in circles. There seems to be a real softly softly approach to suspects. They all know each other and they seem terrified of stepping on toes. We've just been speaking to a pregnant woman whose possible lover was murdered and Swift seemed more concerned about her breaking up the victim's marriage than being a possible murder suspect.'

Helen laughed. 'Sounds like Gran. She always told Dad she'd kill him if he brought shame on the family with a dalliance as she called it. I think he really believed her right up until he was married. Mind, she was horribly religious, bless her.'

'I suppose we should be glad things have moved on these days.'

'I heard you've got Stephen Collins down there. From what I hear they didn't hit him hard enough.'

'Oh God, Helen, I'm just keeping everything crossed that the sod survives. The bloke who hit him is an ex-copper. His wife's got Alzheimer's, and there's no family living locally, or even any proper friends that we can find. He adores her, despite everything. The thought of what could happen to the two of them all because of a scumbag like Collins... I just don't want to think about it.'

'It sounds like you've got the opposite ends of the human being scale with those two. Oh, sorry, got to go, Parki's making obscene gestures,' Julie could hear Helen laughing. 'He says it's sign language for Chestnut Road.'

'Thanks for that.' Morgan rounded on her as soon as she got back to the office. 'It's taken two of us until now to process the kids.'

'Don't mention it.' Julie walked past him and sat down at her desk. Rhys, opposite her, stifled a smile.

'So where have you been?' Evans was talking at the back of her head.

'I'm sorry, Constable, are you talking to me?' She stowed her bag under the desk and switched on the computer.

'Is this the way they do things in the Manchester Police, flying solo, not sharing information?'

'Manchester Metropolitan Police is an extremely professional organisation which is more—'

'So you're saying we're not professional?' Morgan's voice was rising steadily now and Swift looked up from his desk. Rhys tried but failed to attract Julie's attention.

'If the cap fits, DC Evans.'

'Kite, my office. Now.' Swift was standing in the doorway, his mouth a grim line. Morgan Evans smirked as she stood up.

'Not quite the attitude for teacher's pet, is it Kite?'

Swift stared at him as Julie crossed the office.

'Evans, go and buy me a sandwich from across the road.' Evans scowled like a petulant teenager. 'Now, Evans.' Swift watched him leave, and then closed his door quietly behind him.

'Sit down, Kite.'

'Sir, I'm sorry. He just…'

'Part of the role of sergeant is to manage staff sympathetically.'

'Yes, Sir, I know, but—'

'No buts, Sergeant. I know Evans doesn't help himself. If he bothered to apply himself he could be an outstanding officer, and one day the penny will drop and he'll grow up.'

Julie opened her mouth to speak, but Swift stopped her with a gesture practiced to perfection on point duty. 'In the meantime, I shall expect you to rise above any petty bickering. Evans has to earn your respect, Sergeant, but unless you can earn *his* respect, the future of this team is at risk.'

Julie blushed. 'Yes, Sir. I'm sorry.'

'I suppose you know by now that he failed his exams?'

'Yes, Sir.'

'Then for God's sake cut him a bit of slack. He still thinks he's been badly done to.' Swift sighed. 'Right. What did you find out at the hospital?'

'Maybe we could wait for Morgan to come back with your lunch, Sir, and I can tell the whole team.'

'Good answer, DS Kite.'

The ballistics report confirmed that the gun was the one which had fired the bullet which had killed Gareth Watkin. The photograph showed an angular black pistol which reminded Julie of those she'd seen in Adam's beloved gangster movies. She scanned the report. 'TT-33 look-alike, probably a Polish copy, a PW wz.33, manufactured between the late 1940s and late 1950s.' There was also a photograph of a magazine with three bullets missing and another of the third bullet, fired in the lab into a block of gelatine. The ragged trace in the smooth surface showed how the bullet would have ripped into Gareth Watkin's temple and onwards into his brain. Julie turned the page as though that would obliterate the picture in her mind of a solicitor in a smart suit and waxed jacket with his head blown apart, his eyes clawed away by birds.

But they were no nearer to finding out who had shot Gareth Watkin. If only they could work out who had driven him from the Metropole car park.

CHAPTER THIRTY-SIX

Swift was in Builth, attempting to find out whether anyone at the solicitors' office had known about Gareth Watkin's proposed business liaison, despite Jessica Southam's assurances. Julie knew Swift was still furious with Southam, her dismissive attitude, the fact that she could treat Dic Jones so badly without a second thought, maybe even break up a family just because that was what she wanted. But what about Gareth Watkin himself? Was he any less to blame? Did the fact that he was dead absolve him from all responsibility for his underhand business activities? Was it just Swift, or was this out of date thinking endemic in mid Wales? She tapped her pen against her teeth.

'As bad as my Rhian, you are?'

'Sorry?' She looked up to find Rhys standing by her desk.

'I keep telling her, it won't do your teeth any good, *cariad*. You got time for a coffee, you look knackered.'

'Yeah, go on then. I could do with a dollop of caffeine.' She threw the biro onto her desk and followed him down the corridor towards the canteen. Maggie passed them, on her way back to her office.

'Sergeant Kite, have you got a minute? I've got some information on that suicide note.' She lifted a plastic wallet out of a tray on the end of her desk. 'It was written on an old-fashioned daisy-wheel printer. Came out of the ark. Other than that there's nothing I can tell you. It's not been written on the laptop from Penrhiw, not unless someone up there is a computer expert and managed to delete every trace.'

208

'Thanks, Maggie. Can we get the computer back to them now then?'

'Yep, there's nothing more I can do with it. The one from the office went back there with DI Swift just now. There's no trace of the suicide note on that either.'

'I'll pick it up in a few minutes, but thanks for that.' Julie took the bagged note from her. 'I don't suppose you found anything on the laptop relating to last week's correspondence that Gareth had deleted?'

'Funnily enough, I have. But it's all pretty boring stuff, the sort of thing you'd expect from a solicitors' office to be fair. I'm just printing it out now and you can have it.'

'So why would he have deleted it all? Was there any mention of Jessica Southam on there?'

Maggie shook her head. 'There was a snotty e-mail from Catherine Jones, slagging Gareth off for not following company procedure. But then she's the boss's wife, isn't she, so maybe that goes with the territory?'

Julie walked slowly into the canteen, rubbing her temples. This bloody case, it was like plaiting fog.

Rhys had bought coffee and bara brith for both of them. He'd chosen a table in the corner, by the window, well away from the other tables. 'You look as though you need cheering up.' He pushed a plate across the table. 'Never fails for me.'

She managed a smile. 'Sometimes it feels like being on a different planet. I just don't seem to be able to read things the same as I could at home.'

Rhys nodded. 'My wife's from Shrewsbury. I know it's nothing like what you're used to, but it took her a long time to get the hang of things. She says when everyone knows everyone else you can feel a bit left out of conversations. It's not deliberate, they just forget that you don't know everything that they do.'

'I know it'll take a while. It's just that I don't seem to be able to work out what sort of people they are. Does that sound mad?'

'I think I know what you mean. Rhi and me, we went to Tenerife on our holidays last summer. We got well and truly stitched up with a dodgy car hire firm. See, if we'd been here, I'd have known the guy wasn't right just by looking. I suppose it's just what you're used to.'

'So why is the DI so upset about this woman who was trying to set up a contract with Gareth Watkin? Why is it all her fault? He seems to think she tempted poor Gareth into a liaison against his wishes.'

Rhys broke a corner off his bara brith and chewed thoughtfully. 'I think he can be a bit Chapel at times. Fire and brimstone, you know. Maybe he thinks she's a Delilah. And don't forget, the boss was really good friends with Gareth Watkin for years. Until the foot and mouth outbreak.' He grinned. 'He's a good bloke though old Speedy, as straight as a die. You could rely on him a hundred percent.'

Julie drained her cup and put it back on the saucer. 'Do you fancy a trip out to Penrhiw. You can let me know if there's something obvious I'm missing.'

Eurig Powell was tall and lean with a shock of white-blonde hair and a fringe which flopped into his eyes. The fringe, thought Swift, was a good defence mechanism when he didn't want to look at you.

'It can't hurt him now, Eurig,' Swift said.

Eurig sat down behind his desk and spread both hands on the leather-backed pad of green blotting paper. 'I promised,' he said.

'Anything you can tell me might help me to find out who killed him.' Swift lowered himself into the visitors' chair and waited.

'He was a good friend, as well as a colleague.' Eurig looked up at Swift and his internal battle was etched on his face. 'I don't want to say anything that would make matters worse.'

'They can't get much worse for Sarah. If we don't find out who shot Gareth then she will remain a suspect.'

'You can't be serious. Sarah? Oh come on, Craig, you know as well as I do that she worshipped him.'

Swift shrugged. 'So tell me about it.'

Eurig put his head in his hands, rubbed his temple with his thumb. 'He was trying to go into business with Jessica Southam, the actuary. They'd been talking about it for several years, on and off. I thought when he was ill …'

'Go on.'

'I thought she'd run a mile. Ms Southam isn't the sort of person to play Florence Nightingale or even Betsi Cadwaladr.'

'I know. I've met her.'

'Then you'll know exactly what I mean. And she did stay away, all the time he was in hospital, all through the chemo.'

'And once he'd been nursed back to health she swooped.'

Eurig nodded. 'Something like that. I think she'd decided he was the only solicitor who she could work with. She was the same with that poor fiancé of hers when she realised her biological clock was ticking. Suddenly he wasn't up to scratch. Mind you,' Eurig looked up at Swift and frowned, 'he had his marching orders over a year ago now. The rumour was he couldn't come up with the goods.'

Swift sat straighter in his chair. Of course. 'It couldn't have been Gareth's child, could it?'

Eurig shook his head. 'It definitely isn't Gareth's. He and Sarah really wanted another baby. They're both besotted with kids, they always wanted three. The hospital said there was a miniscule chance that he could still father a child, but he went through loads of tests and it turns out it wasn't ever going to happen.'

'So there's never been anything more than a business relationship between Gareth and the Southam woman?'

Eurig shook his fringe away from his face. 'No, Craig. There was never anything like that between them. She wanted him for his mind, but she was getting more and more demanding. Until the start of this year she was writing to him at work, phoning the office. Bryony was in a really difficult position, fielding all the phone calls and letters. If Dic had found out, or Catherine, there'd have been absolute mayhem.'

'So Dic didn't know?'

'Good God no. You know what he's like. He'd have excommunicated Gareth if he'd known what was going on. Besides, it would have put Dic in a really difficult position with the rest of the family, especially with Catherine being Ella's sister.'

'So you're absolutely sure Dic doesn't know.'

'I promise you, Craig, there's no way. Please don't tell him if you don't have to. If Sarah chooses to say anything to him and to Catherine then that's her choice.'

'You don't think this Jessica woman had anything to do with his death?'

Eurig's eyes narrowed just slightly as he considered the question, but he shook his head. 'She was so keen on the idea of working with him. She wanted to move him up to her new flagship office in Cheshire – Alderley Edge I think it was. He'd kept putting off the day he had to tell Sarah about the move and Southam was livid. Sarah was happy enough about the new company, but moving – that was a different matter, she really didn't want to go. Her dad's on his own now and not in the best of health, and she wants the kids to keep their Welsh. She'd have a hard time managing either of those in Cheshire. Jessica thought he was just dragging his feet. She wrote to him last week or the week before with an ultimatum, demanding that he confront Sarah, and that if he didn't she would.'

So Julie was right about Gareth moving away from Penrhiw. That would have caused all sorts of problems. Swift stood up and offered his hand to the solicitor. 'Thank you. You know the form, Eurig, if there's anything else you remember, phone me. Any time.'

Eurig sat down heavily. His fringe had flopped back over his face by the time Swift reached the door.

A faint breeze wafted the shrubs in front of the bungalow and from the fields came the call and echo bleating of ewes and lambs. Julie could have closed her eyes and felt the warmth of the spring sunshine on her face, but the sound of the front door being wrenched open broke the spell. Sarah Watkin was less than pleased to see DS Kite and DC Williams.

'What is it now?' She stood squarely on the doorstep with no intention of letting them inside the house.

'We've brought your computer back.' Rhys smiled. 'Shall I bring it in?'

'I can manage, thank you.' Sarah took the laptop from him and turned away.

'Mrs Watkin, do you have an old-fashioned daisy-wheel printer?' Julie asked.

Sarah sighed a small, petulant sigh. 'Yes. The kids use it. I need to work out how to change the ribbon, it ran out the other day and Gareth used to…'

'Could we have a quick look?'

'What exactly is it that you're looking for?'

'We just need to know if it was the printer that…' Rhys stopped himself. 'Did Gareth use the printer at all?'

'No. He had his own in the study. The old printer was too slow for him. We've had it for donkeys' years, but it does for the kids.'

'Could we have a look?' Julie asked.

'I could change the ribbon for you?' Rhys smiled again.

Sarah hesitated. 'Oh go on then. It's in Seren's room. This way.'

Julie picked her way through toy tractors and balers, small plastic cows and a tiny trailer. These had to be Dylan's. Seren was too old for farmyard toys. In Seren's small bedroom there was a copy of *Little Women* on the chest of drawers along with a large packet of pencil crayons and a sheaf of ruled printer paper. An ancient desktop computer was connected to a huge printer, probably both cast-offs from the office in town. 'If Seren were to use this computer, would she know how to use the word processing package?'

'She does use it, just for notes and things. She's a great list-maker is Seren.'

'Could we have a quick look at her documents?'

'There's something wrong with the programme. She can print them out but it won't let her save them. It's not worth getting it looked at, it's so ancient.'

CHAPTER THIRTY-SEVEN

'This is Sergeant Kite now.' Brian Hughes was talking to a plump, middle-aged woman who was holding a white envelope inside a clear plastic bag. 'Sergeant, this is Mrs Beswick. She's a neighbour of Gordon and Eileen Price's.'

'What can I do for you, Mrs Beswick?' The woman seemed agitated, eager to offload the envelope.

'It was Eileen. She wanted me to give you this.'

Julie took the envelope from her. It had been opened. The top was a ragged line as though it had been ripped in a hurry.'

'I was round there today, sitting with Eileen for a bit. She went to get a photograph album, to show me what their Bobby looked like when he was a kitten. I've seen them all before. She forgets, you see, but I don't let on. Anyway, she found this in the drawer. She'd forgotten all about it she said, but she wanted me to bring it to you. She asked for you by name. You must have made quite an impression on her, Sergeant.'

Julie took the letter carefully from the envelope, holding it in a tissue. It was dated 15th April, written from Strangeways Prison.

"Dear Mr Price, I wanted to write and ask if we might meet. I have waited a long time to see you, and have had more than a little time to ponder on my actions in my previous life. I was a different person then. I have learned to live with what I did, but I have to speak to you to beg your forgiveness. I intend to make my way to see you upon my release and I hope you will allow me to explain. *And God shall wipe away all tears from their eyes; and there shall be no more death, neither sorrow, nor crying, neither shall there be any more pain: for the former things are passed away. Revelation 21:4.* Yours in Christ, the erstwhile Stephen Collins."

'I hope it wasn't too important.' Mrs Beswick turned to leave. 'Eileen does put things in odd places, bless her. There was an unopened packet of back bacon in that drawer with weeks' worth of post, and some cutlery.'

Julie watched her leave and reread the letter, still standing in reception. If Gordon had seen this maybe he wouldn't have thought the second note was threatening. What on earth possessed Eileen to file the thing?

'Anything interesting?' Swift was updating the whiteboard as Julie walked back into the office. 'I had an enlightening chat with Eurig Powell.'

'This is more than a little enlightening too, Sir.' Julie manoeuvred the note into a plastic wallet and handed it to Swift. 'The Prices' neighbour brought it in just now. She said Eileen found it in a drawer when she was looking for a photograph album.'

Swift's face ran a range of emotions from surprise to disbelief. He checked the date. 'Oh for God's sake. What's *erstwhile* supposed to mean? So what's he calling himself now? She's had this for over a fortnight.' Swift ran his fingers through what was left of his hair. 'If we'd known about this a week ago maybe Gareth Watkin would still be with us.'

'You think so, Sir?' Julie stared at the picture of a smiling Gareth Watkin on the board. 'I have my doubts. But at least we've solved the mystery of the suicide note.'

'How?' She had Swift's attention.

'It wasn't a suicide note at all. Seren wrote it. She's got her own battered laptop and an ancient printer in her bedroom.'

'Why didn't Sarah tell us that?'

'She says she didn't know.' Rhys handed Seren's fragmented note to Swift in its plastic wallet. '*Mae nôl.* It was the dog, Sir. One of the sheepdogs kept running away. Milos had said it was no use to him as a working dog if it couldn't be trusted. He'd said

216

he was going to shoot it when it decided to come home. Seren asked her father to intervene, to ask Milos if she could keep the dog as a pet. She was just worried about the dog and was letting her father know it had come back.'

'And Milos thought it was the cancer that had come back.' Julie followed the lines and bullet points on the white board. 'Why the hell can't people just talk to each other? Seren, Gareth, Milos – even Gordon and Eileen. Why does everything have to be so complicated?'

Swift passed the note back to Rhys. 'Well, we just have to hope Collins wakes up. At least Gordon would be off the hook for murder or manslaughter, and we could interrogate Collins about Gareth's murder. Good work, you two.' He shook his head. 'I know you were convinced it was Sarah.' Swift bestowed an apologetic smile. 'But Collins has to be our prime suspect now. The only, albeit slightly unreliable, witness saw someone small, dressed in black clothes bending over the body and Collins is a weedy little runt with a penchant for black. Sarah has a cast-iron alibi for the time of the murder. Case closed, or at least it will be when we know what's going to happen to Collins.'

Julie continued to stare at the board. 'What about Ms Southam? And do we think Dic or Catherine could have acted to stop her plans for Gareth?'

'I don't know, but Collins was up there taunting us, taking photographs. Why would he do that if he wasn't involved in Gareth's death? It has to be him. We know he was in the car park and out on the hill at the right times.'

'Did Eurig Powell say who else knew about Jessica and her scheme?' Julia asked.

Swift shook his head. 'He's adamant Gareth never mentioned it to anyone, apart from Eurig. He was obviously opting for the quiet life. Right. Who's for a celebratory cappuccino – my treat.'

The room emptied, everyone following Swift down the corridor to the canteen. Only Morgan Evans was left behind, and

Julie who stood deep in thought by the board, gazing at the photograph of the smiling man in the dark suit. 'Who was it, Gareth?' she asked.

'You're not happy.' Morgan sauntered over to stand beside her.

Julie frowned. 'What about the people carrier? It was still there in the car park after the BMW left with Gareth in it. If Collins was driving the Zafira, then who was it who assaulted Gareth Watkin and drove him away?'

'Maybe he had an accomplice who was driving the Zafira. You saw the DVD. Collins assaulted Gareth, drove him out onto the Epynt and shot him. Simple.' Morgan perched on the edge of a desk. 'You're obviously not convinced. Go on then, what's your solution?'

'I'm not sure. I'm just not entirely convinced it was Collins who thumped Gareth Watkin in the Metropole car park.'

CHAPTER THIRTY-EIGHT

Julie dragged the gate open. In the field beside the lane Joe was checking his ewes and lambs. These lambs were a few weeks old now, bolder, gathering in little gangs along the fence line, leaping off the bank and running as fast as they could down the slope. The ewes seemed quite happy to let them play; unaware of what would happen to them in a few short months. She drove through the gate and climbed out of the car to close it behind her.

'You got the person who did it yet?' Joe's quad bike rumbled quietly as he spoke. 'Bad business that, out on the hill.' He watched her, holding her gaze with icy blue eyes. 'Why would anyone want to kill Gareth Watkin?'

'We're making progress.' Julie pulled the gate shut and wrestled with the spring-loaded catch, avoiding his stare.

'Rumour says it was revenge.'

'I shouldn't listen to rumour if I were you, it just muddies the water.' She went to climb back into the car.

'I told you it would be a foreigner.'

Julie sighed. He really did have a problem. 'Don't you mean someone from off?'

'Bloody long way off.' Joe revved the engine and swung the quad bike in a wide curve, racing away up the field. Julie watched him go, scattering lambs in all directions. Why did she feel so isolated? Swift was satisfied with the outcome, everything pointed in Collins' direction, but still... There was something that wasn't right.

Adam was in the kitchen when she got home. There was a large bouquet of carnations and freesias in the washing up bowl and a card in a red envelope propped up against the pepper mill on the table.

'Happy anniversary!' He threw his arms around her and lifted her off her feet. 'This is going to be a good year.'

'Whoah, steady,' she laughed and kissed him as he plonked her back on the ground. 'Happy anniversary to you too. Hope you like it.' From her bag she pulled a card and a wrapped oblong box. 'I know you've got the posh one, but I thought this would be good for taking on your bike rides.'

'Oh wow, Jules.' Adam already had the wrapping paper off the box and was admiring the sleek camera. 'We could go out on the bikes for an hour now if you like – I didn't expect you back for ages.'

'Well, we've come to a bit of a conclusion.'

'Great, first case under your belt.' He undid the lid of the box and lifted the camera out.

'Sort of.' Julie bent to sniff the flowers in the sink. 'I'm not convinced we're there just yet.' She watched him as he looked through the viewfinder, moving around the kitchen until he found her in the camera's little window.

'I've booked a table at that restaurant in Llanwrtyd. I thought we should celebrate. Smile!'

Julie did as she was asked.

Llanwrtyd Wells was a jumble of pastel-coloured cottages snuggled into the valley, which bound the tumbling Irfon River. At its centre, looming in the dusk, was a sculpture of a red kite, its wings outstretched, beak dipping towards its prey. Would the forked tail and curved beak always remind her of Gareth Watkin, the sightless eye sockets, the brain tissue coating the reeds beside him?

'He's very impressive in daylight.' Adam stood beneath his namesake and gazed up at the massive wings, with each guide feather painstakingly picked out. 'I stopped for lunch in the pub over there the other day.' He nodded towards The Neuadd Arms Hotel. 'Found out all sorts of interesting stuff about the town. For instance, did you know that there's a plaque over there dedicated to Screaming Lord Sutch of the Monster Raving Loony Party?' Julie shook her head.

'You and your local history. How long have we been here?'

'But it's mad, this place. They hold the World Bog Snorkelling Championships and a Man v Horse Race, twenty-two miles in the hills, where runners and horses compete against each other. If the runner wins he gets £1,000. Could be worth a go. Then there's the Real Ale Wobble which would definitely be worth a go.'

'Bog snorkelling?' Julie grimaced. 'Full marks for reinventing the tourist trade then.'

They crossed the road to the restaurant. Inside, there were candles and starched white tablecloths, crystal glassware and original paintings in watercolours and oils. They were shown to their table and handed leather-backed menus containing detailed descriptions of the local produce contained in sumptuous meals.

'There's nothing touristy about this place.' Julie said.

'You make it sound like Blackpool,' said Adam. 'It does have its serious side too. Apparently they have a big eisteddfod here.' He closed his menu and picked up the wine list. 'All very cultural, singing, poetry, it goes back over a hundred and fifty years.'

'Adam, have you done any work at all this week?'

'And over that way,' he nodded towards the window, 'there used to be a school for children who were smuggled out of Czechoslovakia when it was occupied by the Nazis.'

'But why would they bring them out here?' Julie closed her menu and smiled at the waitress who was bringing her a large glass of dry white wine. She waited until the waitress was out of earshot. 'Have you heard any of the local gossip about Gareth Watkin?'

Adam rolled his eyes. 'Jules, you're on work again.'

'Yeah. I know. Sorry.' She grinned. 'Do you think I might have OCD?'

'Definitely. Well, Menna's convinced he shot himself. With the note saying the cancer had come back.'

'So that's common knowledge then?'

'Apparently. People are always happy to pass on gossip.' He picked up his orange juice, hiding his expression from her.

'Adam, let's not go there again. Not tonight.'

He put the glass back down on the table. 'Sorry, fresh start. At least we've got the chance to try, unlike Mr Watkin.'

'Do you think she's right, Menna?'

'I don't know what I'd do if it were me. But to have to go through all that again…'

'So the local gossip is that it was suicide?'

'Not in The Trout. The lads there don't think he'd have shot himself, not after all he'd been through and come out the other side.'

'I wish I'd asked you sooner. What do they think then, the chaps in The Trout? Where is the Trout anyway?'

'Beulah. We passed it on the way here. They think he was murdered.'

'So who do they think did it?'

'Two possibilities.' Adam was enjoying himself now, keeping her dangling. 'About a third of them think it's someone in the family, probably Milos or Sarah…'

'Go on,' hissed Julie.

'Have you decided?' The waitress hovered, pad in hand.

'Oh yes I think so.' Adam picked up the menu. 'I think I'd like the Perl Wen cheese and Carmarthen ham to start with, and then…either the plaice with prawns and spinach or the pork with caramelised onions and apricot sauce.' He smiled at her. 'Which would you recommend?'

'They're both lovely.' She was blushing now.

'Then I'll have the pork please.'

'And for you, madam?'

'All that pork,' Julie said. 'That won't help the training, will it?' I'll just have the plaice, thanks.' Julie turned back to Adam, who slowly picked up the wine list.

'Could we order a bottle of wine?'

'You're doing it on purpose,' Julie hissed as the waitress departed. 'Come on, tell me, what do the other two thirds think?'

'Well…'

'Adam!'

'The vast majority of them think it could have been the chap who's in the hospital after a meeting with the ex-police sergeant who lives somewhere on the way to Merthyr.'

'Oh.'

'Not what you wanted to hear?'

'That's what Swift thinks too. How the hell do they know so much, we haven't announced anything about him.'

'Everyone knows what's going on. It's not anonymous like Manchester. I'd never realised before, just how lonely it can be in a big city.'

'Mmm,' said Julie. 'So tell me more about this Czech school.'

CHAPTER THIRTY-NINE
Wednesday, 4th May

Adam's side of the bed was empty. Julie reached out her hand. He must have been up for a while; the rumpled sheet was cool to her touch. Outside the birds were singing – tweets and warbles, trills and little melodies. Why had she never heard the different songs before? Had there been birds in Manchester? There had been scruffy, dim-witted pigeons in St Peter's Square and Piccadilly Gardens, stalking scraps from between the flagstones, their little round eyes fixed as though they were looking far into the distance. She had never noticed birdsong before, drowned out by the constant growl of traffic. How many birds could she even identify – the odd seagull swooping between the buildings and little brown sparrows, squabbling in the soil round the trees in St John's Gardens. How could you even begin to pick out the different songs?

Adam appeared round the bedroom door bearing two mugs of coffee and a plate of toast on a tray.

'It's going to be a lovely day.' He plonked the tray lopsidedly on the mound of duvet next to her and picked up a piece of toast. 'I've just been for a run as far as the main road.'

Julie stretched and pulled herself upright against the pillows. 'You seem to have adopted farming hours since we got here. How can you be so lively at this hour, you're like the bloody Duracell bunny."

Adam threw the curtains open and sun streamed into the room. Julie groaned and reached for her coffee.

'Look at that. Just compare that to the view from the flat.' Cautiously she reopened one eye. The sun was peeping over the hill, serrating the line of conifers on the top. Below, in neatly hedged fields, sheep grazed, still in shadow. He had a point. From the bedroom window of their flat they had seen Elaine's net-curtained windows, a bank of satellite dishes and the high-rise blocks beyond. 'Best thing we ever did, moving here.' He sat down on the bed next to her. 'We'll get there, Jules, we'll get it right this time.'

Swift was whistling. 'Bread of Heaven,' explained Rhys. 'It's a bit of a rugby anthem.' Morgan Evans and Goronwy were sharing a tale of fishing, if the gestures were anything to go by. At least she hoped it was fishing.

'Good news, Sergeant Kite. Jesus doesn't want Collins for a sunbeam just yet, he's regained consciousness.'

Thank God. Just maybe Gordon Price would get away with a short sentence for assault. 'Is he…normal, Sir?'

'I don't think he was ever normal, Julie.' Swift shook his head. 'But the consultant thinks he'll make a complete recovery.'

'Maybe there is something in this praying lark.' Morgan Evans had strolled over to join them. 'I was reading up on the Collins case. It wasn't the first time he'd been accused of murder. He'd have got away with Janey Wilson too if Gordon Price hadn't been on the ball that day. Pity Gordon didn't "accidentally" do him damage when he arrested him.'

'Constable, a word in my office.' Swift was already on his way back to the glass-fronted booth.

'Oh dear. He really does take a while to catch on, does our Morgan.' Rhys watched the door close. Neither of them sat, but even from a distance they could see Swift turning puce and Morgan Evans hanging his head like a small child. 'The boss hates anything that's not by the book, even talk of it.'

Julie saw Swift pointing to the door and Morgan creeping out into the open-plan office. Despite herself she felt sorry for the poor lad. 'But what about the business with Milos Watkin? He was pretty lenient there.'

Rhys considered his words. 'He might look benign and he doesn't like to stir things up locally if he can help it,' Rhys lowered his voice as Morgan approached. 'But he's a damned good copper. Knows exactly what he's doing. All right, Morgan?'

Evans glared at them both and hurled himself into his chair.

'Julie, you're with me.' Swift stared hard at Evans, who sat up straighter and switched on his computer. 'Hospital. Let's go and have a word with this born-again creep, Collins.'

Julie grabbed her jacket and her bag, and hurried after Swift. But on her way past, she winked at Morgan. She was nearly at the door when she heard a shout.

'Sarge!' Morgan Evans was giving her a thumbs up and he wore a rather surprised grin.

Collins still looked alarmingly unwell. He had been transferred to a private room at the end of a normal medical ward and was propped up on a mountain of pillows. There was nothing on his bedside table except a jug of water and a plastic glass, no grapes or get well cards, no barley water or well-thumbed magazines. The skin beneath his eyes was blue-grey, in contrast to the parchment of his forehead. If she were to reach out and touch him, Julie expected the skin to feel cool and taut, like an embalmed body. His top lip was raised in what seemed like a sneer, but once he began to speak she knew it was because his mouth was dry, making his words stick to his tongue. Despite herself she reached over, poured half a glass of tepid water and handed the glass to him.

'Thank you, officer.' The voice was little more than a whisper.

'Mr Collins, what can you tell me about what happened to you on Friday?'

'Very little, Inspector.' Collins held out the glass as though it was too heavy for him and Julie removed it from his hand and replaced it on the bedside table.

'Do you remember where you were?' Julie had to fight to keep an abrasive edge from her voice, to try to sound solicitous. She knew Swift was still making his mind up about her.

'No, Sergeant. The day remains, for the moment, a complete blank.' Collins smoothed the sheet with a hand bruised by the cannula which was still attached to a drip beside the bed.

'What about last Monday? Can you remember anything about that?' Swift stared down at Collins. 'Can you remember where you were on that day?'

Collins stared back at Swift. 'I was driving from Manchester on Monday.'

'Really? Then the evidence we have must be wrong. Our information is that you drove from Manchester on Saturday.'

Collins' eyes flicked towards Swift, but he carried on smoothing the sheet and did not speak.

'So where were you going?' Julie's voice was still soft.

'There were people I had to see,' said Collins.

'Could you tell me more about that?' Swift was barely concealing his impatience. 'To catch up with friends, was it?'

With difficulty, Collins turned towards Julie. 'I think I'd like to rest now, Sergeant, if that's permitted.' He closed his eyes. Swift's lips tightened into a grim line.

'Certainly, Sir. We'll come back and see you when you've had a rest,' Julie said. The ghost of a smile animated Collins' face, and then it was gone.

Outside on the corridor Swift released his pent-up aggression by slamming a pound coin into the waiting jaws of the coffee machine. 'Thank you, Sergeant.'

'Sir?'

'Thank you for reminding me that Collins is to be classed as a victim, at least until we can charge him with murder.' He reached down for the cup of grey liquid proffered by the machine and scowled, but sipped it cautiously. 'I just can't believe he's changed.'

'Not after seventeen years in prison, Sir?' Julie pressed the button marked 'hot chocolate'. 'Maybe he's had therapy.'

'Therapy!' Swift spluttered coffee. 'I'd have given him therapy, and it wouldn't have involved do-gooders and namby-pamby bloody social workers. He blushed. 'I'm so sorry, Julie. That was less than professional. God, I hate the way that lowlife in there makes me feel. I need a PC outside his door to keep an eye on him until we can interview him under caution, don't want the sod tottering off into the hills.'

'Careful, Inspector. Your blood pressure must be ridiculously high.' Kay Greenhalgh slowed as she passed and winked at Julie. 'And that stuff won't do you any good at all.'

'Any port in a storm, Doctor. Be thankful it's not single malt, which would be my preferred option right now.'

Greenhalgh looked at her watch and shook her head. 'I hear your assault victim has regained consciousness.'

'I think I preferred him the way he was.' Swift dropped the half-drunk coffee into the bin and scratched his ear.

'I'd say he was incredibly lucky,' said Greenhalgh.

'And so was his attacker,' Julie said. 'At least he won't be going down for murder.'

Frank Parkinson was still trying to impress her. Julie knew that, but there was no harm in humouring him was there? Not if it meant she could save time, circumnavigate the system, just a little. He didn't mind anyway, he'd always helped wet-behind-the-ears DCs, turned them into proper, no-nonsense investigators with an eye for the truth, or lack of it. She tapped her teeth with her pen. Morgan Evans was scowling at his computer screen, checking out the spate of stolen cars in Brecon. The DI was probably right. Would she have got this far without Sergeant Parkinson's guidance, nudging her in the right direction, making her think about every question, every piece of information? Maybe she ought to try a bit harder with

Morgan Evans. She checked the clock and dialled the number Frank had given her.

'Could I speak to Officer Deakin please?'

'Speaking.'

'This is Detective Sergeant Julie Kite, Mid Wales Police. Could I just ask you a few questions about one of your recent inmates?'

'You can, who are we talking about?' His accent sounded broad Mancunian. She wouldn't have given it a second thought a week or two ago.'

'Collins. Stephen Collins?'

'Thank you for reminding me, Sergeant. I had hoped I'd never hear about that particular slimeball again.'

'Ah. He was a popular prisoner then?'

Deakin snorted. 'About as popular as a dose of the clap. What's he been up to now?'

'Let's just say he's helping us with our enquiries.'

'I doubt that very much. Helping anyone isn't in his nature and devious is his middle name. Speaking of which, you do know he's in the process of changing his name do you?'

'No, he hasn't said anything. Is it anything to do with witness protection?'

'It's more to do with his latest fetish. The bastard's found God.'

'Ah. And that means what exactly?' She could hear the sigh of frustration at the other end of the line.

'He did a law degree. He was going to sue everyone from the trial judge down to the court usher and the foreman of the jury. He said his trial was fixed, accused the police of malpractice, ill treatment, you name it. He even said the duty solicitor was deliberately working against him and damaged his defence. Then he got into psychology and then after that, for the last seven years or so, he's been studying theology with some crackpot distance-learning university in the States. Apparently he's desperate to convert to Catholicism. Maybe he could do us all a favour and get himself into a closed monastic order.'

'Is it for real do you think?'

'Collins? For real? Highly unlikely. He's the most conniving, despicable, manipulative excuse for a human being I've ever met in my career.'

'No real views either way, then.'

Deakin laughed. 'Fair point, Sergeant. No, I don't think it's genuine. It made my flesh crawl just to look at him. He spent a lot of time in solitary, especially lately.'

'Bad behaviour?'

'At his own request. He said it helped him to study and to contemplate. I've never heard a con say that before. Not that anyone was too upset not to have to share with him. And the governor's latest self-appointed prisoners' welfare advisor is one of these progressive types. Everyone can be healed with the right approach to rehabilitation according to her.' Julie laughed at his impression of a well-to-do lady of a certain age.

'Ah. So if Collins made his way to where he was arrested and charged for the Janey Wilson murder…'

'Then he'd be up to no bloody good, Sergeant.'

'Thank you for your help, Mr Deakin. Just one more thing, what's he intending to call himself now?'

'I think he went through every combination of gospels before he settled on his new moniker, and I wouldn't be surprised if he hasn't got Mark and John down as middle names. It's a wonder he didn't just call himself Jesus H Christ and have done with it.' Deakin let out the verbal equivalent of a scowl. 'Matthews, Sergeant. His poncy new name is Luke Matthews.'

Julie put the phone back in its cradle. So that would confirm Swift's take on the situation then. She stared at the board, at the neatly arranged white cards with their biblical references. So all the notes were his too, including the one stuffed into her gate. She leaned back in her chair and sighed. Maybe she really was out of her depth. New people, new job, new country. Was it too much change at the same time? What if Collins was really plotting something in Llanafan? What would she do if Adam was out or away? It was nearly half a mile to the next farm. It wouldn't do you any good at all to stand on that lane and shout, however loudly you could scream.

'You OK?' Morgan was looking at her.

'Yep. I'm just feeling like a penguin in a flock of sheep.' Morgan raised his eyebrows and burst out laughing. On impulse she heard herself offering to buy him a coffee. 'I want to run something past you,' she said. Morgan looked as though he was on the spectrum somewhere between shocked and suspicious, but he followed her anyway.

'Go on then,' he said as they sat at what was rapidly becoming Julie's favourite table. 'What's bothering you, Sarge?'

The motorcyclist was watching television. His mother showed Julie into the living room where he was watching motorbikes racing across the huge flat screen at ridiculous angles. His leg rested on the low coffee table and looked, to her, as though it was held together with scaffolding and a huge, heavy plaster cast. A pair of crutches was propped against the arm of the sofa and on a straight-backed wooden chair next to him the remains of a sandwich lunch.

'You're on the mend then?' Julie sat down across the room from him, next to the television.

'Getting there.' He hitched himself straighter on the sofa. 'Doc says it's going to take a while. I hope I've got a job to go back to at the end of it.'

'What do you do?'

'Mechanic. For the tractor place over towards Tirabad.'

Julie nodded knowingly. 'So that's why you were on that road last Tuesday, taking a short cut?'

He picked up the remote and switched off the television. The room was quiet. 'I've been having trouble with the insurance company because of it. They say it's not classed as a public road, say they might not be able to pay out.'

'I can't believe that. They're trying it on. Do you want me to phone them?'

He grinned. 'Mam had a go at them this morning. She was well grumpy. Said if my bike had been on the drive or I'd been trialling somewhere I'd be covered. They're playing the card that it was on MOD land and I didn't have permission to be there.'

'Ouch. Let me know if I can do anything.'

'Thanks. It's my own fault for being a total idiot, but I was late for work again, and I'm on a warning for time-keeping.'

'So that's sorted out why you were up there. I'm still not clear about what you saw and when. Could you go through it again once more for me?'

'I had thought about phoning you, but then after that identity thing, when I was out of my head on painkillers. I made a bit of a prat of myself there too didn't I?'

'We were just grateful you came in at all. So, you've thought of something else?'

'I don't know. It'll sound stupid.'

'Go on.'

'Well I'm not sure now, about who I saw. I mean I still think I saw him, the man I told you about, but...' he picked at one of the metal rods in his leg; the metallic pings made Julie shudder. 'I think there were two people, and that one of them was a woman.' He looked up at her like a puppy who knows it's done wrong, but she was smiling.

'Can you remember who you saw first?'

'I've no idea, sorry. One of them was before I lost consciousness for the first time, just after the bike had come off the road, but it's all still jumbled up. Bits keep coming back to me, but it's a mess.'

'What did she look like, the woman?'

'They weren't too different to be honest, I think that's why it's taken me a while to work it out.'

'Related maybe?'

'I don't know, but similar heights, dark hair. Sorry, I did say you'd think I was mad, hallucinating or something. I can't remember the detail. I think my visor was scratched too. Mam won't let me see it, or the bike. Useless isn't it?'

'No, it's not, anything you can recall is useful. Can you remember what they were doing?'

'That's the thing; they were both standing over the body. Not that I knew it was a body then. I couldn't see it from where I was. I could just see them looking at something. That's why I thought it was the one memory, just the one person, not two different people at different times. Sorry.'

'Don't apologise.' Julie pulled a business card from her bag. 'But do promise me you'll phone if you remember anything else. It doesn't matter how small, it might mean something to us even if it means nothing to you.'

'Right. Sorry. I should have phoned you sooner.'

'Don't worry. We've got the information now. That's what matters. I'll see myself out, but call me.'

Before she got to the front door she could hear the roar of motor bikes hurtling round a track.

CHAPTER FORTY

'Where are you?' Swift sounded distracted.

'On my way back from Sennybridge. I've been to see the motorcyclist, to see if he could remember anything else.'

'Can you meet me at the hospital? Collins is asking to speak to me again. He's rounded up a solicitor, God help the poor bloke.'

'He's not going to be called Collins for much longer apparently, Sir. He's changing his name to Luke Matthews.' She heard Swift groan.

'And you know what this means, Sergeant?'

'Yep, all those notes with verses from Luke and Matthew were clues. He's been laughing at us, showing off, seeing how long it would take us.'

'Oh now that's just annoying that is. So he was hanging about for our benefit, up at the farm too.'

'Either that or he was just returning to the scene of his crime. I'm about half an hour from you, should I see you by the shop in reception?'

'Perfect,' said Swift. 'I'll wait for you.'

Julie turned the car round and headed up the hill, out towards the towering sandstone mountains of the Brecon Beacons. Little clusters of buildings picked out the individual farms, and there were sheep as far as she could see; fields full of ewes and lambs like little white seed pearls on pale green velvet. A fortnight ago her patch had been the back streets of Central Manchester, the clubs and pubs teeming with people, the Arndale with its glittering shops and the remnants of the rag trade, warehouses and mills turned into trendy apartments and fashionable hotels. She had spent her precious weekends watching Adam compete in triathlons, cheering him on as he dripped his way out of his wetsuit and onto his bike to hurtle round city streets. They had visited libraries and museums for Adam and markets and the cinema for her. But what now? Without the bustle of the city, without the distraction of friends and relatives they really were on their own. This was make or break and suddenly she realised just how desperately she wanted to make this work. Julie couldn't imagine life without him. She had to forgive him so they could move on.

She stopped at a T-junction where two major roads crossed and looked both ways. To her left, in the far distance, a tractor with a flashing amber light on its roof. To the right there was nothing. Not a single vehicle, just two lanes of empty tarmac. It looked the same as any road in England. The road signs were familiar, despite the Welsh descriptions, the cars parked outside the house opposite was the same make and model as hers, but it was all so foreign, like being on holiday somewhere in the past.

Swift was pacing the polished tiles of the reception area when she got to the hospital. As she reached him he carried on walking, heading for the lifts. 'Let's get this over with,' he said, jabbing at the button.

'How do you want to play it?' Julie asked as the doors opened, releasing a motley crew of patients, visitors and hospital staff.

'Carefully,' muttered Swift. 'We don't want him wriggling free on a technicality. And you can ask the questions.' The lift doors closed, leaving them alone. Swift leaned back against the brushed steel wall, staring up at the concealed lighting in the ceiling. 'I've put two PCs outside his room 24/7 and they can stay there for as long as it takes to get him back to Strangeways. I've been reading up on little Janey Wilson.' He rocked forward and looked straight at her. 'I may have been a little harsh with Morgan. This one's pure evil. No wonder Gordon Price hit him. I'd have done the same if he'd threatened my wife.'

The lift doors opened and a trolley was wheeled past them; two porters and a nurse tending to a small, unconscious child. Swift reached into his trouser pocket and removed a large white handkerchief and dabbed his mouth. Julie's immediate thought was that he was going to throw up.

'Let's take the stairs,' she said, squeezing past a large lady with shopping bags and out onto the second floor. Swift followed, having to jink through the closing doors. 'You OK?'

Swift nodded. 'Just don't read the case notes until this is sorted. I want at least one of us to remain objective.'

Collins was propped awkwardly against the metal of the bed. The nurse who showed them into the room plumped pillows and straightened sheets. 'There you are, Mr Collins. now you look respectable for your visitors.'

Swift turned the comment that almost escaped his lips into a cough and two pairs of eyes turned towards him.

'I'm Detective Sergeant Kite.' Julie held out her hand to the solicitor. 'And this is Detective Inspector Swift. You'll be aware of the background to this case?'

'I gather that my client has been questioned about the incident on Friday, which resulted in his present condition,' the solicitor nodded towards the bed. 'But there also seems to be some question about his whereabouts on Monday and Tuesday of last week.'

Julie looked at Swift, who was staring resolutely at a point on the wall way above Collins' head. 'Where would you like to start?' she asked Collins, and had to lean closer towards him to hear his words.

'I had arranged to see Gareth Watkin on Tuesday.' Swift's gaze snapped onto the shadow of a man in the bed. 'But it seems I was just too late to beg his forgiveness.'

'To beg his forgiveness...' Swift's voice was rising towards a shrill crescendo.

'Where did you arrange to see him, Mr Collins?' Julie asked.

'I was to meet him at his offices. I spoke to a very pretty and obliging young lady there, but unfortunately I didn't actually see him. I did find his farm in the middle of some God forsaken moorland. I don't know the name of the place. My first thought had been to see him there, but there always seemed to be so many people about the place, that I decided not to disturb him.'

'So you didn't speak to him at all?'

'Only in a manner of speaking. I prayed for him. I told him that I lamented his passing.' Collins swallowed. 'And then I asked the Lord to accept his soul.'

'So how do you know he was dead if you didn't see him?' Swift thrust his face towards the pillows.

'DI Swift, if you could…' the solicitor was on his feet.

Swift withdrew and stalked around the bed. The solicitor sat down. Julie smiled at Collins. 'How do you know?' she said. Collins frowned. 'How do you know that he was recently deceased, Mr Collins?'

'Someone told me.'

'Where were you when you heard this information?'

'The young lady in Mr Watkin's office told me of the unfortunate demise of her employer.'

'What excuse did you give her for visiting Mr Watkin?"

Swift turned from the window to look at her, offer a warning perhaps? She waited for Collins, who had gestured towards the glass and jug on the bedside cabinet. As before, she poured water into the glass and held it out for him.

'Bless you,' he said, lifting his head off the pillow to take a sip of water. He subsided gently, his face creasing with pain as he came to rest. 'I said I wanted to avail myself of his services.' Collins closed his eyes. 'No doubt she imagined I was interested in buying a property in this beautiful area.' He laughed, and with difficulty he turned his head so that he was looking at Swift. 'That would be a treat for you, Inspector.' Swift looked back at him, his expression perfectly blank. 'But in fact my reason for seeking out Mr Watkin is much more interesting than that. I am intending to apply to have my wrongful conviction overturned.' He stared straight at Julie, lifting his lips in a small smile. 'With Mr Watkin's knowledge of my case he would have been in a perfect position to help me obtain a pardon.'

'A pardon!' Swift swooped towards the bed once more.

'Inspector, I really must insist that my client is allowed to speak.' The solicitor stood up again and leaned towards Collins, blocking Swift's way.'

'But you were there.' Julie said. 'You were out on the hill the day Gareth Watkin died. I saw you.'

'I think you must be mistaken, Sergeant.'

'You were taking photographs.'

'I have no camera, Sergeant. I am sure you will have checked my belongings quite thoroughly. Did you find a camera among them?' Again, the small, smug smile hovered on Collins' thin lips.

'So you deny seeing Gareth Watkin or making any contact with him since you were freed from prison?' Julie's voice was controlled.

The two suits backed away, the solicitor to his chair and Swift to the window, both fists clenched but by his sides.

'Mr Collins?'

'I have had neither contact with nor sight of Gareth Watkin for over seventeen years, Sergeant.'

'But you also saw him on Monday of last week, Mr Collins. You watched him get into a car in the car park of the Metropole Hotel in Llandrindod Wells.' Collins stared at her again and Julie could feel a shiver run across her shoulders. God, this guy was a creep.

'How do you know, Sergeant?' Collins' voice was a hoarse hiss 'Can you prove any of this?'

Julie looked down at the bed, avoiding his gaze. 'So where did you go after you watched Mr Watkin leaving the car park of the Metropole Hotel on Monday of last week, Mr Collins?'

'Monday. Now, where was I on Monday? Ah yes,' Collins' face

was completely devoid of expression. 'There were other people I needed to catch up with.'

'Other people?' asked Julie.

'Old acquaintances, Sergeant. I forget the details for the moment.' He raised a hand to his head, his fingers brushing the dressing and Julie could almost feel the pain that caused his face to crumple.

Once he had regained his composure he fixed his gaze on her once more. 'I'm afraid I can't help you.'

'So we won't find your fingerprints on the pistol which was used to shoot him?' Swift spat the question.

'No, of course not.'

Collins swallowed with difficulty and the solicitor turned to Julie. 'I think perhaps my client has told you enough for now. At the very least he must be granted a break. He has been extremely cooperative and he needs to rest.' But Collins raised his hand, causing the IV line to catch against the bed rail.

'I need to finish this.'

The solicitor nodded and Collins continued. 'I knew what you'd think. I threatened Watkin at the trial and now I was getting my own back. But I'm not the same person I was then.' He was smoothing the edge of the sheet with his fingers now. 'I just wanted to explain to him.'

'And Gordon Price? Terrifying him and his wife because you wanted to explain that you'd changed?' said Swift.

'I had no idea that Mrs Price was so ill. I just wanted to put the record straight, to absolve Sergeant Price from his part in my incarceration. I also understand now that he had no choice but to arrest me, and that his treatment of me was…understandable in the circumstances.'

Julie cut in before Swift had a chance. 'And how did you find out that Mrs Price is "so ill", Mr Collins?'

Collins stared at her. 'Someone must have told me, Sergeant. My memory is playing tricks on me at the moment, as you can imagine.' He raised his hand and pressed his long, thin fingers to the undamaged side of his head.

Julie stared back at him and glanced at the solicitor. 'So you sent Mr Price threatening letters offering absolution?'

'It wasn't my intention to threaten him, Sergeant, just to talk.'

'What happened at the Prices' house on Friday, Mr Collins? Did Mr Price act in self-defence?'

The solicitor cleared his throat, but Collins waved him away. 'Nothing happened on Friday, Sergeant. I simply tripped and fell in the hallway of the Price's house. Having been spectacularly unsuccessful in my mission to clear my conscience, I then drove to the reservoir intending to take in the magnificent mid Wales scenery to lift my spirits.' He smiled, baring his small, pointed teeth. 'Apparently I had hit my head harder than I realised.'

Julie followed Swift down the stairs and out onto the concourse. There were patients in pyjamas and dressing gowns heading for the X-Ray Department smoking den, visitors with flowers and magazines, and others looking nervously at the signs for the various clinics. An elderly lady was being helped towards the exit. She looked as though she'd been crying forever. Swift overtook her and the porter who had his arm round her shoulder. 'Come on, Kite, let's get out of here.' Once they were outside in the bustle of the car park Swift stopped, closed his eyes and sighed.

'God, I wish I still smoked.'

'Do we believe him, Sir?'

'Who knows?'

'At least it lets Gordon off the hook.'

'It doesn't though, does it. There's no way Collins could have driven himself from the Price's to the Elan Valley. Not with that crack on the head.'

'But if he says that's what happened, if he refuses to testify against Gordon do we have a case?'

Swift shrugged. 'Gordon's not confessed and this creep says it was an accident.'

'But how did he know he was found at the reservoir if he was unconscious when he got there and when he went into the ambulance. He would have known if he'd driven himself though, wouldn't he?'

'Kay Greenhalgh thinks that's a very remote possibility.'

Julie sighed. 'What do you think about Watkin, Sir? Do you think Collins is telling the truth about not having seen or contacted him directly?'

'We have absolutely no evidence to suggest otherwise. It could have been exactly as he said.'

'We need to get back to the Prices' and ask Gordon one more time what happened the day Collins turned up. After the Jehovah-bashing it's more likely that he could have gone for Collins. Maybe he'll have thought a bit harder about things by now.' Julie didn't look at Swift. 'Would you like me to go and talk to him?'

'I'll do that Sergeant. You've done more than your fair share already today.' Swift forced a smile. 'Why don't you go and talk to Bryony and at least corroborate what Collins said about his visit to the office. I'll see you back at the nick.'

CHAPTER FORTY-ONE

Morgan Evans was waiting for her when she got back to the station. Almost conspiratorially, he signalled for her to join him at his desk. She dumped her bag and her jacket and perched on the edge of his desk.

'So what have you found out about Llanwrtyd?' she asked him.

'You're getting better, Sarge, that sounded almost native.' On his screen was an account of life at the Czechoslovak State School in Llanwrtyd Wells between 1943, when it had moved from Shropshire and June 1945, when the Second World War ended. 'I had no idea about this place. Six hundred and sixty nine Jewish children were rescued from the Nazis in occupied Czechoslovakia by someone called Nicholas Winton.' He scanned the screen. 'It says many of their parents were killed in the death camps.'

'Does it say what happened to the kids?'

'Not really, but we know some of them ended up in Llanwrtyd for a while. There's a lime tree they planted in the grounds, look, and a plaque.'

Julie read over his shoulder:

The smallest town in the land remains
Forever the greatest in our hearts.

This lime was planted by the old boys and girls
of the Czechoslovak Secondary School Abernant (1943-45)
now scattered throughout the world.

She tapped her teeth with a biro she'd taken off Morgan's desk. 'Do we have a list of the children who were pupils at the school?'

'No, Sarge, sorry.' Morgan looked crestfallen, but only for a second. 'I could go and visit my Mam's next door neighbour tonight though. He's ancient, and he grew up in Llanwrtyd.'

'Great, that's somewhere to start. Good work, Morgan.'

'Sarge, why did you want to know about the school?'

'Just a vague idea, nothing concrete yet. It has to do with a ring. Or, more precisely, a lack of one.'

Swift's visit to the Prices was to yield little more than they already knew.

'So, are you any further on?' Gordon stood with his arms folded, leaning against his car. The garage was cold, despite the bright sunshine outside.

'You know I can't tell you anything, Gordon. You're lucky you're not still in custody. I thought they might not give you bail.'

'I've done nothing wrong, Craig.'

'Collins has regained consciousness, that's as much as I can tell you.'

'I suppose I should be pleased.'

'You should be ecstatic.' Swift led the way back into the hallway. A black and white cat made a bee-line for him and rubbed its head against his leg. Swift resisted the urge to shoo it away.

'I don't know how you think I could have done something like that.' Gordon was petulant, whining like a schoolboy.

'Don't push it, Gordon. Let's forget the amateur dramatics shall we? The cat's recovered then?'

'Thank God. I don't know what Eileen would have done if he'd…you know.'

'What would Eileen have done if Collins had died, Gordon? If you'd have gone down for life?'

Gordon stroked the cat's head abstractedly. 'What do you think will happen to me?'

243

Swift looked down at his feet and the beige carpet. His eyes strayed to the patch which had been bleached, paler than the rest, and to the door with its invisible blood trail. 'That depends on so many things, Gordon. You know how it works.' Gordon Price nodded. The little cat looked up at him and purred. 'Just take each day as it comes would be my advice,' said Swift. He paused on the step. 'And don't have any ideas about visiting Collins.'

Gordon smiled. 'Of course not, Craig.'

Julie stared at the map on the screen in front of her. Why was she so useless at geography? Any further than France or Spain and she was totally lost. Why did her knowledge of Europe stop at Germany's borders? What happened to the Czech children after the war? How old would they be now? She counted up on her fingers and decided they'd have to be in their eighties probably.

'Sarge,' Morgan Evans stood behind her chair. 'Still on the Czech school?'

'It's a long shot, but there's something I'm not getting about all this. There's a link.'

'How?'

'I don't know.' She closed down the map. 'Maybe I'm seeing connections that aren't there.'

Adam was out when she arrived home. She changed into her running shoes and jeans and set off, walking up the lane. It was almost dark, but Cam must have heard her footsteps and wandered over to meet her. She took a fat carrot from her pocket and poked it over the gate. He crunched through it with no effort, and she curled her fingers away from his muzzle as he sought out the next chunk.

'You could have my fingers off,' she said and stroked his nose. 'I think I've upset your Dad.' She leaned against the gatepost and the horse put his whiskery face over the gate next to her. 'If he'd just stop ranting on about incomers we could have a sensible conversation. Do you know, yesterday he even referred to us as foreigners. Oh shit.' She rolled her eyes. 'You really are a stupid sod sometimes, Julie Kite. Sorry, got to go,' she said to the horse, and she set off down the lane at a run, into the fading light.

Back at the cottage she kicked off her trainers, dumped her coat and raced through to the tiny dining room where Adam had set up his computer. She flicked the switch and watched as the picture of St Peter's square loaded. Only a history teacher would have a background photograph dedicated to the Peterloo Massacre. He was certainly a one-off. She clicked on the shortcut for the genealogy website Adam was so fond of and while it loaded she took a list of names from her bag. Swift would have a fit if he knew what she was doing, but there were too many loyalties involved here, too much obfuscation. She laughed to herself. Finding ridiculous words and sliding them into reports was one of the little games she and Helen had indulged in, to while away the hours spent watching for suspects, parked outside flats and terraces waiting for the slightest movement of a net curtain. Obfuscation had been a favourite.

'Gareth Tomas Watkin' she typed. Tomas – was that Welsh for Thomas? The cursor flashed and a list of options appeared on the screen. She selected England & Wales, Birth Index, 1916-2005. Only one name appeared on the list 'Gareth Tomas Watkin, registered Jan-Feb-Mar 1972, District Builth Wells.' She clicked on 'View Record' and there it was, on the screen. 'Mother's Maiden Surname: Dobransky.' She typed Ella's surname into a new search, All England and Wales, Marriage Index, 1916-2005. There, among the Dobrianskayas and the Dobrianskis, she found Gareth Watkin's mother. Eliška Dobransky. She clicked on 'Find Spouse' – Adam would insist on it for completeness – Brandon Christopher Watkin. Bingo. So siblings, just Katerina – Catherine. And their father – God, the internet was so slow here – their father was Pavel Dobransky, born in Prague. There was no record of his death. So that was a dead end too. What was bugging her about the Czech connection? What if…she picked up the phone and dialled the station. Rhys was on a late; he'd be bored anyway. She could hear the smile in his voice as he picked up the phone.

'Don't you ever stop working, Sarge?'

'Oh God, you sound like my other half, which is not good.' She laughed. 'Could you just check for me, I've already looked at background for Catherine Jones and drawn a blank. Could you put in Katerina Jones, or anything maybe hyphenated with Dobransky in the system for me and check for a firearms licence or anything else.'

'I'll look now. What are you expecting to find?' She could hear Rhys tapping at the keyboard.

'I don't know, I'm probably just clutching at straws, but it's worth a go.'

'No sorry. Nothing. Oh, hold on.' There was more clicking. 'There's Ella's shotgun licence on here though. Well, I never knew she was really called Eliška.

'Don't tell me I've taught you something about the locals.'

'Impressive that is.'

'Anything else on Ella… Eliška?'

'I'll have a look now. What are you expecting to find?'

'I haven't a clue,' admitted Julie. 'Don't worry, it was a daft idea.'

'Oh, hold on… never. I don't believe it. She's in the choir with my Mam she is, and I never even knew about it.'

'What have you found?'

'She was arrested for assault. I can't believe that, not Ella Watkin.'

'In 2001?'

'How do you know?'

'What happened?'

''There was a fight at a funeral. She threatened someone with a shotgun. Well, you think you know somebody…'

'Was she sentenced?'

'Er…' Rhys tapped away at his keyboard. 'No Sarge, the

charges were dropped. They took her gun licence off her for a while though.'

'Thanks, Rhys. I'll see you tomorrow.'

Great, now she had an excuse to go and talk to Ella. Maybe Ella could tell her what Catherine's problem really was with the other partners at the solicitors, and maybe she would even find out whether Ella was still inclined to reckless behaviour with a shotgun. She scribbled a note for Adam, grabbed her coat and her car keys and she was gone.

Morgan Evans listened to the tick of the grandfather clock as the old man attempted to remember. Llewellyn Morris had been an accountant with his own firm in the centre of town. His son ran the office now, but Llewellyn's attention to detail, the balancing and reconciling of every fact, had stayed with him. It was important that he could recall as many of the children he played with down at the Abernant as possible, to relive those difficult times. Evans tried to let him ramble. He had no idea at all what DS Kite was looking for, wasn't even sure that she knew. Maybe Mr Morris would turn up something useful. From the depths of the cottage, Westminster chimes ticked off another quarter of an hour.

'Do you know where they are now, Mr Morris? Where did they go when the war ended?'

Llewellyn Morris looked up at Morgan. 'We never knew, for a long time we didn't know about what had happened to the ones who were sent back to Czechoslovakia.' For a moment the old man looked as though he was on the verge of weeping. He focused on the embers of the fire. 'Many of them had lost their whole family – parents, siblings.' He rocked gently in his chair. 'They had been exterminated, even the children, sent to the concentration camps at Auschwitz and Treblinka, but our friends were the lucky ones. They survived.'

'I didn't know.' Morgan spoke quietly. I just assumed that once they went back…'

'You thought they just got on with their lives, Morgan?'

'It seems such a long time ago.'

Julie realised she had left her phone on the table in her haste to prove her newly-developed theory. Perhaps she should have told Swift where she was going, but he would have made her wait until the morning. There was a light on in the yard as she turned the Fiesta down the last steep slope of the drive. In the headlights the hanging baskets cast long shadows on the ground and she could see the indistinct shapes of three collies chained to their kennels, but the house was in total darkness. She drove down the track to the bungalow and stopped the car. Gareth's black BMW was parked in the open-fronted shed by the side of the track, but there was no sign of Sarah's car. She cut the engine. It was only by the lights from the bungalow that she managed to pick her way along the last few yards of rutted track and into the halo of light that illuminated the garden. She could see Dylan asleep on the sofa and Seren next to him, reading. The television was on but nobody was watching it.

It was Seren who answered the door.

'Hi, remember me, I'm from the police. Could I speak to your Mum?'

'I remember who you are. She's not here.'

'Is your Granny here then? Could I speak to her?'

Seren shook her head. 'They're both out.'

'So who's looking after you, are you here on your own?'

'Seren?' The voice was sharp and with only the slightest hint of an accent. 'Who is it?'

Catherine appeared in the doorway, wiping her hands on a tea towel.

'Oh, I'm sorry to bother you, Mrs Jones.' I've just got a few questions for Ella. Is she here?'

Seren scowled and ducked back indoors, leaving the two women face to face. 'No she's not.' Catherine spat the words at Julie.

'I wanted to know about the Czech school in Llanwrtyd, at

248

Abernant. I was hoping Ella could help me with that, but you probably know just as much about it as she does. Was your father, Pavel Dobransky, or your mother ever a pupil there?'

'I have very little knowledge of or interest in the school and I don't have the time to talk to you now. Would you please leave.' Catherine stared at Julie, her pale grey eyes unblinking in a blank stare, which made Julie begin to feel uneasy.

'Could you tell me when Sarah or Ella will be back?'

'No. I have nothing to say to you.'

'Could I come in and wait for Sarah, will she be long?'

'I don't think that would be a good idea, Sergeant. I would like you to leave.'

Julie opened her mouth to argue when she heard the sound of a shotgun being snapped shut. Catherine had reached behind the door and produced the gun, which she was now pointing straight in Julie's face. 'Get off my sister's land. Now.' Without taking her eyes off Catherine's face, Julie moved backwards and slipped off the step, twisting her ankle. As she buckled and lurched forward the gun went off. Julie grabbed the barrel with both hands and attempted to twist the gun out of Catherine's hands. The last thing she saw was Seren's terrified face, before the stock hit her squarely on the side of the head.

Morgan Evans looked at his watch. Llywellyn Morris must have missed having an audience since he retired and, Morgan had to admit, the stories of his childhood in Llanwrtyd were captivating. But this was never going to lead anywhere, was it? Sergeant Kite had missed the target big time with this one. He drained his cup and inserted himself into a slight gap in the reminiscences. 'So what did happen when the children went back to Czechoslovakia, Mr Morris? Did things sort themselves out after the war?'

Llywellyn Morris sighed and gave Morgan what his mother would have called an "old-fashioned look". 'Afterwards,' he said, spreading his fingers in his lap, 'life in Czechoslovakia was unbearably difficult for ordinary people. From the end of the war, right up until you were born probably, they were spied on by the state. Their homes were bugged by the secret police. They had to queue for hours for food, if they complained or signed a petition they could be thrown into jail.'

'Why didn't they just leave?'

Llewellyn Morris shook his head. 'You couldn't just leave a communist country. Some tried, a few succeeded, but the families they left behind were persecuted.'

'You seem to know a great deal about it, Mr Morris.'

'There was a boy about my own age at the school. We were both good at maths, and of course the language barrier wasn't so much of a problem when you were solving mathematical problems. They spoke excellent English by the time they left.' He smiled at some long-hidden memory. 'This boy returned to Prague. His parents had been murdered in Auschwitz and none of his family survived. But he married and had two little girls of his own. He became a professor of mathematics at the university. Such a clever man.'

'So he was the one who told you about what went on?'

Llewellyn nodded. 'He wrote to me to organise for the little girls to come to Llanwrtyd. We had no idea how long they would stay, but he insisted that they would not be safe to stay in Prague. His wife had been murdered – they thought by the secret police. By this time she and Pavel had made enemies in high places, with their idealistic ideas. He knew the only future for his daughters was to get them out of Czechoslovakia, to send them to Wales, to Llanwrtyd, where he had been happy.'

'But what happened to him?'

'They never knew. The girls' letters to him were never answered. They have always thought that he was murdered because of their defection to the west.'

'Do you know who his daughters were?'

'They're still alive, Morgan. Ella Watkin at Penrhiw and

Catherine Jones from Builth. I remember it took Catherine a long time to get used to being in Wales. Ella was a much happier child, but Catherine was wilful and surly. She missed her father so badly.'

'And her mother, Llew, the poor child missed her mother.' Mrs Morris shuffled round the open door and into the room. 'You couldn't blame her, poor soul. You can't imagine seeing your mother shot right in front of you, can you? And then her father sent her away and she never saw him again. It's a miracle that the two of them have done as well as they have in the circumstances.'

Outside the cottage, Morgan Evans experienced a rare moment of epiphany. So Catherine Jones had seen her own mother murdered and then felt she had been abandoned by her father, when he sent her to Wales. He closed the gate and stepped onto the pavement. So what if she had found out that Gareth was about to leave her too, to disappear off up north to work with Jessica Southam and abandon her and Dic and the firm they had worked so hard for? Would that sort of disloyalty be enough to tip her over the edge? Could it have been Catherine who had murdered Gareth? He went back to the cottage and hammered on the door.

'Mr Morris, I need to ask you something.' Morgan pushed at the letterbox. He could see the old man shuffling towards the door. 'Would you happen to know if Ella Watkin or Catherine Jones knows how to use a gun?' The bolts were drawn back and the chain rattled before the door opened. 'Sorry, Mr Morris, Ella Watkin, could she handle a gun?'

'Ella – yes, of course she can. They both can. But Catherine's the one I definitely wouldn't want to tangle with on the gun front. She took up clay pigeon shooting for a while, before moving on to pheasants.' He smiled. 'She's a crack shot too. I think she imagines she's quite the country lady in her tweeds and her big hat. Why, Morgan? Is there something wrong?'

Morgan had already got as far as the gate. 'Thanks, Mr Morris, sorry, I've got to go.' He was smiling as he pulled his phone from his pocked and dialled Julie's mobile number. He could see Llywellyn Morris still watching him from the doorway. Maybe this would make the Sarge take him seriously. Where the hell was she? He was about to cut the connection when the call was answered.

'Hello.' A man's voice.

'Oh, could I speak to Sergeant Kite please?'

'Who's calling?'

'It's DC Evans, I'm a colleague. I've got some information she's going to find really interesting.'

There was a pause at the other end of the line. 'I'm her husband, and I'm sorry, but she's not here, DC Evans. She's at… I can't read her writing. Does Penrhiw mean anything to you?'

'Mr Kite, does the note say anything else?'

'Only that she thinks she's… hang on… something… it… Would that be cracked it?'

'Mr Kite, has she gone on her own do you know?'

CHAPTER FORTY-TWO

'I think she might be in danger, Sir.' Morgan Evans was running to his car. 'She's found a link between the foreign pistol and Penrhiw Farm.'

'And she's in danger because?'

Evans zapped the central locking and clambered into the driver's seat. 'Because she's gone off up to Penrhiw on her own.'

'So Milos *was* involved?'

'Not necessarily, Sir, sorry, Sir, it's to do with a concert in Rhayader. I have to go. I'm on my way up to Penrhiw now.'

'Be careful, Morgan. I'll organise backup. I'll be there as soon as I can.'

Evans threw the car into reverse and his tyres squealed as he set off up the hill, past the statue of the kite. 'Don't you do anything stupid, Sarge,' he muttered as he roared round the sharp right-hand bend at the woollen mill on the wrong side.

When she came round her feet were bound and her hands were tied behind her back. A single light bulb dangled from the eaves, swinging gently in the breeze and illuminating a vehicle. She was on the ground alongside Gareth's BMW. Catherine stood at the open end of the shed, the broken shotgun over her arm, looking up the track towards the farmhouse. Julie tried to raise herself on one elbow to get a clearer view, but if she moved, the car and Catherine span in front of her eyes. How long had she been here? She was so cold. She lay back down on the concrete, her head pounding. In the distance, the low whine of an engine became gradually distinguishable from the wind blowing through the slatted sides of the shed, and she could see headlights bobbing in and out of view as a car bounced its way down the drive. Please God, let it be someone who could help her.

It was Sarah's car that stopped beside the mad woman with the shotgun. Julie heard the door slam, then a second door slammed and footsteps crunched over the scalpings towards the shed. She kept as still as she could, making herself breathe slowly and quietly. Sarah spoke first.

'What the hell's going on, Catherine?'

'The policewoman. She was snooping. Asking questions about the Gymnasium in Llanwrtyd.'

'What have you done to her?' Sarah stepped onto the concrete floor of the shed, but the voice of a third woman stopped her in her tracks.

'Get into the house. Look after your children. This is nothing to do with you.' There was fear in this voice. 'Go!' Julie could see Sarah's feet under the BMW, the high heels she favoured. Sarah paused, but then turned and walked quickly back onto the track. 'And stay indoors.'

Julie heard Sarah's footsteps receding, the swing of the gate on its rusty hinges. The voice was still urgent, but quieter now. 'So it was you. You killed my son.' It was a statement. 'You murdered your own nephew, my precious Gareth. How could you do that, you stupid, stupid bitch? What do you intend to do with this one? Will you drag her out onto the mountain and leave her there for the raptors to pick at?'

'I didn't shoot her. She's only unconscious. For now.' Footsteps approached the corner of the shed where Julie was lying. 'But she knows too much. She knows about the school, maybe even about táta's gun.' Catherine's voice now, much too close for comfort.

'Put the gun down, Katarina. This has to stop now. I'm going to phone the police.' Footsteps led from the concrete of the shed onto the track.

'You would betray your own sister?' Julie heard the snap of the shotgun being closed once more and Catherine followed her sister onto the drive. 'It's about family, Eliška. It's about our family, not these people. They have no idea what we went through.'

'And now you are destroying our second family.'

'Gareth did that all by himself. Taking after his pathetic father, seeking an easy way out. He left me no option. They have to stay here.'

'There was nothing pathetic about my Brandon, Catherine and Gareth did nothing wrong. He worked hard for his family, for you too. And he was always a good friend to Dic.'

So Catherine must have known about Gareth's plans. Julie's brain whirled. She felt as though she'd been to an all-nighter at Bredbury Hall. Something was digging into her cheek as she lay on the concrete, but she didn't dare move.

'So will you shoot me too, Katarina, will you shoot Sarah and the children?'

Julie lifted her head. She had to stop this, right now. The car moved in and out of focus and she could feel the metallic taste of blood and wondered, for a split second, how many teeth had been dislodged by the blow from the shotgun. It could have been worse, much worse. Catherine had her back to Julie; she was pointing the shotgun towards Ella, but Ella was looking over her sister's shoulder straight at Julie in the corner of the shed. Carefully, Julie shook her head, willing Ella not to give her away. Ella nodded, the merest movement of her head.

'Father wouldn't have wanted this.' Ella's voice was softer now. 'You think he risked his life to get us out of Prague for this? He wanted us to be strong, to make a good life for ourselves here. Otherwise what was it all for? Did he die in vain, Catherine, Did máma? And his own father and mother, did they suffer in the camp for nothing?' Julie could hear the grass blowing gently on the other side of the slatted wall of the shed. Ella put her arm around Catherine's shoulder and, somehow, she managed to put herself between Catherine and Julie. 'They died because the world was different then, *sestřička*. We were the lucky ones.' Ella backed carefully towards Julie, all the while talking to her sister. 'We were the ones who had a second chance to live, in a good place, a place where we could grow, not like poor táta. His second chance was no chance at all. Put the gun down *cariad*, there is no need for anyone else to be hurt.'

Catherine thrust the muzzle of the shotgun into her sister's shoulder and Ella staggered backwards. Catherine pushed her towards the back of the shed, her finger closing round the trigger.

'What do I care any more? My life has been one long betrayal. Why should I listen to you? You have always been happy to treat me as a joke. Oh yes, Catherine Jones, the solicitor's little wife in her perfect house and her top of the range Mercedes, pretending she is important. You never spared a thought for the fact that you were the one with the adoring husband who would have done anything for you, that you had your children and grandchildren, that you were oh so very popular. And as for this interfering bitch, she's too clever by half with her city ways. What does she understand about us, about our lives?'

Catherine raised the shotgun to her shoulder and took aim. 'This is the only way, Ella, believe me. There's nothing left.'

There was a shout and a tremendous clang and a brilliant white light. Ella threw herself in front of Julie, the BMW's alarm went off and the shotgun discharged, one shot taking out the light bulb and a second shot into the dark. Julie heard the shotgun being kicked across the concrete floor and the unmistakable metallic rasp of handcuffs being fitted. In the orange light of the car's flashing indicators, they saw a figure kneeling beside the car and then the blinding white light was directed at them. Ella clung onto Julie, supporting her head away from the rough concrete.

Between the BMW's honking alarm and Ella's quiet sobbing, Julie made out Morgan Evans' voice. 'You all right, Sarge?' In the distance a wail of sirens joined the BMW's chorus and suddenly Julie felt as though her head would explode.

'Morgan? Are you on your own?'

He walked round the car and opened the driver's door. The interior light picked out Catherine and the shotgun lying just outside the shed on the scalpings. The sirens came closer and as Morgan removed the blinding light from his head they could see the blue lights of the police cars, strobing across the blackness. Morgan bent down to untie the baler twine from Julie's feet and Ella attempted to do the same with the restraints around her wrists, but Julie could feel Ella's hands shaking.

'My sister… is she…?' Ella straightened up slowly and looked at the crumpled figure beside the car.

'I don't think she's hurt.' Morgan pointed to where Catherine lay on the ground by the car. He finished untying Julie's hands and helped her to her feet. 'Are you all right?' He flashed his head torch at her face. 'You're going to need a stitch in that Sarge.' He pulled a handkerchief from his pocket and put it into her hand, then guided her hand to the gash on her cheek.

'Good job you were a Boy Scout, Morgan.' Julie attempted to smile and winced as the smile reached her cheek. Suddenly, Ella was shrieking, cursing like a feral dog, kicking out at Catherine and Morgan was running. When the police cars swooped into the yard and out along the lane to the bungalow, he was holding Ella on the ground in a pincer-like rugby-tackle grip, at a safe distance from her sister.

'Evans? What the hell are you doing out here without backup?' Swift picked up the shotgun and broke it. He slung it over his arm and waved a torch into the shed.

'I'm glad he was, Sir. Otherwise we might both have been waiting for Kay Greenhalgh.'

Ella, released from her captor, stood up slowly, leaving a sobbing Catherine on the ground beside the car. 'It's true, Craig. If it hadn't been for Morgan I think we might both be dead by now.'

'But who the hell…' Swift lifted Catherine's arm and pulled her to face him. 'Dear God. Catherine, what were you thinking of?'

'She was thinking of confessing to the murder of my son.' Ella's voice was hard now. Gone was the soft, persuasive edge which had kept both of them alive long enough for Morgan to reach them. 'And how she was even prepared to let poor Milos go to prison for something he didn't do.'

'When did you know, Ella?' Swift looked from one sister to the other.

'I might never have known if Sergeant Kite hadn't been here this evening.'

'You had no idea?'

Ella shook her head. 'Do you think I wouldn't have told you if I'd known who killed poor Gareth?'

'Can you come with us now, Mrs Jones, so we can take your statement.' Julie walked unsteadily towards Catherine.

'You're not going anywhere but the hospital, Sergeant Kite. Morgan, could you do the honours, and don't let her leave until the medics say she can. OK?'

A uniformed officer cautioned Catherine and helped her into the back seat of the police car.

'I must go and tell Sarah we're all right, tell her what has happened.' Ella took the arm that Swift offered. 'Then I will answer any questions I can.'

Swift glanced over his shoulder as he helped Ella towards the bungalow. 'I'll see you two in the morning,' he shouted. Julie was too far away to notice the wink.

'That was a close one, Sarge.' Morgan put his arm round Julie's shoulder and held her upright. 'Can you walk as far as the yard?'

'Yep, as long as I can lean on you. I'm having trouble working out what's horizontal and what's not.'

258

CHAPTER FORTY-THREE

'How did you know where I was?' Julie saw stars with every pothole in Penrhiw's drive.

'I found out about the pupils at Abernant from Mr Morris. Ella and Catherine's father was one of his best friends. He sent his daughters back here, where he'd been safe, when things got tricky with the authorities in Prague. He thinks that Catherine has a bit of a problem, reading between the lines. And he said she was a crack shot in her day. Hard to imagine now though, her being a pillar of society isn't it?' He whistled through his teeth. 'Aren't people complicated? Anyway, I thought if she'd found out about Gareth's intended flit up north, it might have pushed her over the edge. I phoned your place to let you know how clever I'd been and your husband said you'd gone to Penrhiw, so I put two and two together.'

'Thank goodness you did. I really thought my number was up.'

'She wouldn't have shot her own sister though, would she?'

'I wouldn't put money on it. She shot Gareth and left Milos to make himself look guilty with his ramblings.'

'But why?'

Julie pulled down the sun visor and switched on the interior light. Her eye was already beginning to bruise and the cut on her cheekbone looked huge. She groaned and flicked the light off. Morgan grinned, but stopped when he saw the look on her face, lit by the green glow from the dashboard.

'We didn't really get that far. I'm assuming Catherine will provide the detail.'

Morgan swerved to avoid a sheep and went into a hole at the side of the lane. Julie held her head in her hands. 'Sorry, Sarge. You're not going to black out on me or anything like that are you?'

'I think preserving your upholstery should be higher up your agenda.'

Morgan glanced sideways at her and then back at the narrow strip of tarmac. 'How did you know it was Catherine?'

'I went up there just to ask Ella a few questions. I wanted to know about the school and the possible Eastern European connection with the gun, and about Catherine's row with Gareth. I thought it could have been possible that Catherine had found out about his plans. I thought Milos must have been protecting someone, and if it wasn't Sarah… God I've been thick. I hadn't thought for a second that it might have been Catherine who murdered Gareth.'

'Yep you have.' Morgan grinned, then relented. 'I don't know, Sarge, you were almost there. I thought you knew Catherine would be up there tonight.' He indicated and turned right onto the winding road which would take them down into Brecon.

'And how would I know that, Morgan. Telepathy?'

'There was a concert tonight. Rhayader Male Voice Choir were up at the Leisure Centre.'

'And?'

'Gareth and his father were both in the choir. Ella never misses their concerts, and Sarah always goes with her, doesn't she?'

'Of course she does.' Julie closed her eyes. 'And that meant that Catherine would be up at Penrhiw babysitting the kids. Obviously.' She sighed. 'I know the Welsh have always insisted that this is a different country, but now I believe it. I'll never get the hang of this.'

Morgan laughed. 'You will. Maybe I forgot you weren't local, just for a minute there, Sarge.'

'Thank you.'

'What for?'

'For everything, Morgan. For everything.'

Morgan shrugged. Julie knew she had embarrassed him, but she was too tired to think about it.

'How did you connect the Czechoslovakian School with Penrhiw?'

'If I'm totally honest, it was Adam – my husband. He's a history teacher. He has to know where he fits into a place historically like the rest of us buy a map. He told me about the school. The only connection I had was the pistol from Eastern Europe.'

'I would never have thought of that in a million years.'

'You would.' She shivered and pulled her jacket around her more tightly. 'Maybe it's like the scenery, you just notice it more when you're used to seeing something different. What I can't work out is why she would want to assassinate her nephew and leave those poor children without a father.'

By the time Adam arrived to pick her up, her cheek had swollen and both eyes were developing bruising. She could tell he was avoiding looking at her and she wondered just what she must look like under the brash neon lights. Instead he held out his hand to Morgan Evans and introduced himself.

'Thank you for looking after her.'

'He did more than look after me.' Julie attempted to smile, but winced as the steri-strips pulled at her skin. 'If he hadn't been there…' Adam's expression made her edit what she had been about to say. 'Let's just say if it hadn't been for Morgan things might have been much worse.'

'Oh God, Jules.' He wrapped her in a hug and Morgan Evans looked away and coughed discreetly.

'Have you got transport, Mr Kite?'

'Yes, thank you. A neighbour gave me a lift to Penrhiw to pick up the car. I didn't know what to think when they said you'd been hurt. I thought you might be… '

'Then I'd better be off. Goodnight both.' Morgan stood up,

nodded at Adam and looked down at Julie. 'God, Sarge, you look rough.' He grinned. 'See you tomorrow is it?'

Adam sat down next to her on the bed and carefully kissed the top of her head. 'I was imagining all sorts. Maybe I was wrong to drag you out here, I just thought we could wipe the slate clean, have a fresh start somewhere new. You'd have been safer in Manchester.'

'It's just different.' She leaned against him, felt the warmth of him. 'Statistically this area's got one of the lowest crime rates in the whole of Great Britain.'

'Trust you to sniff out a murder on your first day.'

'Just lucky I guess.'

'Julie Kite?' A nurse carrying a large brown envelope bustled into the cubicle. 'You were very lucky, nothing's broken. You can go home, but take it steady for the next 48 hours. If you feel dizzy or confused, experience double vision or memory loss then come straight back.'

'Don't worry, she'll have me to answer to and we'll be back like a shot.'

'Very funny.'

'Sorry, Jules. Didn't think.' Adam grinned and helped her down from the bed.

'Oh, and don't go into work tomorrow.' The nurse smiled as she left the cubicle.

CHAPTER FORTY-FOUR

Thursday, 5th May

Catherine Jones had refused the services of a solicitor. She had also refused to answer every single question which Swift and Rhys Williams had put to her the previous evening. Dic Jones had arrived in reception, was informed that his wife was under arrest and waited patiently until after midnight before walking out of reception and into the night, without a word to the duty officer.

While Catherine was locked in the small, bare cell, her sister had been rather more forthcoming. She sat upright on the sofa in the living room at Sarah's bungalow, her back not making contact with the soft leather, her face betraying nothing. It was, thought Swift, as though she had no emotion left to offer.

'You had no knowledge of your sister's part in the murder of your son until tonight?'

Slowly Ella shook her head. 'No, I knew nothing.'

'Could you tell me what you thought had happened to Gareth?'

'I had no more idea than you did, Craig.' She looked down at the china teacup in her lap and traced the gold edging round the rim with her finger. 'To begin with I wondered whether he had committed suicide. People like to tell me it can run in families.' Her finger was still and she looked up at Swift. 'But it seemed strange that he could go through what he did, the surgery and the chemotherapy, and then put his family through the feelings of guilt and helplessness that suicide leaves behind. He hated what his father did, what it did to the family.'

Swift nodded his agreement. 'You never doubted Milos?'

'No. Milos told me what happened and I believed him. Milos doesn't lie, Craig, you've known him long enough to know what he's like.'

'Did you know Jessica Southam?'

'Do you mean did I know that Gareth was angling after a contract with that woman?' Ella frowned, obviously angry at the question. 'It was a stupid mistake on Gareth's part. He thought we wouldn't get to hear about what he was trying to do with the business.' She stared at Swift. 'There was no other form of relationship, Craig.'

Swift looked at a point on the wall behind Ella. 'Do you think Gareth would have left Sarah and the children for her?'

'No, Gareth would never have left them…'

'And you're sure you had no idea about what Catherine had done?'

'I'm sure.'

'Tell me about your parents, Ella. What happened to them?'

Ella closed her eyes and let out a juddering breath. 'I can't tell you how bad it was in Czechoslovakia in the late fifties and early sixties. I was there, and even I can't believe how terrible it all was. Táta was a professor at the university in Prague, professor of mathematics. He was such a clever man.' She smiled. 'He was so kind and generous. He wanted to help everyone, those who were less fortunate than we were. But the government hated academics. They bugged our flat, watched us wherever we went.'

'So different to what was happening in Wales in the sixties,' said Swift.

Ella nodded. 'Máma hated it. She believed in everything táta was trying to do, but she begged him to stop, wanted him to live a quiet life instead of risking all of our lives for the cause.' She stopped and looked up at Swift. 'I don't even want to think about it.'

'Please, Ella, what happened?' Swift handed her his

handkerchief and waited while she wiped away tears. 'Can you tell me?'

'I was nine years old. We had gone to the market, máma, Catherine and me, to try to buy bread. There were policemen everywhere. We got split up in the crowd. I was holding máma's hand. She had stopped to talk to a neighbour, a woman from one of the flats across the street, when two policemen walked towards us.' Ella's knuckles were white from pressing Swift's handkerchief into her fist. 'There was a bang and máma was lying in the gutter. There was blood everywhere and I was still holding her hand.' She stopped talking again and closed her eyes.

'What happened next, Ella?' Swift was next to her by now, his arm around her shoulders. 'Can you tell me?'

'The neighbour grabbed me and we ran. As fast as we could.'

'And what about Catherine? Where was she?'

Ella stifled a sob. 'She was running in the opposite direction, away from us, but I could see the look on her face, the blood splattered on her dress. I'll never forget that a long as I live.' Ella handed Swift's handkerchief back.

How, thought Swift, would you ever recover from seeing something like that?

'How did Catherine manage to get Gareth's car back to Penrhiw without you seeing her? I'm assuming you didn't see her?'

Ella shook her head. 'Gareth's car wasn't at Penrhiw. We found it on the track that runs down towards Pen-y-Waen.'

'But why didn't you tell us?' Swift scratched his ear. 'We'd have known it was someone local if the car was left there.'

'As I said, I wasn't sure at that point whether Gareth had killed himself. I thought he might have been walking on the hill. He often went up there when he wanted to think.'

'Ella, are you sure you can't think of any reason why Catherine should want to murder Gareth?'

Ella shrugged. 'She was obsessively jealous of Gareth and Sarah. At every family gathering she would have too much to drink and

265

would accuse Gareth of taking clients away from Dic. Gareth was the younger partner with everything going for him. He was on the rise while Dic was talking about retiring. And, despite what Catherine said about wanting him to retire, she was terrified of losing her status. And Gareth,' she paused, 'had children.'

Swift waited, but she said nothing more.

CHAPTER FORTY-FIVE

It was early, even by Swift's standards, and a sleepless night had not improved his mood. Nor had Catherine's repeated, obstinate refusal to answer his questions. Now it was Morgan Evans' turn to be questioned by Swift. Once again they were in Swift's office with the door closed, but this time Swift was complimentary. Evans, thought Swift, found this just as embarrassing as the dressing-down he'd received two days ago.

'You did well last night.'

'Thank you, Sir.' Evans blushed. 'I was just lucky.'

'You were both lucky, Morgan.'

'Yes, Sir.'

'You know you should have waited for backup?' said Swift. Evans nodded, and looked at the floor.

'It's a good job you didn't, mind. Sergeant Kite might not be around to tell the tale if you'd done things by the book. I take it you two have sorted your differences?'

'She knows what she's doing.'

'She needs someone like you to teach her about rural policing. She's going to find it very different to what she's used to.' Swift opened the door and Evans read the signal. He stood up. 'Just one thing,' Swift said, as Evans walked out into the open-plan.

'Sir?'

'Did you really have to throw a metal bucket at a brand new BMW?'

'I couldn't see what I was doing, Sir.'

'Welcome to my world, Morgan. Welcome to my world.'

'I'll come and collect you after school.' Adam had parked as close to the door of the police station as he could and was blocking a patrol car's exit. Julie hurried out of the car and the hangover-from-hell kicked in again.

'Thanks. Hope you don't get into trouble with the Head for being late.' She slammed the car door but he wound down the window.

'Call me if you don't feel well and I'll come and get you.'

'I will.' She waved and walked breezily into reception, attempting not to limp and without looking back at the mayhem he was causing in the car park's one-way system.

'I heard about Penrhiw.' Brian Hughes ran a quick visual check. 'You shouldn't be here.'

'I couldn't stay at home. A morning was enough, it was driving me mad. Besides, I want to know where we're up to.'

'Well just go steady. From what I've heard you were lucky to get out of there.'

Adam had phoned her parents last night. Her father had wanted to drive down straight away. If she'd still been in Manchester there would have been no question. Dad would have fussed, making sure his little girl really was OK. Mum would have been baking, giant scones and butterfly buns, offering milky coffee on the hour. She felt as though, at the age of twenty-nine, she had finally grown up, and got through something momentous without them.

'Oh what a tremendous pair of black eyes.' Rhys met her on the stairs. 'God, Sarge, you look terrible.'

'I can rely on you to tell it like it is.'

'The boss will do that too I shouldn't wonder.'

Julie sat down at her computer. She had only walked from the car and already she felt as though someone was battering her skull from the inside, trying to get out. She reached into her bag for the painkillers the hospital had given her. She hated taking medication for anything, It was less to do with side-effects than the admission of failure, the sense that she needed help.

'You shouldn't be here, Sergeant.' Swift was beside her desk immediately. 'And you shouldn't have been at Penrhiw. Not on your own.' He was frowning. 'We could quite easily have lost you, and Morgan too.' She knew he was right, she should have told him where she was going, or at least waited for Morgan to get back from Llanwrtyd. She'd put him in danger too with her impatience.

'Yes, Sir, I know, and I'm sorry. But to be honest I didn't expect a mad woman with a shotgun. I was just going for a word with Ella about the Czech School, about her father's experiences during the war. I thought it might have some relevance, with the murder weapon being Eastern European. But I should have thought about how it could have turned out, especially knowing she had a firearms licence.' She sighed. 'I had no idea at all that it could be Catherine though. If only I'd known about the choir concert in Rhayader.'

Swift frowned and patted her on the shoulder. 'I know how easy it is to get carried away with it all. Believe it or not I do remember what it's like to be bursting with all that youthful enthusiasm. But just remember we're a team and we need to work together.' He smiled. 'And, ticking-off dealt with, I have to admit it was a brilliant piece of detective work. Morgan says we have to thank your husband for the connection.'

'I didn't tell him anything about the case.' What if he thought she had compromised anything by talking to Adam? 'He's a history teacher and he'd been talking to someone at school about Nicholas Winton and the Kindertransport and they told him…'

'It's fine, don't worry.' Swift smiled. 'We might never have found out the truth if you hadn't annoyed Catherine Jones.'

'Why did she do it, Sir?'

'She's still refusing to say anything. Dic's asked Eurig Powell to come in this morning and act as her solicitor. Ella's told us that Catherine was insanely jealous of Gareth and his family.'

'Insane or jealous enough to kill him?'

'I'm wondering whether there is a mental health issue. She won't see the doctor, and Dic's positive he doesn't know of any problems. Would you be up to sitting in on the interview?'

'I don't know. If you think it will help.'

'I think it will help you too. You'll have to face her in court, you might as well get it over with.'

Rhys and Morgan arrived in a clatter, Rhys bearing a tray laden with coffee and chocolate biscuits. Morgan carried a large bunch of petrol station flowers. 'You scared us there, Sarge.' Rhys plonked the tray on her desk. 'Thought you townies would be a bit more streetwise than that.'

There was something disturbing about Catherine's stare. The grey eyes were unseeing, unblinking. If she recognised Julie there was no obvious sign. Eurig Powell sat beside her, scarcely able to look at his client. When Swift asked her to give her name for the tape they were all surprised.

'Katarina Magdaléna Dobransky.'

'And you know why you're here?'

'Of course.'

'You have been charged with the murder of your nephew, Gareth Tomos Watkin on Monday, 25th April.'

Catherine Jones said nothing.

'Can you tell us anything about that, Mrs Jones?' Julie emphasised the name.

'My name is Katarina—'

'Your name *was* Katarina Dobransky, Mrs Jones. It was changed by deed poll shortly after your arrival in Wales to…' Julie flicked through the paperwork in front of her. 'Catherine Mary Dobson. And in 1970 you married Dic Jones and became Catherine Mary Jones.' Catherine shrugged. 'You have been married for over forty years, Mrs Jones. Is your marriage a happy one?'

Slowly, Catherine let her gaze travel the width of the table and up to Julie's face. She smiled. 'That depends upon your definition, Sergeant.' Eurig Powell tugged at his fringe. 'We have no children to follow in our footsteps, my husband needs to retire so that we can spend our final years together, but his partners seem not to want to uphold the moral traditions of the company. We could never leave it in their hands, in the circumstances.'

'That's important to you is it, Mrs Jones, the moral tradition of the company?' Julie feigned wide-eyed innocence.

'There are certain standards to be upheld. Even in Britain.'

'It's not like post-war Czechoslovakia though is it? At least here we tolerate freedom of speech and insist on lawful actions. We don't bug apartments and shoot innocent civilians because of their views. Or perhaps we do? Can you tell me anything about that, Mrs Jones?'

'There is no comparison between this incident and what happened to my family in Prague. I expect you think you are very clever. No doubt Ella was only too willing to tell her fairy story about our past. My mother was shot in front of me, Sergeant, when I was seven years old. Shot in the head and then kicked by the policemen as she lay in the gutter.'

'But you escaped, Catherine. You got away.'

Catherine nodded. 'A woman, just a passer-by in the street, she took my hand, scolded me for running away from her and dragged me away from where my mother lay dying.'

'Why was she murdered, can you tell me that?' Julie asked the question as though of a seven-year old child. 'Do you know what she had done?'

Catherine's eyes filled with tears, which brimmed over and down her cheeks. She made no attempt to wipe them away. 'She and my father didn't like what the state was doing. The government was murdering people who didn't agree with their

271

policies, good people who were trying to rebuild Czechoslovakia. You have no idea how bad things were then.'

'And how did you come to live in Wales, Catherine, you and Ella? Did your father come with you?' Julie handed her a rumpled tissue from her pocket and Catherine clutched it in her hand until her knuckles were white.

'Father said he had to stay in Prague. He said there were things he had to do to help the people. He promised to come and find us when then struggle was over.' She shook her head slowly. 'He sent us to stay with people who had looked after him during the war, people we could trust. He was a good man, Sergeant, a man who knew about honour and sacrifice. He sent us away knowing that he would be punished for allowing us to defect to the west. He did that for us, for his family.' Catherine was sobbing now, and Eurig Powell was staring at the table.

'Do you think we could have a break? My client might be permitted to see a doctor?'

'I am not your client.' The words came out in a hiss, low and threatening. 'I don't need your help.'

Swift looked at Eurig and raised his eyebrows. 'Are you asking Mr Powell to leave? I would advise you that you need some sort of legal representation. These charges are extremely serious, Catherine.'

'I was doing the family a service.' She spat the words at Swift. 'The men in Ella's family are no good. That useless husband of hers shot himself because he lost his herd of cows. How pathetic. My father's parents, his brother, his cousins, they perished in the death camps, tortured and gassed in Auschwitz and Treblinka, but he didn't take the coward's way out. He went back to Czechoslovakia after the war was over and rebuilt his life. He married a beautiful, clever woman and tried to change the lives of the people of Prague. He didn't leave his wife and children to fend for themselves when times were disappointing. And look at Milos.'

'And Gareth, Catherine, what had Gareth done to the family?' Julie asked the dishevelled woman on the other side of the table.

Catherine curled her lip into a sneer. 'I don't suppose you can even imagine what it was like for Sarah when Gareth was ill. She had two small children but she never missed a visit. She drove for three hours each day to visit him in hospital. She protected him from the outside world. Not even knowing whether he would survive, not knowing if he would see Seren and George grow up and then,' she leaned across the table until her face was inches from Julie's, 'and then, after all her worry and stress, as soon as he is recovered, he starts plotting a new life with a gold-digging bitch. He has no shame, no thought for what moving away would do to his family, to his partners. He did not deserve to have those children.'

'So you shot him.' Julie leaned back in her chair.

Eurig coughed. 'You are still here?' Catherine didn't even look at him.

'I would advise you—'

'I do not need your advice, Eurig Powell.' She shrugged. 'Yes, I shot him. He refused to see sense. I watched him meet that whore at the hotel. I gave him a chance to end the relationship, but he laughed in my face.'

'How did you persuade him to go with you? He could have walked away,' Julie asked.

'I told him that if he didn't come with me I'd tell Dic he had been having a sordid little affair.'

'You're asking us to believe that Dic had no idea about Gareth's plans?' Swift said.

'That's true, Inspector.' Eurig Powell's clear bass-baritone voice filled the room and the three of them turned towards him, including Catherine. 'He would have thrown Gareth out on the spot if he had known. No question.'

'My husband lives by Catholic values, Inspector. He would never have forgiven Gareth for fornication, and if he had known he was planning to desert his wife and children…' she laughed a shrill little laugh. 'He would have asked him to leave the partnership. And he would have continued to work himself into the grave.'

'But there was no affair, Catherine. It was purely a business relationship.' Swift said.

'And you can prove that can you? You can say that with no doubt whatsoever?' Catherine dismissed Swift with a sneer.

'So, you forced Gareth into his own car, you drove it to the hill and you shot him with this pistol.' Julie pushed the gun, still in its plastic evidence bag, across the table. 'That's quite a weapon. Where did you get it from?'

Catherine smiled down at the gun. 'It was my father's. He was part of a resistance movement after the war.' She reached for the bag, but Julie moved it away. 'He gave it to us when he sent us away from Prague. He told us we must never use it frivolously, but if our lives were threatened, then that would be acceptable.'

'And you felt that your life was threatened?' Swift asked.

'Oh yes, Inspector. Our way of life. All our lives were threatened. They would never have been the same again if Gareth had been allowed to desert us for that *nevěstka*.'

At 4pm and much to Julie's embarrassment, Brian Hughes phoned through to say that Adam was waiting in reception.

'Sorry, Sir, he's being a bit over-protective.' Julie switched off her computer.

'You get off home. I hadn't expected to see you for the rest of the week.' Swift retrieved the flowers from where they had been propped in the waste bin and handed them to her. 'And you were right after all, about it being a woman on the CCTV footage from the Met.'

'Sad though, Sir. The fact that someone had to die over something so trivial as work, or even a possible affair.'

'I don't suppose people on the receiving end of affairs think they're trivial at the time.'

Julie blushed. Did he know – had the inter-force grapevine let her down? 'No, Sir.' She took the flowers from him. 'Goodnight.' She stepped into the corridor and stopped so suddenly that Swift cannoned into the back of her.

'Hand signals, Sergeant, please.'

'Sorry. But what if…' She turned round to face him. 'We thought it had to be a *man* who murdered Gareth Watkin.'

'Well to be accurate, I thought it was a man.'

'So maybe it wasn't *Gordon* Price who battered Collins with his sitting-room door?'

'But who…you're not thinking Eileen, surely? There's no way she'd have the strength to do that sort of damage.'

'Why not? Maybe she wouldn't have the inhibition that goes with knowing what the possible outcome could be. You've seen her; she spends her whole day watching cartoons on the television.'

'But why wouldn't Gordon tell us it was her?'

'To protect her, obviously. He's not admitted belting the creep himself has he – does he strike you as the sort of person who would lie?'

Swift pondered the question, but only for a moment. 'I take your point. Gordon Price was always as honest as the day is long, too honest sometimes. But it wouldn't be honest not to tell us if it was Eileen who hit Collins.'

'We didn't ask him. We asked if he had clobbered Collins. He said no.'

Swift looked over his shoulder at the board. 'You could have a point, Julie. It's definitely worth asking the question.'

'Could it wait until tomorrow? I'd like to talk to Eileen. And Collins before I nick him for car theft.'

Swift grinned. 'I'll come with you. Would you like me to pick you up in the morning?'

'Thanks, but I'll be fine by tomorrow. Night, Sir.'

Swift watched her disappear down the corridor. How long had

it been since he'd been as enthusiastic as his new sergeant? He turned and realised that the whole room had been listening to their conversation. How long had it been since this lot had been so keen to impress. Maybe Gwen had been right. Maybe Sergeant Julie Kite was just what they needed.

CHAPTER FORTY-SIX

Friday, 6th May

It was a beautiful morning. The curtains from the Manchester flat weren't quite wide enough for the low, deep-set windows of the cottage and daylight began to creep into the bedroom. Julie opened one eye and looked at the clock. 5.45am. She had never woken this early in Manchester, not voluntarily anyway. Carefully, she touched her cheek, felt the clotted blood between the strips which held the wound closed. It felt more comfortable now, less raw. Experimentally, she lifted her head off the pillow and was pleased with the results. At last the gnawing pain was beginning to subside. She lay back, watching the little birds on the tree outside the window, listening to the ewes calling to their lambs in the fields. From a way off came the sound of a quad bike and the unintelligible shouts of a shepherd. She could barely remember the constant hum of traffic and the rumble of aircraft on their way to the airport.

So what did she miss about Manchester? She missed Helen, the thought that there was someone out there who knew exactly what you were thinking. Would she ever be able to work as closely with someone else? She turned her pillow round and hitched herself up in bed and was overtaken by a shaft of pain which ran the width of her shoulders. That bloody woman must have dragged her from the bungalow to the shed, which would account for the state of her boots too. Could she have done that on her own? What if… she closed her eyes. Forget it, Julie. Let it go.

What else did she miss about home? There was the humour, the sarcasm-as-a-second-language comedy of the North. She missed being able to walk to the shops and not having to plan food shopping like a military operation. She could hear a woodpecker drilling into the electricity pole by the gate, the faint echo as the sound, like automatic fire from a toy gun, was bounced back by the steep slopes. Maybe she could get used to this, learn to live with the lack of traffic, the feeling that life here had stood still for forty years. Even the kids at the High School were polite, with none of the big-city swagger. She'd watched them, talking as easily to old people as they did to their mates, helping the primary school kids onto the bus. She yawned and stretched experimentally. Maybe Morgan Evans wasn't so bad, maybe she could train him. Like a sheepdog. She laughed out loud.

She heard the latch on the kitchen door, heard Adam creeping up the stairs and into the room.

'You're awake. How are you feeling?' She knew he was genuinely concerned, but she hated the feeling that she wasn't quite in control of her body.

'I'm fine. Better. Have you been out on the bike?'

'I went for a run. I've found a bridle path that takes you right to the top of the hill over there.' He nodded towards the window. 'You have to see the view from the top. It's like being on a plane, you can see for miles.'

'Maybe not this morning.'

'Your horse was waiting for you, hanging over the gate.'

'He's a good listener.'

'You do like it here don't you?' He looked so worried that she laughed.

'I'm learning. It's just so different.'

'But different in a good way?'

'Both places have their good points. It'll just take me a while to get the hang of it, get used to how things are done, but yes, I like it. I didn't expect to, that's all.'

Adam sat down next to her on the bed. 'We'll be OK, Jules.

We'll work things out.' He reached for her hand. 'Your Mum and Dad want to come and visit. They think I can't look after you.'

'It would be nice to see them.' She squeezed his hand. 'But they're wrong.'

At the Prices' neat little house, the remnants of breakfast were still on the kitchen table. Triangles of toast with a bite out of the middle but the crusts untouched, jammy spoons and the milk jug with its crocheted, beaded shawl. Gordon Price looked wearier than ever as he filled the kettle and attempted to tidy the table.

'What happened to you?' He stared at Julie's face, and slid the uneaten toast into the bin, flicking at the crumbs on the table with a tea towel.

'I walked into a shotgun butt.' Gordon pulled a chair out and Julie sat down.

'It looks painful.' He turned his back on them and counted teabags into the large brown pot.

'Excruciating,' agreed Julie. 'It's only today I've been able to drive.' Gordon appeared not to have heard her.

'Have you had any more thoughts about what happened on Friday last week?' Swift walked over to the sink to stand beside him.

'No, Craig. I told you what happened. Collins must have tripped over the step. He left the house and drove away in a grey people carrier.'

'He must have been in quite a state,' said Swift. 'And he drove away?'

'You don't believe me.'

'I don't believe he could have driven with that head injury. And we have forensic evidence that puts you in the driving seat of the Zafira.' Swift tapped his fingers on the draining board. 'I think you drove him over to the Elan Valley and left him there, unconscious in the car.'

'I didn't hit him, Craig.' The kettle clicked off and Gordon poured the boiling water onto the teabags in the pot, then put cups and saucers, sugar and the little milk jug onto a tray. Swift gestured towards the sitting room and Julie stood up.

'Can I take Eileen her tea?' she said. Gordon hesitated, looked at Swift's face and removed two cups and saucers from the tray.

Eileen was watching the television, another children's programme, someone dressed as a clown wearing a yellow suit and enormous orange boots. There was a gaudy plastic flower in his lapel. The cat was sitting on her knee, purring in time with every stroke of Eileen's hand. Julie put the two teacups down on the small table next to her. 'I need to speak to you about the man, the one you thought had hurt Bobby.' Julie knelt by her chair as she had before. 'About when he came back when Gordon was here.' Eileen began to rock and the cat jumped from her lap. 'Can you remember that day, Eileen?'

'He wanted to hurt Gordon. I saw him. They were fighting in the garden.' When Eileen turned to look at her, Julie could see the fear in her eyes, the panic beginning to overwhelm her.

'And what happened then, Eileen, when the man came into the house. Can you remember?'

But now Eileen was laughing at the clown on the screen, who had tripped over his own feet and landed in a heap. 'He fell over.'

Julie sighed. This could take hours. 'Not the man on the television, Eileen, what happened to the man who came into your house?'

'What man? Do you work with Gordon?'

Julie reached for her tea.

CHAPTER FORTY-SEVEN

The uniformed officer who had phoned Swift was still on the corridor outside Collins' room when Kite and Swift got to the hospital.

'Has anyone other than medical staff or his solicitor been to see Collins in all the time that you've been here?'

'No, Sir, only medical staff or police personnel.'

'When you say police personnel, you mean serving officers, do you?' The constable paused for a second too long.

'It was only for a couple of minutes, Sir.'

'And we are talking about Gordon Price here, Constable?'

'Yes, Sir. He said his wife was concerned about Collins. He just wanted to see him so he could reassure her.'

'Of course,' said Julie. 'That's how Collins knew that Eileen was "so ill". Gordon must have told him.'

Swift closed his eyes. 'And that's when they agreed the events in Gordon's hallway. Brilliant.'

'Collins is still making progress?' Julie asked.

'He's just waiting for the consultant apparently, then he's off.' The constable was grateful for the diversion.

'Is he discharging himself?' Swift looked through the window at Collins, who was dressed and lying on the bed reading a newspaper.

The officer shook his head. 'Nope. Apparently he's fine. Still complaining of a headache, but one of the nurses told me he's enjoying being waited on and they need the bed. You look like you need it more than he does, Sarge.' He grinned and Julie gave him the look which Helen had called her 'interview stare'.

'Mr Collins, you're leaving already?' Julie pulled the newspaper away from his face. 'It must be a miracle. Praise the Lord.'

'Good heavens, Sergeant. Have you been falling over too?' He folded the newspaper and recrossed his legs. 'You should be more careful.'

'This was about as accidental as your injury.' She walked round the bed so that he had to crane his neck to see her. 'Is your memory still playing tricks?'

'There's nothing wrong with my memory, Sergeant. As I have said to you already, I simply tripped and fell whilst trying to talk to Sergeant Price.'

'Did you speak to Mrs Price at all?'

'She was there, yes. I wanted to apologise to both of them for any inconvenience I may have caused them at the time of my trial.'

'Inconvenience?' Swift, who had been watching cars manoeuvring in the car park, wheeled round. 'Inconvenience? Do you realise what your threats have done to her? You call it inconvenience…'

'And did they accept your apology, Mr Collins?' Julie asked. 'Mr and Mrs Price have forgiven you, have they?'

'And I them, Sergeant. Live and let live. Let bygones be bygones. *And their sins and iniquities will I remember no more.*' He smiled his rodent smile and straightened the sheets with his slender fingers. 'Hebrews Chapter 10, Verse 17.'

'And why were you spying on Penrhiw Farm?' As Swift leaned past her Julie could see the vein standing out on his temple.

'Spying, Inspector? That's a very emotive word.'

'We know you were there on at least two occasions. Were you attempting to beg Gareth Watkin's forgiveness too?'

Collins wiped spittle from his cheek. 'That's very nearly assault, Inspector Swift.'

Julie was aware of white coats outside in the corridor. 'Mr Collins, why were you at Penrhiw Farm?'

'That's obvious, Sergeant.' Collins was playing to the gallery as the consultant and his students entered the room. 'It was to reassure Mr Watkin that I forgave him for his lack of professionalism when I was arrested. He was quite a junior solicitor at the time, I believe. Unfortunately,' he smiled at his audience, 'I was too late. Poor Mr Watkin was already dead.'

'And the notes you sent us, *Mr Matthews*?'

Collins smiled his rat smile. 'Ah you have discovered my alter ego. I was simply attempting to bring a little enlightenment to the heathen masses.'

Swift turned and shepherded the whole gaggle of white coats back towards the door. 'Give us two minutes, doctor, and we'll be out of your way.' The consultant stared and two of the students smiled behind their hands, before they trooped back out into the corridor. Swift closed the door behind them.

'According to our timings, you saw Mr Watkin being driven away from the hotel in Llandrindod by a woman.' Julie waited for Collins to comment, but he stared at her, a beatific smile plastered in place. 'Why did you not tell the police what you had seen?' Collins threw his head back and laughed, a hollow, mirthless laugh that made her scalp crawl.

'I'm afraid my conversion has not been that complete, Sergeant. Helping the police is still very much against my religion.'

'And that would be the reason you threw the pistol away from Gareth Watkin's body into a pool of water?' Swift eyed him from the safety of the doorway.

'Why else? I have never used a firearm in my life and presumably you already know from forensic information gained without my consent, that I did not fire that gun.'

'And the motor cyclist?' Julie was losing patience, wanting to curtail Collins' floor-show which was purely for the benefit of the waiting medics. 'Your new love of mankind doesn't extend to injured bike riders who might just have been bleeding to death in a ditch?'

Collins narrowed his eyes and hissed through bared teeth. 'And you'll charge me with what, exactly? I could see that a vehicle was already making its way towards poor Mr Watkin. A red Land Rover. I left the driver to do the decent thing.' He smiled again. 'Besides, I had absolutely no idea where I was and would have been completely unable to provide directions to the emergency services. It all looks the same up there to me. 'As for charging me with anything petty, I wonder whether the Prices would thank you for that particular course of action?'

'You…' Swift lunged towards the bed but Julie pulled him away.

'He's not worth it.' She pushed Swift away from the bed and a slight smile lit up her face. 'Mr Collins, Manchester Metropolitan Police are anxious to speak to you regarding the theft of a motor vehicle. The theft would, as you are aware, breach the conditions of your parole. Could you tell me whether you were acting on divine orders when you drove it away from outside the toilets in Heaton Park last weekend.'

'As I have said, Sergeant, I still find myself unable to help the police with their enquiries.' Collins raised his lip into a sneer, but as he did, she could see beads of perspiration forming. He wiped his top lip with the sleeve of his jumper.

'So you won't mind an additional charge of wasting police time?' Swift was back by the bed, like a terrier goading a much larger dog.

'This is harassment,' said Collins, squirming away from Swift's face as well as he could. The click of the door handle made Swift turn and Collins rolled away. The flash of white coat at the door distracted Swift long enough for Collins to get off the bed and stand by the window.

'Get him away from me, Doctor. You saw him, he tried to assault me.'

'It was just a misunderstanding.' Julie was standing beside Collins now. 'Wasn't it, Mr Collins?'

Collins smiled at Swift. 'An apology from Inspector Swift will be sufficient.' Swift stared back.

'If you could give us another couple of moments, Doctor.' Julie smiled, the doctor looked from Collins to Swift and back again.

'Are you all right?' he asked.

'I'm going to be fine,' said Collins.

The doctor returned to the corridor, but stood with one shoulder leaning on the glass between them. He was watching. Swift had retreated into the corner, his bulk wedging the door closed. 'What really happened at Gordon Price's house, Collins?' There was no reply.

'Mr Collins, what happened?' Julie asked. Collins shook his head and sat down on the bed. He glanced at Swift, glowering in the corner, and then at Julie. She could almost hear his mind working before he spread out his long, pale fingers on his knees and stared at them as he spoke.

'I simply tripped over the step and hit my head on the door. As for driving away, well all I can suggest is that I must be fitter than you give me credit for.' Collins smiled. 'The exercise regime at Strangeways is first rate.'

'Come on, Sergeant, I've had quite enough of this.' Swift headed for the door. As he yanked the handle and flung the door open, the consultant almost fell into the room.

'But Inspector,' whined Collins, 'I'm still waiting for that apology. Or perhaps you will yourself be looking at a charge of harassing a witness.'

'Sergeant.' Swift was already halfway through the door and into the corridor. Julie followed him, weaving through the gaggle of white coats.

'But Sir, shouldn't we…' She realised that a couple of the students were enjoying the entertainment.

Swift slowed only to speak to the uniformed officer before Julie caught up with him. 'But Sir, couldn't we at least arrest him for harassing the Prices? What if he goes after Gordon and Eileen again?'

'I hate to agree with the evil sod in there, but he didn't actually do anything to them, did he? Look, I understand what you mean and Collins is a hateful specimen, but what good would it do?'

Julie stopped walking and stared at Swift's retreating back. 'On the other hand, Gordon could be charged. If Collins reports him and with the forensic evidence against him in the Zafira he could be the one who ends up in custody. That's not…'

'Not what, Julie? Not fair? The CPS wouldn't take Collins to court for harassment, and the forensic evidence in the Zafira is slight. Two of Gordon's hairs on the headrest, that's all it was. The defence would argue that Collins had picked them up from the carpet at the house when he fell and transferred them to the car himself. Nobody can remember seeing Gordon or Eileen in the Elan Valley and we don't know how they got back home from there if they left the Zafira there with Collins in it. Collins has insisted it was an accident so neither of the Prices will be charged with assault. Both Collins and Gordon Price swear that Collins drove himself to the Elan Valley.'

'But he couldn't have. I should know. If he'd been hit as hard as the hospital said there's no way he could have driven all that way.'

'I know it's not much, but we're actively tracking down anyone else who was threatened at Collins' trial. So far four of the jury members are dead, but there were no suspicious circumstances and the deaths were all way before Collins was released. Maybe he was telling the truth about why he was here, maybe he has come to repent. Sometimes, Sergeant,' Swift held the door to the stairs open for her, 'things just aren't as black and white as we'd like them to be. Besides,' Swift smiled and punctuated it with a wink, 'Collins will be back in Manchester before he knows what's hit him.'

Julie laughed and reached her phone out of her pocket, checking for messages as they walked downstairs. 'Bloody hell.' She held the phone out to Swift. 'It looks a bit more black and white now.' Helen's text was two hours old but straight to the point.

If you know where Collins is, lock him up and throw away the key. Joseph Lazarus found tortured and kicked to death in Prestwich. Body's been there over a week, poor old sod. Search warrant out for Collins. Be careful. H.

Swift handed the mobile back to her and turned on his heel, taking the stairs two at a time.

'Steady on, Sir.' Julie ran after him, back out onto the corridor. 'Who's Joseph Lazarus?'

'He was one of the key witnesses at Collins' trial,' gasped Swift. 'He saw Collins talking to Janey Wilson in the front garden of her parents' house, just before she went missing.' He slowed to a walk and punched her on the arm. 'We've got him.'

The white coats were still in Collins' room and he was smiling for his audience. Swift flung open the door, which slammed into the wall. The consultant's mouth was a thin line as he rounded on Swift. Swift held up his hand to stop him. 'Is this patient fit to be released?' The consultant stood his ground, determined to regain his status in front of his students.

'I would be obliged if you would permit me to examine my patient, officer.'

'If Mr Collins is well enough to leave the hospital, then I will be happy to relieve you of any further responsibility, Doctor.' Swift smiled. 'We will look after him now.'

'I really must object, Inspector. Your harassment is becoming somewhat problematic.' Collins smirked and raised one eyebrow at the pretty trainee doctor standing beside him.

'Well, let's give you something to really object to, shall we, Mr Collins.' Julie pushed through the students and, with a practised flick of the wrist, she had her handcuffs out of her bag and Collins' hands tethered before he could protest. 'Stephen Collins, I am arresting you on suspicion of the theft of a motor vehicle. You do not have to say anything, but it may harm your defence if you do not mention when questioned something you later rely on in court. Anything you do say may be given in evidence. Do you understand?' She smiled down at him and he leered in response.

'On the other matter, Mr Collins, the murder of Joseph Lazarus, you are wanted for questioning by Manchester Metropolitan Police. It will, of course, be our pleasure to offer you our company until they get here. PC Pritchard will make sure you are accompanied to the police station to await their arrival.'

There was a gasp from the students, and the two closest to the bed backed away.

Collins watched them and smiled slowly. '*He that is without sin among you, let him cast the first stone.* John, Chapter Eight, Verse Seven.'

Swift leaned against the Volvo in the hospital car park. 'You did well in there, Julie. I don't know that I'd have managed to stay so calm.'

'It was touch and go, Sir. Trust me.'

'Well, I'm grateful. I could have embarrassed myself without your professionalism.'

'It looks as though Gordon was right to be terrified then?'

Swift nodded. 'God knows what might have happened if Collins hadn't tripped over the step, eh, Sergeant?'

'Do you think he really did trip?'

'Not a chance. My guess is that Collins went along with Gordon's story so he could exact an excruciating revenge on Gordon and Eileen at a later date, which wouldn't have been nearly so effective if one or other of them had been banged up.'

'And if Catherine Jones hadn't been so hasty with a pistol, then Collins might have done her job for her too.'

'I wonder what would have happened to Gareth if Collins had got to him first.' Swift closed his eyes. 'I don't even want to think about it, not after what he did to Janey Wilson.'

'And poor old Joseph Lazarus. I wonder what he did to him?' Julie asked.

Swift reached into his pocket for his handkerchief. 'I've no doubt we will find out in due course and in graphic detail.'

Julie leaned on the car next to Swift. 'I still can't believe that Catherine killed her own nephew over something so trivial.'

'You've been at this game long enough to know that people kill for reasons that look stupid, even pathetic, but they get caught up in petty squabbles or get fixated on something until it gets totally out of hand. We've all seen it before. The psychiatrist thinks she never got over being sent away by her father and felt as though she was being abandoned again.'

'But he was moving to Cheshire to improve his prospects. It's not a million miles away, is it?'

Swift shrugged. 'Who knows. Whereas Collins is just an evil, violent…'

'Quite, Sir.' Julie walked round the car to the passenger door. 'Thank God it's over.'

CHAPTER FORTY-EIGHT

There was just one more thing Julie had to do. She turned right out of the police station and through the town, up the hill past the cathedral and on towards the Epynt.

Sarah Watkin had just got back from picking the children up from school. There were bags of shopping in the hallway of the bungalow and a muddy, wall-eyed collie in the porch.

'Sergeant. What can I do for you?' She looked weary, but turned and led the way into the kitchen. 'Tea?' She flicked the switch on the kettle. 'You look terrible.'

Julie nodded and sat at the table with its colourful cloth with scenes of tractors and lambs encapsulated in the plastic.

'Will you be all right?'

Sarah shrugged and held the tea caddy clutched to herself. 'Time will tell. You have to keep going for the kids don't you?' In the other room she could hear Dylan laughing at the television.

'You weren't aware that Catherine knew?'

'About what?'

'That Gareth was going into partnership with Jessica Southam and you were intending to move up to Cheshire.'

Sarah put the caddy down and pulled out a chair and sat down. 'Nobody knew, especially not Catherine. We knew she would have been incandescent. All she wanted to do was get Dic to retire, so they could spend more time together. How could we have ever imagined she would do something like this.' She sighed.

'But it was all decided, you really were going to move away?'

290

'It was going to be the biggest gamble of his life – of our lives. I really didn't want to go. I'd even considered staying here with the kids and letting him move up there on his own. You wouldn't believe the blazing, screaming rows we had about it. Stupid. Gareth was struggling with it too, if he was honest. He didn't want to let Dic down. Dic had always been very good to us, but there just wasn't enough work for all of them, and what there was just didn't seem interesting enough for Gareth somehow. Dic was adamant he didn't want to retire, so when the chance of starting a new practice came up, with all the business Jessica Southam could give Gareth, well, it was just too good to ignore.'

'But Dic knew that Catherine wanted him to retire.'

'Catherine's never been an easy woman, Sergeant. The thought of spending all of his time with her… Well, let's just say I think he was putting off the fateful day.'

'And did you talk much about the partnership with Gareth, apart from the rows?'

'We talked about nothing else in the few weeks before…' Sarah stood up and turned her back once more as she busied herself with mugs and milk jug.

'Did Catherine babysit for you very often during that period?'

Sarah kept her back to Julie but was suddenly very still. From the other room they could hear shouting, then Seren appeared in the doorway, holding an exercise book and a pen.

'Mam, can I go and use Dad's office to do my homework? Dylan is being a pain.'

Slowly Sarah looked round at her daughter and nodded. 'Yes, *cariad*. That's fine. Tell me, did you talk to Auntie Catherine about Daddy's work, about his new job?'

Seren had already turned to leave and she looked back at her mother over her shoulder, wide-eyed and pale.

'It's all right,' Sarah said. 'You're not in trouble. It would just help Sergeant Kite to tie up a few loose ends, that's all.'

'Well,' Seren twisted the pen in her fingers. 'A couple of weeks ago, the night I wasn't very well and you came home early, Auntie Catherine was really angry. She asked about the pregnant lady we saw in Abergavenny, and she wanted to know if Daddy was friends with her. I thought she wouldn't be quite so cross with Daddy if she knew it was only about work. She was really interested. She wanted to know where we would all live.' She walked over to her mother and took hold of the sleeve of her shirt. 'Did I do something wrong?'

Sarah shook her head. 'No, *cariad*. It's fine. Don't worry about it. You go and do your homework now. Tea won't be long.' Seren smiled at her mother and left the room. They heard the door of the study being closed before Sarah moved. 'Thank you,' she said.

CHAPTER FORTY-NINE

The road snaked across the moorland, barely visible in the bright sunshine and the sea of waving ferns. From his perch high on a sandstone outcrop, the buzzard watched the car as it zigzagged along the narrow strip of tarmac, then pulled into the side of the road and fell silent. The door opened and a figure got out of the car, leaned against the bonnet and turned its face into the late afternoon sunshine.

Julie could hear the bird as it flew over her, high on the thermals above the steep drop. She opened her eyes. It was a buzzard. A huge great thing, but without the characteristic v-shaped tail of the kite. Below her she could pick out the chimneys at Penrhiw, just visible over the steep brow of the hill, and in the valley to the west, the small stone houses of Llangammarch, huddled round the tumbling river. She could smell the fern and the peaty earth, the waft of sheep-dropping and clear mountain air. Way down in the valley a quad bike growled its way around a small flock of sheep and three collies raced to keep them together; it was like watching a pool of quicksilver trying to find its own way.

Julie snapped open the brittle biscuit of a fortune cookie and pulled out the slip of paper, letting the biscuit crumbs fall to the ground. She smoothed the paper and read the words printed on it. *A journey of a thousand miles begins with a single step.*

She pulled her mobile phone from her pocket and dialled Helen's number, but before it connected she ended the call, tapped her phone on her teeth and dialled again.

'Are you all right?' There was an edge in Adam's voice, concern, which he knew she hated. 'I've just got in,' he said, forcing carefree calm. 'There's no traffic at all. Can you believe it only takes me quarter of an hour to get back from school, not a bit like it was in Manchester.'

'I've felt better,' she said, watching the dogs push the sheep through a gateway and into a new field. No. Not at all like Manchester. A big blue tractor trundled its way to the top of the hill and the driver raised his hand in a wave. It was Milos Penrhiw and she waved back.

'Are you still there?' As the sound of the tractor faded she could hear Adam on the other end of the phone.

'I'm still here,' she said. 'I'll see you in a few minutes.' She closed her eyes and felt the warmth of the sun on her face, heard the cry of the buzzard as it rode the thermals above her.

'I'm coming home.'

Jan Newton grew up in Manchester and Derbyshire, spending her formative years on the back of a pony, exploring the hills and moorland around her home. She lived and worked in London and Buckinghamshire for 19 years until moving to Wales in 2005, where she learnt to speak fluent Welsh. Jan has won several writing competitions, including the Allen Raine Short Story competition, the WI Lady Denman Cup, and the Oriel Davies Gallery competition for nature-writing. She has been published in *New Welsh Review*. *Remember No More* is her first novel.

www.jannewton.net

ABOUT HONNO

Honno Welsh Women's Press was set up in 1986 by a group of women who felt strongly that women in Wales needed wider opportunities to see their writing in print and to become involved in the publishing process. Our aim is to develop the writing talents of women in Wales, give them new and exciting opportunities to see their work published and often to give them their first 'break' as a writer. Honno is registered as a community co-operative. Any profit that Honno makes is invested in the publishing programme. Women from Wales and around the world have expressed their support for Honno. Each supporter has a vote at the Annual General Meeting. For more information and to buy our publications, please write to Honno at the address below, or visit our website: www.honno.co.uk

Honno, 14 Creative Units, Aberystwyth Arts Centre
Aberystwyth, Ceredigion SY23 3GL

Honno Friends

We are very grateful for the support of the Honno Friends: Jane Aaron, Annette Ecuyere, Audrey Jones, Gwyneth Tyson Roberts, Beryl Roberts, Jenny Sabine.

For more information on how you can become a Honno Friend, see: http://www.honno.co.uk/friends.php